The Unseen Witness

Published by Brolga Publishing Pty Ltd
ABN 46 063 962 443
PO Box 12544
A'Beckett St
Melbourne,VIC, 8006
Australia

email: markzocchi@brolgapublishing.com.au

Copyright © 2016 Grant Peake

National Library of Australia
Cataloguing-in-Publication entry

Peake, Grant, author
The Unseen Witness
ISBN: 9781925367584 (paperback)
Subjects: Detective and mystery stories.
A823.4

Printed in Australia
Cover design b Working Type Studio
Typesetting by Tara Wyllie

BE PUBLISHED

Publish through a successful publisher. National distribution, Macmillan & International distribution to the United Kingdom, North America. Sales Representation to South East Asia
Email: markzocchi@brolgapublishing.com.au

THE
UNSEEN
WITNESS

Power and vanity meets danger and death

GRANT PEAKE

My thanks to all those who have encouraged and supported me to continue writing. With gratitude, Grant Peake

CHAPTER 1

A SUDDEN FATALITY

Detective Inspector Ben Driscoll was feeling quietly confident as he drove his triple black Mercury Park Lane Brougham along Oceanview Drive.

He had purchased the four-door hardtop last year in '68, updating from the Chevrolet wagon that had served his family faithfully for ten years. The interior upholstery was a wine-red colour with scrolls intertwined in the vinyl, and boasted ample comfort with a powerful 428 cubic inch 7-litre engine. There was plenty of room for his wife Noreen and their three teenage daughters.

Glancing up into the night sky as he drove on, Driscoll was bedazzled by a myriad of stars that decorated the heavens above. The moon was a glow of brightness as it hung in a state of regal supremacy. The smell of the ocean wafted through his open window. This brought back memories of summer days with Noreen and the girls at the beach – not that Ben was an excellent swimmer or surfer, for that matter, but he did like to splash around and play on the beach with his beloved daughters.

Driscoll's mind now focused on the letter he had received about a month ago, kindling his keen interest in an unsolved case from many years ago. Why the letter was mailed to him, he could not fathom, but his curiosity was sparked.

Having done some background research on the case, Driscoll had stumbled across some vital information. Then had come the anonymous telephone call, which had led him to make this visit tonight to Seascape Apartments in Oceanside Waters. The instructions were to meet his informant at apartment 3A. Normally he would have been accompanied by his offsider, Detective Sergeant Karl Peterson, however, Driscoll had not divulged any details of the letter or telephone call to Peterson or anyone else.

Preferring to work alone, Driscoll had taken a bold risk to attempt this incongruous meeting. The anonymous caller had given Driscoll very clear instructions: 'Meet at the Seascape Apartments in Oceanside Waters, apartment 3A ... come alone.' It was difficult to tell whether the muffled voice was male or female. The individual informed Driscoll that they had information relating to a death from many years ago. Managing to track the call, with the assistance of the boys in the back room, Driscoll had been told that the call originated from a phone box at the corner of South Flower Street and Olympic Boulevard, Los Angeles.

The Mercury continued cruising along Oceanview Drive and was approaching its intended destination. Oceanside

Waters was a well-to-do beachside suburb on the outer perimeter of the sprawling city. Driscoll was anticipating a breakthrough in this mysterious case that the police had never been able to solve.

Ben Driscoll slowed the vehicle down and turned off the headlights as he drove into the parking lot of Seascape Apartments. The time was just before 9 p.m. He was right on time for his rendezvous.

He got out of the car and carefully closed the driver's door, but left it unlocked. Stubbing out his cigarette, he gazed around the parking lot. There were only four other automobiles in the parking lot this night: a bright yellow VW Beetle bug with white wall tyres, a weary looking red and white Buick Skylark from the mid-1950s and two different late model white Pontiacs. The parking lot lights lit up the area well.

Driscoll peered around him – all seemed quiet. From what he could see, there was no one else around. Pulling his hat down firmly on his wide head, the detective slowly made his way to the stairs, which led up to the outside corridors of each floor.

The apartment building was of recent construction and had six floors in all. Its shape was semi circular – a different shape to most apartment blocks that Driscoll had seen. Each apartment had been designed to obtain unobstructed ocean views, with long wide windows. A blue and white colour theme had been used to emphasise the ocean, which was only a short distance away. The bedrooms and living areas faced the ocean whilst the apartment entries and kitchens faced over the large expanse of pool and sun lounge area.

Choosing to ignore the elevator, Driscoll made his way up the stairs. This would prove to be a fatal error, one which would have dire circumstances for our lovable main character Driscoll. At the second floor, Driscoll hesitated, halting his ascent. Not accustomed to climbing stairs, Driscoll had become breathless. Pausing his progress, Driscoll was alert to any sound.

What was that sound he had heard? Driscoll was breathing heavily now. His heart was pounding in his ears. A sweat had broken out on his forehead and was now trickling down his ruddy face. He reached into his jacket, his right hand touching his police issued automatic pistol positioned in the gun holster.

A heavily built man of 46 years of age, the 5 foot 6 detective was somewhat overweight and not as fit as he used to be. His wife, Noreen, was a good cook and encouraged her husband to savour her new recipes, along with their three growing daughters.

The only sound Driscoll could hear were the crickets calling each other in the warmth of the June evening. Taking his hand out of his jacket, he held onto the railing with both puffy hands for support. His breathing was getting heavier. After a few moments, he wiped his forehead with a white handkerchief and then loosened his necktie for some relief. Feeling that he could carry on, Driscoll put the handkerchief back into his trouser pocket and inhaled some air into his lungs. A prolific smoker, Driscoll was in need of a nicotine fix, but overcame the desire, and collected his emotions. Sensing that he was overreacting, Driscoll continued up to the third floor landing, in the direction of apartment 3A.

Having reached the third floor balcony, Driscoll could now see the opalescent glow of the pool below him. The water was glistening in the moonlight and the lights surrounding the pool added brightness to the outdoor furniture and diving board. Now focusing his attention on his quest, Driscoll looked behind him. Seeing no one, he began walking along the corridor, his eyes searching for apartment numbers. Soft music and laughter came from apartment 3D, while apartment 3C was ablaze with light – apartment 3B, however, was in total darkness. As Driscoll approached 3A he noticed that it too was in darkness. Not even the slightest bit of light shone from the crack under the apartment door. He found this to be quite strange – the mystery telephone caller had distinctly said to meet in apartment 3A.

While Driscoll stood deliberating, a hand had emerged from the door of apartment 3B holding a lethal gun. The weapon was an automatic with silencer. An arm held the lethal instrument with amazing calmness. The target was just placed in the right position. The black leather gloved finger curled around the trigger of the weapon, waiting for its prey to be ensnared in the delicate web that had been laid with startling skill.

Driscoll walked back towards the balcony railing, contemplating his next move. The lights from the ceiling above silhouetted his bulky frame. His eyes fixed on the door of apartment 3A – unaware of the extreme danger lurking in the murky shadows of apartment 3B.

The entry to each apartment was recessed and afforded our assassin the coverage they required to carry out their despicable deed.

Detective Inspector Ben Driscoll never made his move, the only move he made was to fall backwards over the balcony as a result of the two rapid bullets fired in succession that smashed into his large, hairy chest. Death had been instantaneous. His body somersaulted down into the pool, where his bulky mass made an enormous splash.

All was silent again.

Driscoll lay face down in the pool, his oozing blood creating a soft red discolouration in the azure blue of the rippling crystal water.

The deadly assailant had withdrawn back into its hiding place, a smirk appearing on the face of our unknown killer.

FIVE WEEKS LATER

It was just after 7.30 a.m. A bright clear sun heralded some heat for the day ahead. Already the sun's rays were intensifying, as Private Investigator Paul O'Shea unlocked the business suite, walked through the reception area and strode into his office.

Seating himself in his black vinyl chair with rollers, complete with headrest extension, if desired, and footstool, with the touch of a lever at the right side of the chair, O'Shea opened the *Los Angeles Tribune* newspaper. Quickly losing interest with all the latest news, O'Shea turned to the sports pages and began to read the results of the baseball. His team, the Baltimore Bears, had been thrashed by the Chicago Cougars, 31 to 9. O'Shea scowled at the scores and closed up the paper, placing it away from his sight. *Not going too good this year! We need to lift our game to make the finals,* thought O'Shea to himself.

Having been a private detective investigator for the last six years, O'Shea had done quite well for himself. He had purchased this office on the third floor of the Parkside Business Centre – as well as a two-bedroom apartment at Beachcomber Sands, a relatively new coastal settlement just north of the commuter belt of the rapidly expanding city. It provided convenient access to the Pacific Freeway for his commute to West Hollywood. When his marriage to Barbara had been annulled, Paul was awarded the house in Brandon Vale as part of the marriage settlement. Paul had been quite surprised, but then given Barbara's lavish taste for bigger and better things in life, she told Paul that the house was not good enough for her to live in.

Barbara had been swept off her feet by a tall, rich Texan who had money and oil flowing from his ears and eyes. Paul simply could not compete with the lavish lifestyle the greasy scumbag had offered to Barbara. 'Money is no object for Hal,' Barbara had rudely informed Paul. 'His place is far better. You can keep the dump!'

So Paul decided to sell the house and set himself up as

a private detective. He had served the Los Angeles Police Department for 16 years and then resigned – promotion was not coming his way. Even though O'Shea held the title of Detective Sergeant, this was never enough for Barbara.

They had married young, Barbara 19 and O'Shea 21. He had prospects of moving through the ranks, but with so many guys all hankering after the same ladder, promotion had been slower.

Barbara had expected Paul to be the Police Commissioner the first week they were married, but her expectations were quickly dashed as the years wore on. Ever conscious of her voluptuous figure, she would not entertain the thought of having children. O'Shea would have liked a family, but that was not going to happen with Barbara around.

Strong willed and very sure of herself, Barbara was constantly climbing the society tree, wanting more and the best life had to offer. Even if O'Shea could not afford it, Barbara still had her way.

Finally, after much pestering on the part of Barbara, O'Shea had succumbed to her pressure, and they had moved to the new housing estate at Brandon Vale. A large home with a good-sized block and pool, Barbara wanted to entertain and show off their new wealth. Paul's nerves were at fever pitch with Barbara's constant spending. Clothes were stuffed in the floor-to-ceiling wardrobes. Paul's wage was stretched to capacity to make ends meet. Barbara had no intentions of ever working. "Charge it, honey", she would tell her female friends, "that's what I do."

O'Shea was not even aware that Barbara was having an affair with the Texan chap, Hal Rothbartson III. It was only one night coming home earlier than expected, that Paul caught them out having it on in their front bedroom. Barbara's pink silk panties were draped around her shapely neck whilst hairy Hal savoured the merchandise lower down. Squeals of delight echoed down the passage as O'Shea made his way to the master bedroom, wondering what all the commotion was about. He certainly discovered the reason why very promptly. Shame was something that Barbara never possessed, nor ever would. Her reaction was one of, "So what, it's happened. Get over it!". Paul realised later that Barbara's taste for men had been going on for some time, right under his nose. Fortunately Barbara had moved to Dallas, Texas with her new beau and the promise of a more alluring lifestyle beckoned her there.

Now at 41 years of age, Paul felt he could move forward in his life. Any love for Barbara had now been extinguished, after the shock of Barbara's infidelity had hit him like a brick. Fatuously devoted to Barbara, O'Shea had found it very hard to come to terms with the marriage break up. He had no suspicions at all regarding the affair. Many of their friends had taken Barbara's side and deserted Paul. "Poor Barbara, left all alone each night. It was only natural that she wanted some male company. Paul brought it on himself, no one else to blame", was the catch phrase bandied around their circle of insincere and shallow friends. One friend who hadn't deserted Paul, however, was Detective Inspector Ben

Driscoll. Now Ben was dead, shot at point blank range those few weeks ago.

Gradually over time, O'Shea accepted the marital break up and became immersed with his new vocation as a private investigator. He could understand perhaps the longing for a man's company, as he was always working late hours. And for what? A kick up the backside and 20 years of wasted life, just working to keep Barbara in everything she desired.

O'Shea reflected for a moment and brought his wayward thoughts back to reality, and looked down at the package sitting on his shiny veneered black desk. The brown paper package was addressed to him, and marked "Private and confidential". The package had been hand-delivered by Detective Sergeant Karl Peterson yesterday.

Peterson was probably around 40 years in age. He could have been older but his long, yet pleasant baby face, and wavy black hair, gave him a younger appearance. He was quite tall and had broad thick shoulders. Smartly dressed in a tan suit and dark brown shoes, Peterson seemed a self-assured guy; but as O'Shea reasoned to himself, it was a good thing these days in the force.

According to Peterson, the package was located in Ben's locker at Los Angeles police headquarters. O'Shea was not previously acquainted with Peterson, who became Ben's understudy detective when he resigned from the police force.

'If it is of any help, and strictly off the record, the bullets that killed Ben were from a 765 automatic. We think it was silencer equipped, as no one heard the shots. These were issued to special agents of the British Secret Service,' Peterson had said when leaving O'Shea's office.

O'Shea raised his eyebrows, and said with amazement in his voice, 'The British Secret Service! Surely their not caught up in all this?'

Peterson replied and shrugged his shoulders. 'Your guess is as good as mine. Just remember, I didn't tell you anything! I know that Ben and you were close. We are still clutching its straws. The residents of the apartments said they neither saw nor heard anything.'

On that note, Peterson nodded his head and departed from the office.

The handwriting was unmistakably that of his good mate Ben Driscoll. O'Shea had decided not to open the package straight away – after all, it probably did not contain anything of importance. He had left the package on his desk, ready to open the next day.

O'Shea's mind wandered back to when he was told of Ben's untimely death a few weeks ago. He had been devastated to learn of the sudden death, assassination style, of his former colleague and close pal. When O'Shea had been in the police force, both men had worked closely together as a team. They shared each other's ideas and often spoke about their families. Ben had been a rock of support when O'Shea's marriage had broken down. Noreen, Ben's wife, had also been very compassionate. But then, that was Noreen. A stay-at-home mother, her life centred around Ben and their three teenage daughters. An excellent cook and homemaker, Noreen was worlds apart from Barbara. The two men had maintained contact, with the occasional meal at Ben's River Glen home on the weekend.

Having no siblings, Paul was very much on his own. He had lost his parents some years ago – his father from a sudden heart attack and his mom from pneumonia. Knowing of Paul's situation, Ben warmly welcomed Paul into the family.

O'Shea opened the top right hand drawer of his desk and took out the large letter opener with the black onyx handle. Slitting open the package, Paul extracted a handwritten letter from Ben, a buff coloured envelope and a tape, labelled "Maryanne". O'Shea read the letter first. Its contents were straight to the point but gave concise details of the intentions of the writer.

O'Shea opened the envelope and took out a large piece of paper and another white envelope. It was a message that had been pieced together using magazines and newspapers. The letters had been cut out and pasted onto a thick piece of white paper, almost like blotting paper.

Maryanne Myles Morrow did not commit the murder. Look north to find your answer.
- TT

Paul turned the sheet of paper over, nothing on the reverse. *A very curious message,* he thought.

The envelope that had contained the letter had been retained by Driscoll. It was postmarked Hollywood and dated May 4, 1969. No address was specified on the back of the plain white envelope, however, the addressee details of Detective Inspector Ben Driscoll, c/- Los Angeles Police Department, was typed. The typeset seemed to be from an older typewriter. The letter 'r' was blurred on the words Inspector, Driscoll and Department.

Turning his attention to the tape, Paul reasoned that some information may be forthcoming regarding this Maryanne. Walking over to a tape recorder placed on a smaller desk against the white painted wall, O'Shea placed the tape into its slot and pressed the play button. Within a few moments the clear deep voice of Ben Driscoll became audible.

'Hello Paul …'

This was a little unsettling for Paul O'Shea, as Driscoll always referred to Paul as 'O'Shea'. A large, hard lump formed in his throat.

'I want you to listen carefully to what I have to say and then destroy this tape immediately …

As my letter to you states, about a month ago, I received this envelope in the police mail. No sender's name on the envelope. Having done some research about this Maryanne Myles Morrow, I find that she was a prime suspect in an unsolved murder case from 1922. Yeah, I know it's along time ago, but the case was never solved. So a man by the name of Charles Osborne was shot to death in his Hollywood bungalow on the night of August 4, 1922. Medical examination states that he died between the times of 6 p.m. and 9 p.m. He was a producer for First National Pictures Corporation and apparently was well thought of by his contemporaries. Osborne was also strongly opposed to the use of narcotics, which was beginning to make massive inroads in the motion picture industry. There were a number of suspects, all had alibis … except for Maryanne Myles Morrow, an actress. She reportedly had visited Osborne that evening some time around 7 p.m. and left around 8 p.m., but no one saw her or can verify her whereabouts. The only person to confirm Morrow's movements later that evening was a Maybelle Normansen. She claims that Morrow came to her home some time after 9 p.m. and departed around 10.45 p.m. Morrow was unable to explain her movements after leaving Osborne at 8 p.m. and then arriving at the Normansen home at around 9 p.m. On this basis, the police charged Morrow with the murder, but the case never came to trial due to insufficient evidence. There is no trace of Morrow now, after exhaustive searching of records. Normansen has since died.

I have not told a soul about this tape or the letter I received. I am unable to determine who this "TT" is, but I have left the envelope there in case it is of some use.

Why the secrecy, you may ask? Well, old pal, I have had a number of strange incidences occur since I got this letter. A tyre was slashed on my automobile and a handwritten note was placed under a wiper telling me to 'back off'. I have been followed by a man, but he manages to slip away whenever I get close to him. No idea who it is or what he looks like. Then around a month ago, I was pushed from behind at a crosswalk, while waiting to cross the intersection at North

Highland Avenue and Hollywood Boulevard. My life could be in danger, so I have taken this precaution to supply you with the relevant details to follow on, where I may have to leave off.

I trust you to carry on this quest, buddy. I have had a telephone call earlier this evening to meet some one at apartment 3A, Seascape Apartments in Oceanside Waters at 9 p.m. No name was given. Hopefully, I shall learn some more. Should anything happen, please be there for Noreen and the girls. I know you will, but I just want them looked to ...'

There was a slight pause before Driscoll spoke on, his voice sounded emotional now.

'Thanks my friend for many good years we spent on the force. I hope that I am wrong in doing this, but my instinct tells me to be prepared. This tape was prepared on June 6, 1969 at 7.27 p.m. Your pal, Ben Driscoll.'

O'Shea switched off the tape recorder. This had been recorded the very night Ben had been shot. Paul O'Shea was momentarily smitten with grief and then anger. *Who murdered Ben in cold blood?*

The police had no leads regarding the shooting.

O'Shea had indeed visited Noreen and the girls on a number of occasions, to offer advice and solace. Noreen had been grief stricken and the girls were equally distraught with the loss of their loving father. Their lives had revolved around Ben and he had adored "his girls'", as he affectionately referred to them.

Ben Driscoll had been a family man, but had been cruelly cut down. Ben's police pension would provide an income for the family but it would never bring back the one they cherished. Paul O'Shea was now determined to take this case on and bring to justice whoever had carried out this killing of Ben.

CHAPTER 2
STARTLING REVELATIONS

Deciding to have his secretary come in and see the contents of the package, O'Shea popped his head out from his office door.

'Donna, can I see you please?'

Looking up from her desk, and seeing her employer's sombre face, Donna put her right hand under her chin, and replied in a sexy tone. 'Of course you can, but I warn you, I am expensive!'

O'Shea dropped his head and placed a hand on his forehead, a smile emerging on his face. 'I asked for that, didn't I? You know what I mean! Come on,' he said, pointing toward his desk. 'Or I will have to give you the biggest smack you have ever had?'

With a cheeky grin, Donna made her way toward O'Shea's office. She swept past her boss and plonked herself down on the black swivel chair opposite the desk.

'I am yours to be smacked ...' she whispered in a husky and alluring tone.

O'Shea grinned widely as he walked around his desk and sat down.

Donna had been working for O'Shea since the inception of the private detective agency and had proved herself to be very intelligent and useful to O'Shea. Gorgeously endowed with appealing facial features, high cheekbones, rich chestnut coloured hair and a curvaceous body, Donna was still single after a failed romance some years ago. Heartbroken, she decided to pack up her life in New Jersey and relocate to the sunny climes of the west coast. Always a girl of resolute nature, she was not a lady to be easily trodden down. Donna had emerged from her shattered liaison a renewed woman, thankful that she had picked herself up and made a new life. It was not the failure that had affected her emotions so much, but the getting up, that had been the most difficult. Donna had blossomed as the victor over tragedy. Having given 11 years of her life to a man who gave her worthless promises, and then by chance finding out that he was a cheat and a bigamist, well, that took the wind out of her sails. After all, she was not a spring chicken anymore. Donna was 38 years old but had told O'Shea she was 26 when applying for the job. Donna's younger looks had held her in good stead – but that was six years ago. Donna had not revealed her background to O'Shea, only telling him that she had moved from Jersey City.

Paul O'Shea had accepted Donna immediately for the position of secretary, no questions asked. Her references and qualifications were glowing, O'Shea realised that he would be a fool not to hire her.

That's what Donna liked about O'Shea. He took everyone at face value and treated you as an equal. No judgment was dealt out or show of superiority displayed. Sure, he was the boss, but O'Shea gave due consideration to Donna's input when discussing his work. Underneath their working relationship, Donna had come to like O'Shea, a lot more than words can express on these pages. However, as is often the case with the male, O'Shea was blind to Donna's feelings. Not intentionally by any means, it's just that O'Shea was always involved with his detective agency. Deep in O'Shea's subconscious feelings, he still harboured a candle for Barbara, the woman he had lost. That chapter of his life had ended, yet Paul had yet to accept this. No play, no fun makes a dull boy. Donna had witnessed the emotional period that Paul O'Shea had experienced and had cheered him up with her lively manner and care free, vivacious attitude. Suffice to say, Donna Weston knew firsthand what O'Shea was going through.

'Well sir, what's the matter? You look positively down in the dumps. A wonderful morning like this too, I might add.' She smiled beguilingly at O'Shea. Donna only used the terminology "sir" when she perceived that her boss was in need of cheering up. 'Come on, spit it out. Don't keep a girl waiting.' She gave him an enquiring look and crossed her smooth long legs and waited for a reply. Pencil perched above her right ear and notepad on her lap, Donna was eager to hear what her boss was about to tell her.

'Read the letter and message, and then listen to this tape,' instructed Paul with a lowered tone in his masculine voice.

Donna read the letter from Driscoll and then passed the note back to Paul. 'From Ben Driscoll … so … he was involved in something?'

'Listen carefully to the tape.' O'Shea said before turning the tape recorder on once again.

Enthralled with the words of Driscoll, Donna frantically scribbled on her notepad. Her mind was racing with thoughts, but she was also aware that O'Shea was coming to terms with the contents of the package, especially the words of his old mate, Ben Driscoll.

O'Shea sat on the edge of his desk, listening with intent to the words recorded by Driscoll. He wished that Ben had approached him earlier about all this, then perhaps this tragic event may never have unfolded.

Once the tape had finished, O'Shea switched off the tape recorder machine and sat down in his chair.

'This package was delivered yesterday when you were out at the post office. Ben's offsider, Karl Peterson brought it in. The package was found in Ben's locker.' Paul's face was serious and he appeared to be lost in thought.

Why did it take so long for the package to be delivered? Did Ben have a locker? I can't remember him ever having a locker? Not while I was working with him. Perhaps they just didn't do anything about it. I suppose with the police funeral and the murder investigation being instigated, the package had simply been forgotten.

Shaking his head slightly, and bringing his thoughts

back to the present, O'Shea was considering what course of action should be taken. 'On the face of all this, I reckon we will have to do some in depth investigation regarding this Osborne case. See if you can find out who benefited from his death, anyway, you know the drill. Check out any witness statements and see if they are still alive and kicking. A list of names …'

Donna took notes as he spoke.

'We also will have to locate this Morrow dame, if she is still alive. Whoever killed Driscoll, had lured him to those apartments on purpose. That phone call was a deliberate ploy. Then there is that cryptic message from TT. That requires some thinking. Ben was a good pal to me and I want to find out who is behind his death. Noreen deserves an answer too. A hunch tells me that there is a lot more below the surface, than what meets the eye Donna. Are you okay with what we have to do?'

Donna lifted her pencil from off her notepad and nodded. 'Of course, boss.'

'I want to take a look at the apartment block where Ben was killed … just snoop around and get a feel of the area. I may stumble on something, who knows?' concluded Paul O'Shea, as his eyes levelled with his secretary sitting opposite him. 'Apparently the police haven't got any leads on Ben's murder, just that the murder weapon used was a 765 fully automatic, probably with silencer attached. According to Karl Peterson, those weapons were issued to agents of the British Secret Service.'

Donna was quick to respond. 'Wow, that sounds like

something out of a James Bond movie! Someone took great care not to create a disturbance … but yes, I agree with you about the message from "TT". More work to be done on that. I will check at the City Library for any newspaper articles from the time of the Osborne murder and see if I can dig up any information on this Morrow woman. There must be something about her. Still, I suppose it all depends if she was a real star of the era or just a hum drum second rate actress. There were loads around then before the talkies came on the scene. I will get started now, boss … if that's okay with you?' said Donna with an air of finality, getting up from the chair and looking over to her employer.

'That's fine with me, Donna. The quicker we get this started, the better. I have a gut feeling that we could be opening a can of worms with this one!'

'Oh, by the way, what about the Andersen case you are working on – don't you want to carry on with that too?' asked Donna questioningly.

'Mrs Andersen can wait,' Paul replied stiffly. 'Anyhow, she has gone to Las Vegas to play the slot machines or whatever. If Mrs Andersen's husband is cheating on her, then the least she could do would be to pay me a deposit to get things moving, but no, she's chosen to go to Las Vegas instead!' Paul's reply was brusque.

'Fair enough, boss.' Donna did not argue the point. Given O'Shea's reaction regarding the tape from Ben Driscoll, Donna could sense some excitement around the corner.

Stepping out of O'Shea's office, Donna checked her

appearance with her compact mirror, and was preparing to leave. Notebook and pen in her bag, she got up to depart.

'Say we meet back here at midday, Donna?' asked O'Shea.

'Sure, see you then.'

Donna relished the interest and variety this role had given her. Never imagining being given a degree of trust, this had fired Donna's intense desire to give her best and prove her reliability to her boss.

O'Shea walked over to the coat stand in the corner of his office and proceeded to put on his sports jacket. Straightening his loose tie and tucking his blue shirt in his trousers more securely, O'Shea was ready to drive to Seascape Apartments. O'Shea then remembered Ben's express wish to destroy the tape.

'I had better destroy that tape before we leave the office!' O'Shea called out to Donna. 'We don't want that falling into the wrong hands.'

Paul removed the tape from the recorder and then walked into the small kitchen that connected to his office. He placed some old newspaper in the base of the stainless steel trash can and dropped the tape on top. He gently poured a small amount of kerosene onto the tape before lighting a match and dropping it into the trash can. Instantly the tape ignited and commenced to melt.

Satisfied that the tape was suitably destroyed, O'Shea walked out into the reception area.

'All done, tape destroyed,' remarked Paul.

'Good,' Donna responded, her brown handbag slung on her shoulder and a business-like look on her face.

Together Donna and Paul walked out of the office and down the corridor to the elevators.

The time was just nearing 8.30 a.m. Standing outside the elevator, waiting for one to arrive, Donna noticed that Paul's tie was all askew and the collar of his sports jacket was caught up at the back.

'Hey, come here … your tie is out of whack and so is your jacket,' Donna offered as she reached over to give Paul's slim line black tie a tug.

Caught totally off-guard and losing his balance, Paul found himself clinging onto Donna's waist for support. Their faces had met and their body language gave one the impression that a lot more was going on.

As fate would have it, an elevator arrived, pouring out its occupants who would walk to their various points of employment. The two figures of Donna and Paul locked in an embrace, right outside the elevators, brought much comment from the arriving workers. They all stopped their procession and gawked.

Donna was quick to respond. 'Well, what are you all looking at? This is just the dummy run!'

'Absolutely disgusting, they can't wait to get at each other!' an elderly woman cried out. 'Now in my day … ' Her resonant voice trailed off as the group decided to leave the scene of sordidness.

Paul was blushing now but he certainly had a smile on his handsome face. Not overly tall, just 5 foot 9, he was quite fit and agile. Clean-shaven with light brown hair, Paul had managed to keep a younger looking appearance for a man now in his early forties. Yes, there were a few lines around his eyes, but this only added to his charm and maturity.

Donna was laughing with merriment as the pair entered the elevator to descend to the ground floor.

Fixing himself up in the elevator and wiping lipstick off his face, Paul emerged ready to drive to Seascape Apartments.

***

On the drive to Oceanside Waters, Paul was thinking over the events so far.

Why was Ben chosen to receive the package? That needed an explanation. The message from "TT" was also unusual. Normally the writer of these messages seldom revealed any clue to their identity. However, this person had ... but why? Did they want to be known somehow? Then the mystery telephone caller, requesting Ben's presence alone. The set up killing was curious, not to mention downright cowardly. The poor guy didn't have a chance ...

Driving down the Pacific Freeway, Paul O'Shea drove his pride and joy, which he recently purchased last year. Always liking the Ford Mustang, Paul could only drool over them. Barbara's expensive tastes had kept any thought of buying a new car for himself, right out of the equation. Barbara made sure her automobile was updated regularly to keep up with her society knockabout friends.

Having been inspired by the blockbuster film, *Bullitt*, starring Steve McQueen in 1968, the Ford Mustang automobile had made a huge impact on the American public. Paul O'Shea had seen the movie on one rare occasion that he had a whole weekend to himself. Barbara had gone away for a few days to visit her mother in San Francisco, allowing O'Shea time to himself. It was sheer bliss.

Now that O'Shea had some surplus funds, he had ordered his dream car last year, when the Ford Mustang Mach 1 was released to the public in August, '68. These new machines with optional engines, were advertised as the '69 Mach 1 models. Paul had chosen the 351 engine with a 4 valve carburetor and took delivery in November '68. The exterior colour was shiny black with a distinctive red stripe running down the side doors and back panels. The Ram Air Induction was specially fitted at Paul's request. The interior was also finished in black with red inserts in the vinyl. The sloping back window had black louvers as an optional extra. Paul had a telephone installed in the centre console. It would be handy when trying to contact Donna at the office. Plus, as a means of staying ahead of the pack, Paul had a specially fitted telescopic camera inserted into the aerial, which allowed images to display on a screen above the centre console. He could see who was following Mach and take appropriate action. The wide tyres were specially reinforced against nails and other sharp objects that Mach was likely to encounter. As a final accessory, Paul had made to his specification, two additional concealed exhausts, set alongside the two main exhausts. These special stainless steel exhausts were not as long, but were equipped with gas. At the touch of a button on the dash, harmful gas was emitted in a cloud of swift moving vapour. All in all, Mach 1 was quite car for it's time.

As the Mach 1 rumbled along towards Oceanside Waters, O'Shea was asking himself who actually lived at apartment 3A.

Turning off the Freeway, Paul drove into Oceanview Drive and within minutes was turning the Mach 1 into the parking lot of Seascape Apartments.

Walking over to the main entrance, O'Shea decided to check out the names on the tenant directory. Sometimes these were provided but perhaps with this place, being a bit high class, this information may not be available.

Opening the glass swing doors of the entrance foyer, Paul could see no board on the blue and white painted walls displaying names. *Damn,* he thought. He paused for a moment, and looked back to the empty wall. *There's no apartment directory, so I wonder if Ben came into the foyer or went straight to the stairs to go up to apartment 3A? Surely he would have thought twice. I guess he was anxious to meet this elusive telephone caller regardless. Hmmm,* he speculated to himself. Paul's eyes suddenly fell upon a small passageway leading off to a door at the end. The sign on the wall read "Janitor", with an arrow pointing down the passageway.

Paul walked down the narrow passageway and came to a blue and white painted wood door. Knocking loudly, Paul waited for a response.

No answer.

'Hello, is anyone there?' Paul called out. He could hear something, or someone, moving around inside.

The door slowly opened. There stood a small man, probably in his early fifties, from Paul's guess.

'Yeah?' the weedy man said in an annoyed tone. He had on dark trousers, an off-white singlet and, surprisingly, a kaleidoscope tie hanging loosely around his scrawny neck. Grey chest hairs sprung out like wire from the man's shallow frame. A cigarette drooped from the mouth and a can of beer was held precariously in his right hand.

'Hi, I wonder if you can tell me who lives at apartment 3A?'

'Who wants to know?' the tiny man hissed.

'Look pal, either you know or you don't know. Would this help?' Paul took out his wallet and waived a ten dollar bill in the face of the sweaty man.

'Might help a bit!' Grabbing the note from O'Shea, the chap sucked some more on the cigarette and changed his posture so that he was now leaning against the door frame of the room. He stared at Paul, looking him up and down suspiciously.

'So, who lives there?' Showing his business card to the not-so-helpful janitor, Paul awaited an answer.

The janitor shoved the note into his right trouser pocket. 'What's it to you? Nosing around here, like some lousy cop! Private Investigator, huh? What's this all about anyway?' The man's speech was drawled and he was unsteady on his slipper clad feet. He looked down quickly again at Paul's card, and appeared to become unsettled.

'Come on, don't give me that, pal. You know who lives there, spit it out!' barked Paul at the hapless creature before him.

'No one! Now get lost!' snarled the janitor, as he moved back into the room and tried to slam the door – but Paul was too quick.

'Oh no you don't, bud!' Paul grabbed the left arm of the janitor and spun the man around to face him.

The janitor was stunned and his cigarette dropped from his lips. Paul began to twist the bony arm around the janitor's back. The man howled in pain.

'Alright, just let go my arm!"'

Paul continued to hold the arm in a tight clasp. 'Come on, you know who it is!' Paul boomed through clenched teeth. 'Give me the name, or I will break this arm of yours, pal. Don't think I won't, 'cause I will. Got it!'

The janitor was beyond struggling any more, his strength was diminishing. His face was distorted with agony and had become red. The beer can had also been dropped onto the carpeted floor of the room.

'A guy came here a day before that detective was killed.'

'And ...' encouraged Paul, still holding the janitor's arm with a vice-like grip.

'He gave me some green bills to keep my mouth shut. He wanted the key for apartment 3A ...' The janitor had to pause for breath. 'That apartment was vacant, so I gave the guy the key. That's all I know. I swear, man!' He tried to move forward but Paul kept up the pressure on the man's arm.

'Did this guy give you a name? What did he look like?' Paul was furious and was not going to give up until he had extracted the maximum information from this deadbeat.

'I don't know his name. He didn't tell me. I didn't ask him.'

No I bet you didn't, you sleazy rat. The dough was all you were interested in, thought Paul.

'Okay, what did this guy look like. Come on, don't hold back or I will wring this arm off its socket, buddy boy!' shouted Paul.

The janitor was now beginning to double over in extreme bodily suffering. His balance was failing and the arm was aching with a gnawing pain he had never experienced before – or would want to for that matter. Saliva began to ooze out of the man's twisted mouth. 'He … he was tall … but I c-c-couldn't see his face clearly … ''. The man stammered. "He had sunglasses on, so I couldn't get a look at his f-f-face.'

Paul proceeded to hold the arm firmly.'What else? Quick, or I will break the arm, man!' growled Paul. Not one to be messed around with, Paul still knew the tactics from his police detective days.

'He drove a white Chevrolet Camaro.'

Nothing more was forthcoming.

'Did you see him come back the night of the killing?' asked Paul with a curious tone in his voice.

'No, I didn't! I was watching the t-t-television. There was a program on about the a-a-astronauts who were going to land on the moon.' The helpless janitor gasped for breath and then spoke on. 'I w-w-watched that till after 10 … th-th-then went to bed.'

Before Paul could ask anymore, the janitor pleaded with Paul to release his arm.

'Please pal, let me go. I don't know any more, honest!'

The features of this lean man were disfigured with pain. He was going to collapse now, the knees suddenly gave way and the limp body fell to the ground.

'What about the key? Did this guy return the key?' snapped Paul.

The janitor was moaning now. His thoughts were racing. He wondered when Paul would give up.

Paul prodded the slumped body of the janitor in the ribs. The man gave a shudder and rolled over, face down on the carpet.

'You have not answered my question, Mr Janitor. Was the key returned?' said the persistent Paul.

'No, it wasn't! Leave me alone, I've done nothing wrong!' the janitor screeched, hot tears streaming down his pink face as he lay on the ground shaking.

'Because of you, an innocent man lost his life that night, you low life bastard,' Paul hissed. 'I hope you rot in hell.'

With that, Paul saw an opportunity. Stepping over the body of the janitor, now completely unable to function, Paul wondered if there was a duplicate set of keys somewhere in the foul smelling room. *Swell*, he thought as his eyes fell upon a board on a wall with keys.

Moving over to the wall, Paul could see that the keys were in fact duplicates for the apartments. Taking the keys for apartment 3A, Paul was about to leave the room, when something told him to pick up the keys to apartment 3B. He propped the janitor up against the wall and then walked up the stairs to the apartments.

Fortunately no one was around – the coast was clear.

Opening the door of 3A, Paul went inside and began to check for any clues of a previous visitor. But everything seemed to be normal –the bed was made up, the shower was dry and the towels were still fresh. *Nothing here, better check out 3B*, he thought.

Paul stood at the door of 3B. He paused for a moment, looking around for any sign of life – negative.

Walking through the apartment, Paul satisfied himself that whoever lived here must be at work. Everything appeared to be in order. *Hang on a minute,* thought Paul. *What about the kitchen trash can?* Peering into the trash, Paul could see that it was clean and totally empty. Mystified, he went into the bedrooms; checking for clothes and other personal items. The bathroom was clear of toiletries. *Absolutely clean as a whistle,* he thought. *This place hasn't been used either. So we have two apartments next to each other, and both vacant. Interesting.* Paul's mind was ticking over fast.

Just as he went to exit the apartment, his eyes latched onto a small table near the entry door. *Well, well! What is this?* he mused. Paul picked up the spent cigarette stub in the ashtray. It was a dark brown colour, possibly a small cigar. Embossed into the paper was a symbol which looked like five tiny stars. He smelt it. *Yep, it sure is a small cigar. No trace of lipstick, so could be a male smoker.* Paul took out of his jacket a small plastic pouch. Placing the stub into the pouch, and sealing it up, he put the pouch back into his jacket. *Evidence left behind by our assassin, no doubt,* he concluded.

As Paul locked the apartment, he made a mental note of the vicinity. Standing in the recessed doorway of 3B, Paul realised that if the perpetrator were hiding in 3B, the person would have a bird's eye view of Ben standing further along the balcony, closer to 3A. Instantly, Paul was perplexed. *Why wasn't this cigarette stub picked up for analysis by the forensic boys? Surely 3B was searched as well!* he thought. *It doesn't make sense at all. They must know that both apartments are vacant.*

Paul knew that he could not squeeze any more information out of the janitor, so he hurried down to the entrance foyer and left the keys on a sofa. He had no intention of taking the keys back to this horrid little money-grabbing mole. With purpose in his steps, he walked over to his car.

As Paul drove the Mach 1 out of the Seascape Apartments complex, our dubious janitor was making a phone call. Having recovered enough strength to drag himself over to the desk, Mr Janitor was successful to reach the telephone and dial a number, with his right hand. Just as well he was right handed, the left arm was utterly useless.

A familiar voice answered the phone.

Stuttering like a jilted clown, the greedy janitor blurted down the receiver, 'Someone h-h-has been here asking q-q-questions. H-h-he's a private detective, calls himself Paul O'Shea. I-I-I think that he went to search the a-a-apartment. I didn't tell him anything, honest, I didn't!' wailed the shaking man. The whimpering man thought that Paul had only searched apartment 3A. Not checking the duplicate keys taken from the board, was a big mistake for the clumsy janitor. However, our other "friend" had some better ideas …

'Keep your cool, I will be over shortly to sort things out,' said the calm and sinister sounding voice on the other end of the line. 'In the meantime, have a drink on me. I have a little reward for your loyalty.' Clicking knuckles, the malevolent mastermind on the receiving end of the call prepared to make their journey to Seascape Apartments.

Within a short space of time, Mr Janitor was sleeping permanently. A bullet through the head had really sorted him out well. Such a nice reward from our evil genius.

CHAPTER 3

TT EXPOSED

It was nearing midday when Paul and Donna met again back at the office.

Opening up the sandwiches Donna had bought for them both to devour, Paul started to eat ravenously.

'Well, firstly how did you get on, boss?' enquired Donna, sitting in Paul's office.

'Take a look at this,' Paul muttered, his mouth full of beef and ketchup sandwich, 'I found this in apartment 3B.' He placed the plastic pouch in front of Donna. 'Someone was in the apartment, and yet *that* was left behind when the forensics scaled the apartment. According to the dozy janitor, apartment 3A is supposed to be vacant. Well, I find out that apartment 3B is also vacant! Seems odd doesn't it?'

'It does indeed,' agreed Donna, pursing her lips.

'Surely they would have seen the stub in the ashtray. So, I ask the question. Was that apartment actually searched or not? I'm sure you get my meaning ... ' Paul sat back in his vinyl chair.

'Hmmm … could that stub have been left by the killer? Yet, that was five weeks ago! So the police didn't check the apartment?' asked the curious Donna, taking a bite of a cheese and tomato sandwich.

'Seems like it. Ben was killed near the entrance to 3A, so I think our killer was positioned in 3B. Whoever it was, must have known that those apartments were vacant.' Paul then proceeded to tell Donna what the janitor had told him, not mentioning the duress he placed on the seedy character. Changing the subject from Seascape Apartments, Paul turned his attention to his trusty secretary. 'How did you get on, any light on this Morrow woman?'

'Yes, I have had quite a successful morning. Before I go on, we're going to visit a sister of this Maryanne Myles Morrow at 9.30 a.m. tomorrow. Her name is Felinda Bentine, she's the eldest sister of Maryanne. Lives at Cricklewood, at a place called "Lorraway". I have the address with me.'

'Good stuff, Donna,' nodded Paul.

'Apparently Maryanne Myles Morrow was the fifth daughter of Hendon and Myosotia Bentine. Both parents had been on the stage and starred in silent films. There were other children as well, but I'll get to that later.' Flipping over her note pad pages, Donna spoke on in an excited tone of voice, 'Maryanne changed her acting name. She kept Maryanne, but took Myles from her maternal grandmother and Morrow was her mother's name. Now from what I can piece together from newspaper articles and other records from the time, Maryanne was supposed to be in a relationship with Charles Osborne. Maryanne worked at First National Pictures Corporation as a highly sought after actress, where Osborne was a producer. Apparently she went to his bungalow in Hollywood on the night of August 4, 1922. She states that it was about 7 p.m. and then departed at around 8 p.m. The next time we have her whereabouts is at the home of Maybelle Normansen, where she arrived just after 9 p.m. and left around 10.45 p.m. So there's gap in Maryanne's movements …'

An intrigued O'Shea leaned in a little closer.

'That could easily have given her the opportunity to come back to Osborne's home and kill him. Maryanne was not living at her parent's home, she rented a bungalow on Beverly Boulevard. It seems that Maryanne did not go back to her home after leaving Osborne. No one saw her or can verify her movements. The police charged her with Osborne's death, but the case was dismissed on the grounds of insufficient evidence. So no trial was instigated –'

'Interesting …' Paul cut in.

'Yes, very … but the stigma that followed caused Maryanne's popularity to harshly decline. She made her last film in 1924 and has never been heard of since. Although, there was a rumour that Maryanne was seen in 1928 at a celebrity dinner for the silent screen stars. The dinner was acknowledging the stars who had come through the silent era, with the advent of the talkies taking over …' Donna paused and glanced up at O'Shea. 'Well, many disappeared overnight but some did make the transition to sound quite well. I did check the Registry of Births, Deaths & Marriages but can find no record of Maryanne whatsoever!'

Eyebrows lowered, Paul stroked his chin as he listened carefully to his clever secretary's detailed report. Having finished his sandwiches, he opened his bottom desk drawer and took out a large packet of popcorn. Opening the bag, Paul took a handful of popcorn and began to consume it greedily.

Donna flicked a page over in her note pad. 'Now, regarding Osborne ... he was very opposed to the use of narcotics, and he made himself pretty unpopular with some people in the film industry. He was 53 years of age, single and had become a mentor and confidante to the much younger Maryanne. Osborne's entire estate was left to Maryanne Myles Morrow, including his home.' Donna waited for Paul to comment.

'So she did have a motive for murder! Money or revenge, perhaps? Another lover comes along, so Maryanne kills Osborne. However, if Maryanne knew about Osborne's Will, then surely she would realise that would incriminate her for his murder. You have to think it through from both angles.' Paul was thinking out loud.

Donna, realising that Paul had ended his words, went on with her details. 'Anyway, I took the bull by the horns and looked up the telephone directory, and saw that the name Bentine was still residing in the Hollywood area. So I took the plunge and phoned, and spoke to Felinda. She did seem stiff and unwilling to talk, but in the end, she did accept my request to come and talk with her about Maryanne.

Felinda has not had any contact with Maryanne, nor does she know where she is.' Donna stopped her speech and gave Paul a direct searching gaze. 'I think we may have stumbled upon our mystery writer "TT", boss!' stated Donna with enthusiasm.

'Yeah!' Paul sat bolt upright in his chair and waited for Donna to continue.

'After Felinda was born, there were twin daughters, with the names of Tryphena and Tryphosa. The next was Clara, then Maryanne and the youngest was Alyssa. All the girls were involved with acting, but Maryanne and Alyssa were the ones to show the greatest potential. So my hunch is that "TT" is none other than Tryphena and Tryphosa.' Donna seemed pleased with her deduction.

'Could well be. It does fit in, but why would the twins send the note to Ben? He didn't even know they existed,' replied Paul O'Shea, scratching his temple. 'With any luck, the twins may still be alive and can shed some light on the situation. Of course, it may not be them at all. We don't even know where they live! They could have married and changed their name.'

'Yes, I know. It is a long shot, but it was just a thought that came to mind when I read about the twin's names,' replied Donna. 'I've made some copies of the newspaper articles and other records, in case you wanted to read them yourself. Quite a lot of publicity about the murder. There are some photos of Maryanne. She looks really beautiful. Pity all this scandal blighted her career and obviously her life too,' finished Donna, with some meaning in her well-spoken voice.

Paul picked up the articles and saw a publicity shot of the lovely face of Maryanne Myles Morrow, sitting outside with her sisters and parents, at the family home of Lorraway in 1920. All the girls were very desirable ladies. The family appeared quite at ease, enjoying an afternoon lunch under the shade of two large umbrellas.

O'Shea read briefly the record of the coroner's report and sundry newspaper extracts, relating to the death of Osborne. The press had a field day with Maryanne Myles Morrow, referring to her as a "cold blooded scheming killer", right down to mentioning that she was a "revengeful lover". A warrant had been issued for Morrow's arrest, and she was subsequently charged with murder. The case was eventually rejected, after much wrangling from the lawyers, who represented Maryanne. No trial was allowed. It was not any wonder that Morrow had decided to disappear from society, after such vicious and unsubstantiated comments had been emblazoned across the tabloids.

After discussing some more details, Donna gave O'Shea a list of the possible suspects at the time of the Osborne murder.

'Apart from Morrow, there was a man called Norman Lindsay, a Costume Manager at the same studio, who had called on Osborne the night of the murder, just before 6 p.m. Osborne's manservant, a Buswell Clancy, verified that Lindsay left the home after a short stay, around 6.15 p.m. I checked on Lindsay, he died in '32. I haven't been able to trace Clancy. An actress, by the name of Clarene Cremorne, also went to the Osborne home, some time after Lindsay, but left at around 6.45 p.m., also verified by the manservant. Once again, I haven't been able to trace Cremorne, but she could have had another name. You know how they changed their names to be more agreeable to the public?'

Paul nodded his comprehension.

'Then a couple arrived just as Cremorne was leaving, a Mr and Mrs Nathan Hummerstein. They were there only about 15 minutes and then left. This was likewise confirmed by the manservant. Nathan Hummerstein died in 1947 but I can't seem to trace Mrs Hummerstein. Her first name was not specified. Anyway, not long after the Hummersteins left, the manservant was given the night off by Osborne and he left the home to go out with his girlfriend to the movies. Morrow came alone to see Osborne at 7 p.m., and departed, according to her statement, just before 8 p.m. Osborne was still alive. Morrow's whereabouts cannot be corroborated after 8 p.m., and before she arrived at the home of Maybelle Normansen around 9 p.m. Morrow was unable to account for that time period, hence the police were sure that Morrow had come back to the Osborne residence, and shot him twice through the chest, as he sat on the sofa in the front living room. If it wasn't Morrow, then who was it that came unannounced and shot Osborne some time later? Whoever it was, he knew, to let them into the house!'

O'Shea sat forward. 'Good work Donna, you've covered a

lot in that time. Gives us something to work on. Let's hope that this dame Felinda Bentine can shed some light on Maryanne!'

'I have my doubts about her, boss. She seemed pretty cagey to me on the phone, but I could be wrong,' replied Donna with doubt in her voice. Donna went back to her desk to complete some paperwork and follow up some telephone answer messages.

O'Shea reclined back in his chair, and gave some thought to this unusual set of events. *Why had this mystery person TT, suddenly mailed this message to Ben Driscoll? Such a lapse of time had past since the murder took place. I know it is a stab in the dark, but we will have to try to determine if any of those remaining suspects are still alive, after 47 years. That was probably quite impossible!* Paul thought with a wry smile on his face.

Having read the various accounts regarding the case, the afternoon was drawing on, and Paul's mind was in need of a break. Also, his eyes needed respite from the reading he had done.

'Plenty to read in all that lot, wasn't there!' exclaimed Donna from the far corner of the office.

'Sure was,' replied Paul, stretching his arms.

'The police were ready to nail Morrow with the murder. I guess I can see their reasoning. Morrow could not verify her movements after leaving Osborne's house.'

Donna had been pondering whether to ask Paul home for a meal. There was something else that she wanted to discuss with Paul, so a meal was the perfect pretext to invite Paul home. As her mother used to say, 'Honey, the only way to a man's heart, is through his stomach! Believe you me!'

'How about you come to my place for a meal tonight? I'm cooking Mediterranean chicken rollups with steamed Spanish rice, and cherry soufflé for dessert. Does that appeal to you?'

Paul was completely taken back. Donna had never asked him to her apartment before.

'W-well yes …' he stammered. 'That sounds great. I'll bring some red wine.'

'Okay, deal. See you at 7? Oh, don't be late otherwise I'll eat it all myself, I'm starving!' Donna giggled.

What to wear, what to wear, Paul thought as he rummaged through his clothes – not that he had much to choose from anyway.

Finally stepping out in a loose fitting navy blue and white striped bowling shirt, navy blue trousers and white loafers, O'Shea took on the appearance of a "man about town".

Stopping off to purchase a bottle of Cabernet Merlot from the liquor store, Paul drove the Mustang to Donna's apartment situated in Cedar Grove.

The night was splendidly adorned, as Donna and Paul sat out on the balcony. The stars shone down their brilliance and the moon was resplendent in all its translucent glory.

The air was scented with the aroma of jasmine trailing over the balcony railings and delighting the senses of all who breathed its magic perfume.

During the course of the delicious meal, Donna was chatting away and ensuring that Paul had ample to eat and drink. She wore an elegant halter neck dress of the softest lime shade. The neckline was lined with white piping, as were the short sleeves. A simple pearl necklace hung around her neck and she had white sandals on her feet. Donna had placed her hair into a bun, and swirled the mass into a high ball. A ribbon of the same lime shade, supported her much admired hair. She had placed a frangipani flower into her hair as well. The fragrance was very pleasant and added a calming effect to the evening. It was the first occasion for Paul to really see who Donna actually was! Not just the secretary he had hired, but a real lady who had emotions and displayed caring qualities, that he, shamefully, had never noticed before.

After the completion of the meal, the couple were relaxing in a swing chair on the balcony, staring out onto the waving palm trees that lined the road beneath them. The gentle breeze, and the aroma of the distant ocean was quite distinct, providing a sensation of wondrous peace. Each had their own thoughts to linger over.

The record player was softly playing the Nancy Sinatra hit from the 1967 film, *You Only Live Twice*. The words were poignant to both of them, as each listened intently to the meaningful lyrics.

You only live twice or so it seems
One life for yourself and one for your dream
You drift through the years and life seems tame
Till one dream appears and love is it's name.

Donna was the first to break their silent reverie.

Turning her luscious head towards Paul, she softly touched his hand that was close to hers. Taking Paul's hand gently, she looked up into his soulful grey blue eyes. 'Paul, there's something that I have been meaning to talk to you about for some time, but I have never got around to it … '

Paul moved his body slightly, and focused his eyes onto Donna's face. The shadow of the moon had softly covered one side of her face. Her radiant features had arrested Paul's intense attention. Paul could see that Donna was quite earnest.

'What's that?' asked a curious Paul.

'Well, firstly. I told you I was 26 when applying for the job. I was actually 32. I thought you would want someone younger, so I lied about my age … ' Donna's eyes searched Paul's face for a sign of annoyance, but saw nothing like that at all.

'Well, that is alright, Donna. I would have employed you anyway, with your references! I was not concerned about your age.' He turned her face towards his and they stared at each other as though the whole world were miles away, and just they existed for this moment.

'Paul, there is something else I would like to talk to you about. Hear what I have to say …' She placed her finger over his lips.

Donna then opened her heart to Paul – telling him of her failed romance and the real reason why she had moved from New Jersey. Paul listened to Donna's explanation with intentness. As Donna was ending her discourse, her mood became quiet and melancholy. Swallowing hard, Donna spoke on. 'My mom gave me some advice when I thought my life was in ruins. She said, "Donna, remember that yesterday is a cancelled cheque, you won't have that prospect again. Tomorrow is a promissory note, your dreams and hopes are just beyond your reach, but today is cash. Spend it wisely!". I think you know what I am trying to express Paul. Barbara is gone, that life is past. Now is for living. We can look at the closed door so long that we fail to see the door that has been opened for us.' Donna had tears in her hazel eyes, and pressed Paul's hand into hers. Paul then saw the meaning of these words, and kissed Donna passionately.

The moon was so delighted that it shone its eternal magnificence upon the couple. The stars twinkled and a far away asteroid spun stardust, like gossamer threads, through the luminous heavens, leaving a trail of striking dusty brilliance.

CHAPTER 4

A MEETING WITH MILLICENT MAUD

Wednesday morning was heralded with a sunrise like no other. The sky was painted with colours of rich vermillion and vivid violet. Cumulus clouds warned of an approaching storm and flocks of migrating birds were silhouetted across this scene of painterly skill. Flying in perfect formation, their mission was to make use of the strong currents in the clouds, and travel to safer lands. Bands of yellow sunshine streamed down like arrows from the firmament and lit up the ground with welcoming warmth.

O'Shea and Donna were en route to their destination of Cricklewood, and their appointment with Felinda Bentine.

Cricklewood, was one of the original settlements in the very early days of Hollywood. Only the elite and wealthy could afford the grandiose homes and elaborate gardens. They built mansions to out do their neighbours and display their wealth. Now, not many of these illustrious homes still remained. Majority had suffered the fate of being demolished, due to the large scale cost to keep these homes in pristine condition.

The Mustang drove through the open ornate gates of Lorraway and into the quartz pebbled driveway. The residence was a jewel in the crown of "Hollywood Royalty", no expense spared and lavishly cared for. It was indeed an imposing building. Seven pink marble Corinthian columns supported a massive archway and tiled roof. A silver blue 1965 Lincoln Continental with suicide doors, was parked at the far side of the house. The Georgian style sash window frames were painted a bright and stunning Prussian blue colour. Mellow stonework had been expertly maintained. The building was two storey, with attic windows, each with their distinctive blue gables. Above the portico was a plaster plaque, set into the stucco background, displaying "A.D. 1909".

'Wow,' muttered Paul under his breath as he alighted from his Mustang. 'This place sure is something.'

Donna was equally impressed, as she focused on the immaculate gardens, with formal hedges and statues of ladies in alluring poses, strategically placed in various beds.

Swathes of vibrant blue agapanthus heads swayed in the gentle wind. An arbour of white rambling roses were planted in a lawn area. The intoxicating sweet smell was evident to anyone near their proximity. Other herbaceous borders were proclaiming their array of colourful blooms and structure.

Walking up to the double cedar front doors, Paul pressed the buzzer, and stepped back in expectation. Within seconds, a man opened the right hand door - his face plastered with disapproval, and perhaps displeasure as well. His tall frame was imposing and gave an impression of being somewhat sinister too.

Paul introduced Donna and himself, and mentioned their appointment with Miss Felinda Bentine.

'Wait here,' came the sharp reply.

Donna could see that the butler's right hand was moving constantly, as though he was unable to control its involuntary movements.

Paul raised his eyebrows at the retreating figure. Donna was also surprised at the sour reaction. This butler, as he was attired, certainly made you feel unwelcome!

'Follow me,' the butler offered coldly upon his return.

Donna and Paul were ushered indoors to a light and airy foyer. The pale lavender walls had niches containing busts of various Roman deities and gods. The cornices surrounding the room were painted the softest hue of green. The effect was calming, yet quite striking. The plaster ceiling was embellished with Greek mythological gods and goddesses, casting their eyes onto the onlooker below.

'This way!' The butler's voice was authoritative and brisk.

Donna and Paul were led down an enormously wide hallway. A thick, long antique carpet runner adorned the centre of the wood floors. As the butler walked ahead of them, the couple noticed he was limping slightly, as if injured in the right leg.

Now stopping at an exquisitely carved wooden door, the

butler opened it and indicated for Donna and Paul to enter. He departed and glided away noiselessly.

Standing at a wide bow window was a tall angular looking woman. Her face was long and the empty emerald green eyes resembled large marbles in their sockets. The facial appearance was not unattractive, but the mouth was etched with severity. Paul dubbed her "Sour face Adios". She was plainly dressed, in a brown tweed skirt, white blouse and open pale green cardigan. The quality of the garments was clearly evident, even though the wearer gave the clothes a hint of restraint. Light brown pumps were placed on her oversized feet. A strand of pearls hung around the neck. A light pink lipstick coloured the thin lips.

Possibly in her early seventies, thought Paul quickly, *but not someone to cross swords with!*

The lady walked closer to them.

Moments before, Felinda Bentine had much to contemplate, as she stood gazing out the drawing room window, waiting the arrival of her visitors. She had told herself she would play it safe and keep things close to her chest. Raking up the past about Maryanne – the little minx had caused enough furore. Felinda didn't want any more muck flung about. She stared carefully at Paul, trying not to turn up her nose at his hand-me-down suit and a dreadful cut. Her eyes then fell on Donna. She quickly raised her eyebrows, noticing Donna's low-cut blouse and mini skirt. Not impressed with the couple in the slightest, Felinda was determined to have them out of her house as soon as

possible – they wouldn't return to her lair in any hurry.
Paul immediately introduced Donna and himself.

'Mr O'Shea, do be seated,' was the blunt reply. No
handshake was forthcoming.

Felinda Bentine did not introduce herself, well, after all,
everyone knew Felinda Bentine – from the field mouse at
the front gate to the roosting pair of birds in the chimney!

Giving Donna yet another "once over", eyeing her from
head to toe, the austere woman seated herself in the wing
back chair opposite Paul. Donna was left standing. No offer
of another chair was forthcoming, although there were
plenty of other chairs scattered around the expansive room.
You could cut the air with a knife, silence enveloped the
room like a devouring claimant.

Adjusting herself in her chair, Felinda Bentine finally
spoke again. 'What is it that you wish to discuss, Mr O'Shea?'
She gave Paul a discerning look, but was certainly on guard.

Realising that he had better "bite the bullet" and get
straight to the point, Paul chose to ask about Maryanne.
'We are trying to locate Maryanne, your sister. It seems that
someone may know her whereabouts. Do the letters "TT"
mean anything to you, Miss Bentine?' Paul watched the face
of Felinda Bentine with careful scrutiny. There was a very
slight twitch of the upper right eyelid, but it was gone in an
instant. *Ah ha!* thought Paul. *Some recognition!*

'No, I can't say that I know those initials at all,' came the
lying reply.

Paul could tell Miss Bentine was fully aware just who

TT was. He chose his words carefully. 'It's just that we have reason to believe that Maryanne may still be alive … I'm sure you would wish to know where Maryanne is after all these years, Miss Bentine?'

Playing the game with expertise, the woman opposite Paul was shrewd and calculating.

'What has instigated the enquiry into Maryanne's disappearance, may I ask?' came Miss Bentine's brittle words.

'Information has come to light that may help in locating Maryanne,' Paul replied, not revealing too much.

'That is very interesting, given the fact that Maryanne has not been seen for heavens know, how long! And you think that you can trace Maryanne after all this time? One scrappy bit of information, from some person calling themselves "TT"! Well good luck to you, that is all I can say, Mr O'Shea!' was Felinda Bentine's incisive reply. Pulling her head back to face Paul, she gave a look of utter smugness.

Okay, the bitch is playing hard, so I have to dig in deeper, thought Paul. 'I didn't say that it was a person,' he then said with some firmness in his voice.

'Well, you implied that it was!' Miss Bentine snapped back, her eyes boring into Paul like sharp needles.

Donna fidgeted a little, watching the game of cat and mouse unfold.

Not good, pal! Have to cool it a bit, thought Paul. Smiling now, and letting the lady opposite him have the upper hand, Paul enquired about Maryanne's involvement with the Osborne murder. 'Surely the police are better equipped than you to ask me about that! That is all in the past. It was quite clear that Maryanne killed Charles Osborne, and then flitted off to some remote destination to escape retribution! How would I know where she is?'

With that juncture, Miss Bentine tutted and pursed her lower lip.

Shit, I have to get this conversation back on track or I am finished with this dame, thought Paul. 'Sorry, Miss Bentine. What I mean is, what can you tell me about Maryanne from her younger days?' Paul played his charm. 'After all, you are the only one who would know everything about Maryanne, her friends and what she did and where she went.'

The appeal to emotion played dividends, and Felinda Bentine opened her locked up feelings. Well, what a treat she decided to dish out!

Dealing with a staff matter first, with startling effect, Miss Bentine called out to the maid that lingered in the corner of the over dressed room. 'Parker, there is no need for you to stand there like some morbid and morose ninny! Mr O'Shea will not be staying long, so you can leave!'

'Yes ma'am,' Parker muttered and then hurried from the room.

Settling into her chair, Felinda Bentine appeared to be quite pleased with herself, and began her lecture.

'Maryanne was dearly loved by my parents, I must stress this, before I proceed. We were all provided for exceptionally well, any thing we wished for, was given to us abundantly. My father was a film producer, and before that he was a talented actor. Mother was also an exceptional actress in live theatre and later on film. I am the eldest, so naturally a lot was expected of me, and more so, when my beloved parents never came to terms with the tragic death of Alyssa. She was just 19, had only been married five months to dear Grayden Plantoleggia, when diphtheria took her very quickly. Grayden took his life just a week later, so overcome with the loss of Alyssa. My parents then immersed themselves in their own world of Roman and Greek deities and the Greek tragedies. Acting out their parts was a way of consoling themselves with the loss of Alyssa. She also had been an actress of some repute, but the star attraction was always Maryanne ...'

Paul leaned forward, listening carefully to Felinda's every word.

'The monetary aspect was now my responsibility as became the running of the house too. My parents were well off, but could not cope with anything apart from acting. Sadly they both died within a month of each other in 1927. I did have one brief claim to fame, when I starred opposite Rudolpho Vincenzo, in the silent film titled, *The Maid from Ancona* in 1920. It was shortly after this that Alyssa died, and my life changed dramatically. Maryanne was a born natural for the stage and then silent films. My parents encouraged her to perform and had her tutored as well. Always a flirt where men were concerned, Maryanne fell in love with a lad by the name of Johnny Appleseed. She had starred opposite him in a film, that was hugely successful in 1919, and the pair were feted up and down the country. Maryanne played Venus, who falls in love with Adonis, played by Johnny. Johnny was the same age as Maryanne, but had developed a liking for cocaine. He carried a pouch around with him, had the stuff for breakfast, lunch and dinner. Sprinkled it on his cereals, I understand. Talk about being a cereal killer! Stupid boy. Revolting diet! Well, of course he turned up his toes and raced off to heaven without a care in the world, leaving Maryanne in the lurch, as men always do, I might add. Maryanne was heart broken! So she starts jumping backyard fences in search of another heartthrob! Then she meets Charles Osborne, her saving grace! This was after the death of "cocaine Johnny", sometime in early '21.'

Paul raised his eyebrows, but chose not to say a word *Get off my neck, you old dame,* he thought. *I want to spit! Was Miss Bentine jealous of Maryanne? Quite possibly. Having her own career cut short to take over the running of the house plus consider her parents mental state. That was a lot for her to undertake. Were these real happenings, or just some artful scheme of words to deflect me off course? She is literally amazing this woman. No shame or consideration for others, total disrespect!*

During this discourse, Donna still standing, had been taking notes.

Without any warning, Felinda Bentine turned her attention to Donna. 'As for you,' she said with a vicious tone, 'I would suggest you cease making those ridiculous notes. Mr O'Shea is more than capable of coping with matters himself, without the likes of you standing there like some silent sentinel. And what's more, get rid of that pencil, biros have been invented. I suggest you get yourself one quick smart! As for that obsolete note pad which came out of the ark, throw it in the trash. You certainly won't be in the running for "Miss Efficiency 1969", I can tell you that! Now hop outside and go play on the swings with Tryphena and Tryphosa. Make yourself useful out there!'

Donna's jaw hung down almost to the ground in total shock at these spiteful words.

Paul went to get up from his chair, but Donna whizzed out of the room with her handbag. Fury was in her face, but she had managed to control her emotions.

'Insolent little hussy, that one! I can tell them a mile off. Watch her, she is dynamite!' spat the "Queen of Lorraway".

Paul was not going to let that comment go unanswered. He spoke rapidly in a terse tone, 'I do not think your words are appropriate, nor warranted. Donna is my secretary, and was doing as I instructed.'

'Well, suit yourself, Mr O'Shea. Can't say I warned you!'

Glaring at each other, seated in their respective chairs. Paul was still at the mercy of this wretched creature.

Felinda Bentine was rather pleased with herself – no way would they return.

'You were relating about Charles Osborne ...' Trying to get the conversation back on track was going to be difficult. Paul was angry, but knew he had to hear some more details. Or was it just all piffle?

Felinda recommenced her story with great aplomb. 'Charles Osborne became like a father figure to Maryanne, she adored him and hung onto his every word. Single he was, absolute rubbish! They say that, men do, just to convince an innocent and halfwit girl like Maryanne into believing they are the right one. We tried to talk her out of it, but no, no, nothing would do! She had to have Charles, hell or high water! Well he indulged Maryanne, I admit, and gave her expert advice for her acting roles. Then that night came when Maryanne went to his home …' Felinda looked to the ceiling, as if searching for words.

'Yes …' urged Paul.

'Whatever happened,' huffed Felinda, 'we will never know. She must have had a gun with her, or Osborne had the weapon. She does the deed, and then flutters off, and is unable to account for her movements for a considerable time period. Everyone else had alibis, so naturally the police arrested Maryanne. I think Osborne wanted to ditch Maryanne for someone else. Maryanne would have been so distressed, overcome with the thought of losing Osborne, she shoots him, cold hard dead in the market! Well not literally, but you know what I mean, Mr O'Shea? As for her whereabouts, I do not know. Maryanne has never made any contact since the scandal, and that was in 1922!' Sitting back in her comfortable wing back chair, Felinda Bentine was satisfied with her account of Maryanne. She eyed Paul with total disdain, but displayed a very conceited attitude. A smile of the utmost insincerity was plastered on her face.

Gee, this woman does not like men. Was she jilted by some

man? Well, he did himself a favour! thought Paul, trying to suppress a smile. O'Shea quickly recalled the other three sisters. Altering the subject away from Maryanne, O'Shea raised the topic of the other sisters. 'Do Tryphena and Tryphosa still live here? I gather so from your earlier comment. What happened to Clara?' Paul was curious to see Felinda's reaction to these questions.

'Of course Tryphena and Tryphosa live here! What did you think, that I had done away with them? They are simple girls, Mr O'Shea. Some would say delinquent, others would say eccentric scatterbrains. I look after them, they are well provided for. I can assure you that!' replied Felinda in a stern, reproachful tone 'But sadly, as for Clara, she died when she was only 25 years old. Consumption, hmmm …' Dropping her head down, Felinda was supposed to be tearful, and drew out a white handkerchief from the sleeve of her cardigan, dabbing her nose. Raising her head, Felinda carried on, 'Yes, very sad. Died in Switzerland seeking treatment.'

One last punch, just to rattle this bitch! thought Paul. 'Is it possible to speak with the twins?' he grinned.

'No, it is not in their best interests,' Felinda said in a tone of rebuke. 'The girls adored Maryanne, and as for mentioning her name, it would be very upsetting for them. Now good day to you!' Her words lacked any personal warmth. 'Jedson, will you show Mr O'Shea out, please?'

Paul had enough information for the time being. His head was pounding and he longed for some fresh air. He was pleased to leave this house, it held a dark secret, he was sure of it.

Felinda Bentine sat back and put her head against the chair back, and gloated over her morning's work.

Paul had not noticed the shadow that lingered in the curtained alcove, right near where the "friendly banter" had just taken place. The right hand twitching during the course of the discussion, if you could call it that.

Butler Jedson appeared from behind the curtained alcove, and escorted Paul from the home.

Felinda Bentine's thoughts were running rampant with the utmost bitterness imaginable. At all costs, she would do all in her power to thwart any further probing regarding the horrendous events that caused disgrace and shame to the Bentine name. Sitting on her throne of heavenly grace, she began planning the necessary moves to secure secrecy. Walking over to the large window, she could see Tryphena and Tryphosa speaking with the nuisance pair.

'Right, we will put a prompt halt to that!' she muttered under her breath. 'Jedson!' she called as she hurried out to the hallway. 'Go break up that party at once!'

Out of the house went the obedient puppet-cum-servant to perform his mission.

CHAPTER 5
MEETING TT

Donna hurried outside the home, feeling degraded and furious at the same time. She had only walked a few steps when she was met with an unusual sight. Sitting on the bonnet of the Mustang were two women. They were both waving their hands and kicking their legs, which were encased in patent leather black boots.

'Hello, you must be one of the visitors that were expected.'

Donna increased her pace, and stopped in front of the ladies. 'Hi, I'm Donna.'

One of the ladies said in a friendly and excited manner, 'I'm Tryphena.'

'And I'm Tryphosa,' came the words from the other lady.

Both women displayed smiles of warmth and humour.

Donna realised instantly that these were the twins. They were identical, even down to their clothes and voices. Neither had aged and were remarkably young looking. Clear unwrinkled skin and dancing blue eyes, with a definite twinkle. They were both dressed as though they were members of Mod Squad. Short red leather hot pants with white sleeveless tops. Their dyed red hair had been brushed up into a fizz effect and held by intensive layers of hairspray.

'We like fast cars, this one is hot stuff!' said Tryphosa.

'Hope he doesn't mind us sitting on the bonnet, it's lovely,' Tryphena chortled.

Donna drew closer to the ladies and said with a hushed voice, 'Are you TT?'

'Clever girl, yes we are! Did you see the letter we sent to Ben Driscoll? Tryphosa did it all by herself! Our nice cut out message, wasn't that special, all those colours?' chuckled Tryphena, giving Donna a mischievous smile.

'Yes, I have, but how do you know him?' Donna asked with urgent eagerness in her voice.

'Oh, that is simple, deary. You see, Ben's mom is a friend of ours from long ago. So we sent Ben that letter to try and help him find Maryanne,' replied Tryphosa with her head tilted to one side.

'Do you know who made the telephone call to Ben telling him to go to Seascape Apartments?' Donna then asked, her thoughts were racing with alarm.

'No, we don't know. But you can bet your bottom dollar that Millicent Maud was behind it! Poor Ben is dead now, and he can't help us …' Tryphosa shook her head and gritted her teeth.

'Who is Millicent Maud?' enquired a confused Donna.

'Our big sister, Felinda, of course. That's what we call her.'

'Hehehe,' they both laughed.

'Thinks she owns us, orders us around. Watches our every move! Parker, the maid, keeps us up to date with what's going on. That is how we found out that you were coming this morning. Otherwise we would never know anything,' said Tryphena in an innocent voice.

By this time Paul had left the mansion, and saw the gathering around the Mustang.

A hand had parted back a curtain, and was closely watching proceedings from a safe distance.

'Hello ladies. Keeping the bonnet warm are you?' Paul wasn't overly happy to see them perched there, but for the sake of the investigation, he had to play along with their fun.

'Hello there. Who are you, pet? He's lovely isn't he?' Tryphena flashed a wicked smile at Donna.

Donna was annoyed with Paul regarding the incident in the house, but endeavoured to recover herself without appearing too hostile.

'Ladies, this is my boss, Mr Paul O'Shea. Paul, meet Tryphena and Tryphosa ... the authors of the letter to Ben Driscoll.'

Before Paul could muster a reply, Tryphena said coyly, 'You must be from Ireland. Are you in the Irish Sweepstakes this afternoon?'

'Well, tell the truth, my forebears did come from Ireland but I am not a good punter, when it comes to the horses,' laughed Paul.

'What a pity, we were hoping for a good tip for the 2.30 this afternoon too,' teased Tryphosa.

'How did you know Detective Inspector Ben Driscoll?' enquired Paul with intense interest.

Tryphosa sat forward on the bonnet. 'We were just telling Donna that Ben's mom is a good family friend of ours from way back. We were hoping that young Ben might be able to locate Maryanne. Why, she just left without saying a word ... we do miss her. Felinda won't tell us, so we have tried many times to find out ourselves, but each occasion Felinda discovers what we are up to, and scolds us. And don't trust that Jedson either. He is a nasty piece of work!'

'Yes, that man is beastly,' confirmed Tryphena.

'Can you tell us what you meant by "look north", in your message?' asked Paul, searching the twins' faces.

They both then looked at each other apprehensively before responding,

'We think that Maryanne is living in Canada,' Tryphena whispered. 'We are having our hair done tomorrow at 10 a.m., meet us there say around 11 a.m., when we are finished. It's that new hairdresser, called Walter, at 66 Sunset Strip, just over the road from 77 Sunset Strip. We loved to watch that program on the TV.' Tryphena put her hand over her mouth and suppressed a laugh. 'Then we can go somewhere and talk some more, alright, dear?'

Without warning, the group who were so engrossed in their discussion, had not seen the approaching figure of Jedson.

'Tryphena and Tryphosa, come with me inside. NOW!' His voice was cool and cutting. Standing there with his left arm pointing to the house, he displayed a menacing impression.

'No we won't! We are quite happy with our new friends, so buzz off!' snapped Tryphena.

Jedson minced no matters, and surged forward, grabbing both women from the bonnet with alarming physical power. Holding the arm of each lady, Jedson began to drag the miserable twins toward the den of iniquity.

They both winced with pain, and had to make swift steps to keep up with the marauding monster.

Paul stepped in to stop the heavy weight Jedson. 'Let them go, buddy. They've done nothing wrong!'

Promptly, Jedson released the arm of Tryphosa, and brandished a long threatening knife from inside his butler's coat.

Paul halted, and said, 'Okay pal, keep your cool! I just don't like the way you are handling the ladies!'

'Go, now!' Jedson demanded. He grabbed the twins by the arms yet again and forced them into the house.

Both twins were whimpering and gave Paul and Donna looks of dire distress.

'What can we do, Paul?' asked Donna.

'Not much, I'm afraid. Let's hope we can meet them tomorrow and find out some more. Come on, let's get back to the office.'

Jedson's twitching right hand was acutely obvious.

* * *

'I'm sorry about the way she spoke to you, Donna. You don't deserve that,' said Paul, gripping the steering with one hand.

Donna was still seething. 'Well, you could have said something to the bitch, instead of just sitting there and letting her get away with it!'

'I did tell her off … after you left," Paul responded in defence.

Paul's genuine look of concern was evident, but Donna was still on the negative uptake.

'Yeah, sure you did!' Donna wasn't even directing her eyes on Paul, but looked out of the Mustang window.

'I did speak to her, honest! Come on, I will stop and buy you a coffee, you need it after that scene.'

'Don't want a coffee, I just want to get back to the office.' Donna was clearly offended.

'Yeah, that Bentine woman is an arrogant bitch. I have met some difficult people in my time, but that one takes the cake! So self opinionated and downright offensive. And what's more, she knew about "TT". Did you notice her response?'

Donna chose to ignore Paul's comment. She reached forward and turned on the car radio. Paul decided it was best to leave saying anything else.

'We interrupt this program to bring you an important announcement,' came the voice through the speakers. 'A body of a man was discovered this morning at the Seascape Apartments in Oceanside Waters. He has yet to be formally identified, however, reports suggest that the man was the janitor at the Seascape Apartments. This death is the second within a space of six weeks, since the body of Detective Inspector Ben Driscoll was found there, brutally murdered on June 6. The police are treating this death as suspicious. If any one has any information regarding these deaths, the police are requesting that they come forward immediately and contact the Los Angeles Police Department. We now return you to the Top of the Pops for 1969.' Music blared out and the voice of Janis Joplin was heard.

Paul and Donna were both astonished with this news.

'Right, we are going to Seascape Apartments. Now! I have a hunch that could point us in the right direction. We'll go in your car Donna – I have a little job for you to do. We shall get back to the office and swap cars. I shall tell you what it is on the way.'

'My car! What for?' asked Donna, glancing over at Paul.

''Cause I'm known, you aren't! That's why. Now listen to what I want you to do …' Paul's foot hit the accelerator, and the Mustang Mach 1 sped with lightning pace back to West Hollywood.

Back at Lorraway, an arthritic hand had dialled a well-known telephone number. Waiting for the phone to be answered the other end, Felinda Bentine doodled with a pen on a pad in front of her.

The phone call was answered by a familiar voice.

'I had a visit from some tiresome tinker this morning …' informed Felinda. 'Calls himself Paul O'Shea, a private investigator, if you can believe that! Had with him some trolloping tramp, supposed to be his secretary. Tryphena and Tryphosa were talking to them outside, but I have the matter in hand …' she paused to listen to the malevolent voice the other end. 'Yes, Jedson checked the car out. It's a black with red stripe Ford Mustang Mach 1, quite new he says. Registration is simply "Mach 1". Probably needs to be driven at Daytona Beach, rather than cause everyone to suffer permanent deafness and all our windows to be shattered!'

The voice at the other end spoke briefly to the "malicious mastermind".

'Very well.' Felinda put the receiver down.

CHAPTER 6

THE PLOT THICKENS

Having swapped cars, Donna drove her pale blue two-door 1960 Chevrolet Corvair to Seascape Apartments. Her treasured "Gerty" had proved to be a very reliable car. Without a hitch, Gerty had got Donna all the way from Jersey City to California.

Travelling along the Pacific Freeway, Donna's mind was trying to piece together all the known facts, especially Paul's visit to the apartments.

'Did you speak to this janitor guy at the apartments, Paul?' Donna asked. She was concerned that Paul could be involved with the death.

'As a matter of fact, I did speak to the creep, but no, I did not kill the guy. Someone got to him after I was there, and I want to know who it was!' Paul's face had a determined countenance. 'We have two murders on our hands now, both are obviously connected. Someone with ruthlessness and brains is behind all this,' Paul resolved. He was absorbed in his own thoughts. *Did the killer see me when I was at the apartments? Was the person or persons present when I manhandled the janitor? I am plucking at straws now. I hope we can get somewhere tomorrow, when we meet with the twins.*

As the car was about to drive into the parking lot to Seascape Apartments, Paul instructed Donna to pull over. He hastily alighted from the car and hid behind some Hacienda bushes, screening the parking lot.

Donna drove in and parked her car. Already having a description of Detective Sergeant Karl Peterson, she had no trouble in identifying the man. Peterson stood next to a parked squad car and was chatting to a uniformed officer. Now Donna had the perfect opening.

With brisk energetic steps, she walked right up to the two men and interjected their conversation. 'Excuse me. I'm Wendy Matthews, from the *Oakland Tribune*. I wondered if I could have some details on the body that was found here this morning, please guys.' She fluttered her eyelids at the two men.

The uniformed officer lifted his hat and smiled, but Peterson was dour and spoke authoritatively. 'The police are not discussing any particulars at the moment, lady. Please leave us.' Peterson stubbed out the butt of his vile cigarette and moved away from Donna.

'But I've come all this way, guys. Please, can't I have something to take back?' she asked with a charming manner.

'Beat it, lady,' Peterson growled back. 'I told you, the police are not issuing any statement yet!' With that, Peterson and the other officer began to walk towards the apartment block.

Seeing the stub, Donna bent down and picked it up and placed it into her powder compact. She knew it would be of interest to Paul – it could be linked to the cigarette stub he had found in the apartment.

While Donna was keeping Peterson and the officer occupied, Paul had spotted a former colleague from his police force days. The plain-clothed detective was standing well back from the apartments, outside another squad car, looking at some paperwork. Taking the chance to hurry over and speak to the man, Paul was successful with his objective. The man was Bruno Capezio. He was in uniform when Paul was on the force, but had obviously been promoted to detective now.

Capezio greeted Paul warmly. It was fortuitous that he was aware that Paul and Ben Driscoll had worked together on the police force – thereby releasing information to Paul quite easily. Paul told Capezio that he was now a private investigator. Expressing his sadness at the murder of Ben, Capezio was equally dismayed at the heartless shooting of such a good officer. When Paul asked Capezio about searching the apartments for any clues, the detective informed Paul that Peterson had assured him that nothing was found in either apartment, when he had searched himself. Alarm bells sounded in Paul's ears.

Then he saw it.

Parked over against the far wall of the parking lot, was a white Chevrolet Camaro.

'Whose car is the Camaro, Bruno? I like the Chevy

Camaro, late model too?'

Capezio replied, setting his eyes on the distant vehicle. 'The Camaro, yeah, nice job that one. Belongs to Peterson, bought it last year. Would love one myself!'

Paul knew that his time was now limited, Peterson was already walking to the apartments. Pleasantries over, Paul fare welled Bruno. On reflection, Paul knew he had taken a risk. *What if Capezio let slip that he had spoken to me! Damn, I had no choice, I had to get that info*, he thought. Ensuring that Peterson would not see him, Paul slinked back to the cover of the Hacienda bushes.

By now, Donna had driven out of the parking lot, and was approaching Paul. 'Get in!' she called out to him.

Paul quickly climbed into the car. 'Let's go, we have work to do!'

Accelerating away from the curb, the Corvair was guided by Donna back onto Oceanview Drive.

As Donna was driving, she told Paul about the cigarette stub, and pushed her handbag over to him to obtain the powder compact. Retrieving the cigarette stub, Paul instantly recognised the gold five star emblem around the filter. It was quite possible that these were specially made cigarettes. Their aroma was strong, probably a blended tobacco. There were a number of tobacconist's in the city, so tracking down which one had made the cigarette, could take a while.

'Have you any idea where this Peterson guy lives? If we can find that out, then perhaps we can track down any tobacconists in the vicinity?' asked Donna.

'Good thinking! We could try the phone book or I may be able to follow Peterson in your car. I'm positive that Jedson would have taken note of the Mach 1, and reported back to base. Peterson is definitely involved with all this, but just finding out how, is not going to be easy,' Paul concluded, giving Donna a serious expression. Looking at his Tissot watch, Paul saw that it was nearing 1 p.m. 'Donna, would you mind if you got a cab back to the office, and I'll go back in your car to Seascape Apartments? If Peterson's still there, I have to follow him, just to see where he goes. If you could check out the tobacconists for that cigarette, we can kill two birds with one stone. Is that okay with you?'

Donna raised her eyebrows and sighed. 'Oh, alright! Mind you are careful with my Gerty, she doesn't like being thrashed around!' Turning her face to confront Paul, she said in a lowered tone, 'Paul, I apologise for the way I spoke to you after we left the Bentine woman. She just really offended me, that's all. I shouldn't have let her get to me.'

'That's quite okay, you have feelings. Think nothing of it, Donna,' replied Paul in a reassuring voice.

Donna pulled over, and let Paul take the wheel of her beloved car, Gerty. She managed to hail a cab back to the Parkside Business Centre.

Turning Gerty around, with a squeal of the tyres, O'Shea was en route to Seascape Apartments. Paul was determined to check if Peterson's car was still in the parking lot.

* * *

Great, the Camaro is still there, Paul thought with a smile before parking the Corvair further down Oceanview Drive.

Walking back on foot, Paul hid behind the Hacienda bushes again. The time was nearing 1.30 p.m. Only one other squad car remained. Capezio was not in sight, only two uniformed officers standing at the entrance of the building.

Time ticked away, still no sight of Detective Sergeant Karl Peterson. Instinct alerted Paul to another presence not far away. Bending low, he parted a branch of the Hacienda bush. There was a figure of a tall person, probably male, sitting on a motorbike. This individual was intently gazing over to the apartments, not more than 50 yards away from Paul. The motorbike had been positioned very carefully away from view of the apartments, but the viewer was in a prime place to observe who came and went without being seen.

Paul could only see this person side on, but it was apparent that it was a male, who possibly wished to remain incognito. They wore a black leather skullcap, dark wrap around sunglasses, a black leather studded Brando biker jacket and black knee high biker boots. His long hair was a reddish-blonde colour, and hung down over his shoulders in ringlets. Paul was concentrating so much on this unknown biker that he failed to observe Peterson appear from inside the apartment building. The biker was the first to respond, and got himself ready to start his bike. Paul then realised that something was happening, and saw the figure of Peterson walking to his Camaro. By this time, Peterson was now in his vehicle, and pulling out of the parking lot. The biker was hot on the trail, but had managed to keep a safe distance from Peterson. Paul had to scramble back to the Corvair. Attempting to start up the car, he stalled the engine, before getting back onto Oceanview Drive. Trying vainly to catch up the bike and Peterson was no use. Paul lost them both as they sped down Pacific Freeway towards the city. Cursing himself for not being alert enough, Paul chose to drive back to the office. At least he had seen this biker guy. Now all that remained, was to identify who he was.

On the way back, Paul was mulling over everything so far. *Tomorrow may prove profitable with the twins, regarding the information they had. Has Donna been able to track down the tobacconist? At least I know that Peterson was involved with this puzzling series of events,* he thought. *This biker guy was watching Peterson like a hawk and Felinda Bentine was definitely covering up something, but what? Or was she hiding a dark secret for another person or persons?* Thoughts were flashing through Paul's mind as he made the journey back to the office.

Stopping off at a KFC outlet, Paul purchased himself some crumbed pineapple and fries. He sat slumped over, chewing away at his food – and his thoughts.

Donna had been busy making phone calls to various tobacconists. After the ninth, she felt exhausted, but there were still four more to try. The telephone book had been unhelpful in revealing where Karl Peterson may live.

Making herself a much-needed coffee, Donna returned to her desk and phoned the next tobacconist on her list.

Ibrahim Al Bazoukia Exclusive Tobacconist and Smoking Accessories was situated in the elite older district of Palm Ridge. Donna dialled the number and hoped that this tobacconist might be the one they were looking for.

After listening carefully to Donna's description of the cigarette, store owner Mr Ibrahim Al Bazoukia was certain that he had this brand in stock.

'Yes, I know the one you are talking about. It has five gold stars embossed around the filter, yes? Good, we are speaking of a blend called "Ruby Glow".'

'That's the one!' Donna chirped.

'Perfect for a gift, my dear. This particular blend is from Turkey. Quite rare and very aromatic!'said the Turkish proprietor.

Donna wasn't too sure about the "aromatic" bit, but played along with the tobacconist.

'Oh, your husband's friend recommended me? What is his name, and I will give you a special discount for business referred?'

With her enormous charisma and beguiling voice, Donna mentioned the name of Karl Peterson.

'Oh, Mr Peterson. Yes, he has been a client for some years,

as is his mother too. No problems at all, my dear. When would you like to collect the cigarettes?'

Scratching her hair, Donna decided on two days time.

'Now what is your name please?' came the inevitable question.

Donna had to think fast, she had forgotten about that!

'My name is Mrs Weston.'

'Very well, Mrs Weston, I shall have them ready for you, good day to you.'

Donna was overjoyed that she had struck lucky. She knew Paul would be pleased. It was very interesting to learn that Peterson's mother also smoked the same brand. She wondered who this woman was.

Yes, if only Donna had known then.

Paul returned to the office to be informed of Donna's success tracking down the tobacconist.

When Donna told Paul that Peterson's mother also smoked the same brand, he was very interested indeed.

Updating Donna with his visit to Seascape Apartments and the knowledge now regarding the search of the two apartments, plus the mysterious biker, Paul told Donna to go home early.

'You have done well, Donna. Go home and have an early evening. We have to meet with the twins tomorrow.'

'Yes, let's hope that is informative. They might just tell us where Maryanne is actually living!' She was still excited with her success.

Collecting her bag, Donna drove home with a happier disposition, than when she had left the Bentine abode.

As all good intentions may hope to be, our tobacconist was not easily fooled by Donna's cigarette order.

Shortly after speaking with Donna, Mr Ibrahim Al Bazoukia, had a brief telephone conversation with Detective Sergeant Karl Peterson.

'Yes, she called herself Mrs Weston … She is coming on Friday morning to collect the cigarettes … Very well … No, I did not mention your mother's name … You agree it sounds suspicious? That is why I thought it best to let you know.'

The phone called ended – Ibrahim Al Bazoukia was satisfied he had taken the right course of action. A smile of deep satisfaction assailed his wide pock marked face.

Donna finished her ironing and some household chores before relaxing in front of the television. She liked to watch *The Mary Tyler Moore Show*, and she was eager to be ready when the show commenced at 8 p.m.

Her dinner with Paul earlier in the week had been a breakthrough for Donna. She felt that he had finally come to terms with life. Perhaps there was now a definite opportunity for them to begin a new life together. However, as Donna's mother used to tell her daughter, "Learn to walk before you run!" Without a doubt, these were wise words.

Meanwhile, at the apartment of Paul O'Shea, he was splayed out on the living room sofa, snoring wildly like a contented pig.

The television was still on. An episode of the new television series called *Hawaii Five-O* was screening. Paul related to the crime theme series, and it brought back memories whenever Steve McGarrett said those famous words, "Book him!"

Paul's thoughts had not been focused on his evening with Donna whatsoever. Trying to piece together all the known facts into a meaningful order, Paul had sunk a few too many beers that night following a can of baked beans and a plate of vanilla bean ice cream. His mind was over worked and stomach more than filled.

A walk to the bedroom was not feasibly possible tonight, and Paul spent the night in idyllic glory on the lumpy sofa.

CHAPTER 7

AN ELECTRIFYING HIT

Morning was a dazzling array of muted colours crossing the heavens, as dawn broke with supreme loveliness. The moon had been wrapped away and the sun shone its splendour upon the waking earth. Sunshine had began to stream into the living room of Paul's apartment, waking him from his slumber.

Attempting to rise from the sofa was initially an effort for the man. Paul moved his neck around carefully and placed some weight on his legs. *Wow*, he thought. *I certainly had too much to drink last night.* Stretching his back and neck muscles gently, he stumbled into the kitchen and began to make some black coffee. *Should I shave? Hell, of course I have to! I am going to meet these twins.* The alpha male was still kicking in. After all, it was only 7 a.m. If only he didn't have to wear a collar and tie!

Donna's morning routine, however, was slightly different.

Up early, having had a nourishing breakfast of Corn Flakes, fruit and frozen grated lemon rind washed down with a black tea, she was now in the shower. Next would be the elaborate task of applying her face and fixing her stunning hair.

Organising themselves, they both made their respective ways to Parkside Business Centre.

Meeting up at the office, the pair discussed the plans for their meeting with the twins. It was arranged that Donna would go into the hairdresser first to ensure that the ladies had their hairdos completed. Paul would stay outside and then they would all walk to the coffee shop to hear what these lively ladies had to reveal. Donna had said that there was a good coffee shop within a short distance at number 43 Sunset Strip.

Ensuring they were on time, Paul got to the hairdresser establishment at 66 Sunset Strip a little early.

The shop front was garishly decorated in gold and black tones, advertising the name as "Walter".

Parking straight outside the shop, Donna waited for a few minutes before entering the shop. Neither of them had noticed a van parked about 50 yards away, further down the bustling Sunset Strip. Paul was yawning and Donna was adjusting her shoe on her right foot.

A man dressed in dark overalls had materialized from the brightly painted shop, carrying a duffle bag. Walking slowly, yet with a definite purpose, the tall figure was heading for the van. Sporting a cap pulled down to hide his face, anybody would assume he was just an everyday tradesman going about his daily task.

Paul had just cast his eyes down the Strip, when he

casually saw the van with the lettering "Hollywood Electric and Cable Company. Phone Hollywood 7413".

Not taking any significant attention to the man or the vehicle, the van had just begun to move away from the curb.

Without any warning, there was a loud bang and a humming noise, and then screaming from inside the shop. Paul and Donna heard the commotion, and quickly sprang from the Mustang and hurried to the shop entrance. A hysterical young girl suddenly ran out from the shop.

'Help, help, somebody please help!' she screeched in distress. She wore a short, tight-fitting dress with black boots.

'What's happened, honey?' Donna asked frantically.

Paul did not wait for an answer, he just ran inside the shop to find another girl hovering over two slumped figures under hairdryers. There was a male in the background, but Paul knew immediately what had occurred.

'Don't touch anything!' Paul warned the young girl.

'I can't make them hear me!' the girl wailed violently. 'What has happened to them? Oh no, please no!' She was dressed in the same outfit as the hysterical girl outside the shop.

Paul drew her aside and asked the male where the fuse box was.

The guy seemed to be far more interested in smoking his cigarette and eyeing Paul than comprehending the question.

"*Where* is the fuse box?" Paul said again sternly.

The young lady hairdresser pointed in the direction of the far wall.

Racing over to the fuse box, Paul lifted the cover carefully, and could see the fatal wiring. Above the fuses was the lettering "Dryers". The wiring had been tampered with.

By this time, Donna had entered the shop with the other hairdresser.

Paul and Donna suddenly realised that the collapsed figures were none other than Tryphena and Tryphosa.

If only we had been here a little sooner, this disaster may not have taken place, agonised Paul inwardly.

The dryers had been their death penalty, designed to exterminate the twins before they could talk. Frizzled to a frazzle!

'Donna, phone the cops now! I'll have a talk to them all.'

While Donna was busy phoning the police, Paul secured the shop.

A middle aged woman, dressed as mutton done up as lamb, was banging on the door. 'I have an appointment at 11.00 a.m.! Open this door!'

Paul gave her the two fingers sign, and her face almost fell off in horror.

Fortunately there was only one other lady in the shop, who had been having her grey hair transformed into "Goldilocks" by the chain-smoking male hairdresser. The lady was relatively calm, and said she remembered seeing a man come in and going to the fuse box for a few moments. She thought that he had gloves on, but did not take too much notice.

'Did anyone see or speak to this man?' asked Paul, looking skeptically at the staff.

'I saw a man came to the counter and said he was from some electric company and needed to have access to the fuse box,' said one of the hairdressers, still shaking with distress.

'Did you know that he was coming?'

The tall male still kept himself from being involved with conversation. Content at puffing away aggressively, and staring at Paul.

'No, we didn't know. I did ask Walter if it was alright to let the man through, and Walter said it was, so I showed him where the fuse box was.' Sobbing again and wiping her mascara-streaked cheeks, the hairdresser sat herself down on a customer chair.

'Did you notice if his right hand was shaking?' Paul asked in desperation.

Her body was now trembling and she sniffled a reply, 'No, I didn't see his hands really. The only thing was that he seemed a bit rude when he spoke to me. I can't remember anything else!' The distraught girl buried her messy face into a tissue.

The other hairdresser said that she had not really seen the man's features but that he was tall and wasn't young.

'And your names, please?'

'Habinella … Habby for short,' replied the young girl as she sunk deeper into her chair.

'I'm Diana,' said the other. 'The guy … he was in hurry … but I was cleaning up my station after the twins' appointment so I was looking down most the time.'

Habby was not that helpful now. The startling reality of the deed had sent her into shock.

'It all happened so quick! Those two ladies came here all the time to have their hair done and now they are dead!' Habby sobbed openly. Goldilocks was now comforting her.

Donna came back on the scene and informed Paul that the police were on their way. She then went over to the huddled group of whimpering ladies.

Playing from the radio was the popular Johnny Cash song, *Cocaine Blues*. Paul strode behind the front counter and promptly switched the radio off. *Well, I had better speak to Walter. See if I can get any sense from him,* he thought, but with some trepidation. *Hmmm, I don't know about this guy!*

Going to the back of the shop, Walter was staring at Paul with lustful eyes of glee. Smoke billowed from his nostrils like a fiery dragon as he leant back against the counter. Walter saw his golden chance, and strode forward to confront the approaching figure of Paul.

Walter's real name was Sperry von Macklenburg, but he had chosen to be called Walter rather than the unusual name of Sperry. Hollow chested and tall, he wore black skintight pants with a white belt and gold buckle. The motif on the buckle was two males entwined in each other's arms and their legs wrapped around each of their buttocks. Red alligator cowboy boots with gold tips adorned the feet. The shirt was a loose fitting floral design, unbuttoned most of the way down the chest. Hanging around the neck was an enormous gold disk on a chunky gold chain. Walter's hair was close cropped and had been dyed peroxide blonde to offset the bushy black eyebrows. His face had been afflicted

with acne. Even today there was a pimple on Walter's chin –
a monstrous zit, in fact – that had broken its contents onto
his unshaven face and oozed down like a spitting volcano.
Not a pretty picture!

Paul attempted to speak to Walter without moving any
closer to the love struck man. Walter had other ideas and
was crafty in luring Paul to move slightly sideways, but
sufficient enough that Paul was now pinned against a set of
cupboards. Paul was trapped.

'Did you see the face of the man who entered the shop?'
Paul asked, peering up to the face of Walter, who must have
been all of 6 foot 3 inches tall in height.

'What have we got here!' Walter moved his body further
towards Paul.

Paul swallowed hard. 'Why did you let the guy have access
to the fuse box, if you didn't know he was expected?'

Walter had placed a heavily ring encrusted right hand on
the shoulder of Paul and began to run his hand down Paul's
arm.

Paul tried to glance over to Donna, but she was trying
to console Diana. He did see that a large screen had been
placed around the bodies of the twins.

Walter's smile was creepy and his breath reeked of coffee
and nicotine. Then the left nicotine stained hand was placed
onto Paul's left shoulder. Walter had drawn himself very
close now to Paul's body and his eyes were bulging like
iridescent glass balls. His upper lip twitched, and was ready
to inflict a direct hit!

Shit no! thought the absolutely terrified Paul. He knew he had to react quickly. Acting upon impulse, Paul gave Walter a severe nose nudge with his head.

Howling like a baby and clutching his face, Walter had now become "Walter Wetnose"!

Stumbling back in acute pain and alarm, Walter keeled over coughing and spluttering, blood gushing from his pointy nose.

Paul hurried away and grabbed Donna by the arm.

'Come on, we are out of here!'

Donna was surprised at the hasty exit and obeyed Paul without hesitation.

'What was all that about! That guy carrying on at the back of the shop! Did you hit him Paul?' shrieked Donna, quickly buckling her seatbelt.

Mach the Mustang gave a roar and rapidly left the scene of death and despair. A small gathering of onlookers had clustered outside the shop, trying to peer inside.

'Nope, we just had a little man to man talk that's all. Nothing to get concerned over, Donna.'

Donna screwed up her face and then saw some blood on Paul's forehead. She chose not to probe any further.

CHAPTER 8
GROPING FOR THE LIGHT

Donna and Paul were lucky enough to just miss the arrival of the police.

Sirens blaring, the two police cars screeched to a halt. Larger crowds now gathered outside the shop, and the media were not far behind.

After the Mustang had got the pair safely out of the vicinity, Donna turned her eyes to Paul. 'This is all very tragic now, Paul. The twins are dead. Someone wanted them out of the way, don't you agree?' Her voice was anxious and very troubled.

'Yeah, you are spot on, Donna. We do have something now to go on, with this guy who entered the shop. Why in the hell did they let him have access to the meter box?' Paul barked out, driving furiously down Hollywood Drive. He banged the steering wheel with his right hand in anger.

'That Diana, she said that the shop is owned by someone

else. That guy you had words with, is only the manager. I guess they thought it was a legitimate reason, Paul. The man was dressed like an electrician apparently, so I don't think they thought of questioning him any further.'

'If only we could have had more time to speak to the twins yesterday, we might have got a lead. I feel sorry though for the twins. They were certainly lovely ladies, who wouldn't hurt anybody intentionally. Felinda Bentine is behind all this, I am sure of it!' Paul replied with a powerful expression.

'Yes, you are not wrong there! Paul, we should have remained behind. We could be implicated in all this now,' responded Donna, with a tone of annoyance and concern, all at once.

'What, and risk Karl Peterson seeing us there! No way! He may not be assigned to the twins' murders, but we cannot take the chance! So, now we have four murders and literally nothing concrete to go on. It's all supposition at the present moment,' Paul said, turning his face towards Donna, as the Mustang Mach 1 drove them back to West Hollywood.

Paul stopped at a Buck's diner in West Hollywood and they had some lunch.

Paul had decided that he would now visit Noreen Driscoll and ask her about Ben's mom. Perhaps the woman was still alive, but he knew he had to cover every possibility to crack this covert operation. Could Ben's mom shed some important light on the proceedings so far? An evil overseer was at work here, and Paul was determined to break their modus operandi.

* * *

Feeling nourished and recovered from the morning's incident, Paul and Donna were back in the Mustang. Their plan was for Donna to go to the City Library and City Records Office again to delve further into the missing witnesses.

Dropping Donna off, Paul proceeded to the River Glen home of Noreen Driscoll. This now gave Paul some time to reflect on the strange and puzzling sequence of happenings, starting with the death of his pal, Ben Driscoll.

Paul now knew that Ben had not been shot by the weapon spoken of by Peterson. That was a definite lie, to get Paul thinking on another tangent. Probably Mr Janitor had been killed by Peterson, or someone associated with him. Jedson, perhaps? Quite likely. Given the way Jedson reacted with the twins, anything was possible. Was Jedson responsible for the murder of the twins? The description could fit Jedson, but without definite proof, it was difficult to say.

Paul drove into the driveway of the Driscoll residence.

Noreen was a fastidious homemaker and loved her garden. Colourful flowerbeds lined the front wrought iron fence and the driveway had an eye catching array of roses, all in bloom.

Paul rang the doorbell, tapping his toe lightly on the concrete while he waited. Noreen opened the front door and was pleased to see Paul O'Shea.

Seating themselves in the immaculate living room, Paul

saw a photo of Ben with Noreen and the girls, placed on a side board. *Probably taken not long before Ben was killed,* Paul thought to himself. Trying to be as diplomatic as possible, Paul tasked Noreen if Ben's mother was still alive.

'Why yes, Lamore and I keep in contact regularly. The girls are quite close to Lamore, and we phone her often. Is something wrong, Paul?' enquired Noreen, wringing her hands.

Paul was aware that Noreen was still coping with the death of Ben, and could not take any further worry or grief.

'No, nothing at all,' Paul answered quickly with a voice of reassurance. 'Would you have her address, I would like to discuss something with her regarding some information I have?'

'Why yes, Paul, I will write it down for you.' Noreen then stopped and looked at Paul with an expression of bewilderment, and said, 'Lamore lives in Canada. I can give you her telephone number too, if you like.'

'In Canada!' Paul replied in amazement.

'Yes, she has lived there for some years, since leaving California. When Lamore's husband died, she shifted from San Francisco a few years ago, and returned to Canada. Lamore loves it there. You see, she was born there before moving to the States and marrying. Is everything alright, Paul? You will tell me won't you?' Noreen's face had an anxious countenance.

Paul sighed and began to carefully recite the details surrounding Ben's death and the comment from Tryphena and Tryphosa regarding Ben's mom. He had to be extremely careful not to reveal too much, but enough to give Noreen a clear picture.

'I have never heard of these ladies, Paul. Ben never spoke of them. Dead you say, that's awful! They knew Lamore!' Noreen was deep in thought, her face was looking at the carpeted floor, wracking her mind regarding the past. 'It must have been years ago, when Lamore was in Hollywood. She never speaks of that time in her life. Ben did say that his mother was a silent film actress, but I never liked to pry into her younger years.'

After spending some further time with Noreen, Paul told her that he would keep her informed with developments. Having the address and phone number for Lamore Driscoll, Paul did ask Noreen not to say anything to Lamore, until he had contacted her mother-in-law. Noreen gave her word; she would abide by Paul's request. She was still emotionally fragile, but for the sake of her three daughters, she was putting on a brave face.

Waving her goodbye from the front garden, Paul felt a pang of sadness for Noreen. She would come through all this, but closure would certainly assist with the healing process.

Back at the office, Paul sat down at his desk with a hot coffee and some homemade chocolate cookies that Donna had brought in. The pair talked over their respective findings.

'You go first, Donna. Mine is a bit simpler than yours,' said Paul, biting into his third cookie.

'Okay, first of all I checked out that name on the van. There is no such company!' Donna looked at Paul in expectation.

'Yes, I thought that would be the case.'

'Now, I have some really startling news for you. You won't believe what I am going to tell you …'

'Well, come on, don't keep me waiting,' said Paul, in trepidation.

'Something told me to do some research on this guy Buswell Clancy. Well, it appears that Buswell Clancy is a nickname given to none other than a Richard Arlington Driscoll, born in Oregon and later moved to Hollywood as a film set worker. This was in the years prior to 1920. How I came to get this guy's name, was that I decided to check on anyone with the name of Driscoll in the Hollywood area in a time frame from 1915 to 1925. I will tell you how I came to check on the Driscoll name shortly,' said an enlivened Donna.

Paul whistled and flung his head back. 'Wow, kiddo, this is great news. What else did you find out, super sleuth?' he grinned at Donna.

'This is the interesting part …' replied Donna excitedly, with a nod of her lovely head. 'Driscoll was working for the same film company as Osborne and Maryanne. Now according to a newspaper, called the Hollywood Headlines, now defunct, a small article refers to Charles Osborne's death in 1922. It states that his manservant was a Richard Driscoll, who Osborne affectionately nicknamed "Buswell Clancy". Osborne must have given him a job as manservant. So Richard and Ben's mom must have met some time during the early twenties or thereabouts. They married and along came Ben.'

"That is extraordinary! This was the guy who accounted for the visitors to Osborne's home that fatal night, except Maryanne. He must have left to take Ben's Mom to the flicks, just prior to the arrival of Maryanne,' reasoned Paul.

'Regarding Clarene Cremorne, no go I'm afraid on that name. She is referred to in a few editions of *Film Pictorial* and *Movie Goer* in the early twenties, but after that she seems to disappear – quite an elusive person to trace. Oh, there was only one picture of her, so I photocopied it. Here …' Donna slid the copy across to Paul to peruse.

'Hard to say from this photo, it is a bit blurred isn't it?' replied Paul, squinting his eyes.

'Yes, not the best photo unfortunately. Now, Mrs Golda Hummerstein died in 1961 in the US Virgin Islands. So that tidies up a loose end! That is all my news!' ended Donna with a flourish.

'Right, now me …' said Paul. Telling Donna of his discussion with Noreen and obtaining Lamore's contact details, Paul was now ready to make a telephone call to McLean in Saskatchewan, Canada.

Lamore Driscoll was hesitant at first when she heard

Paul's voice on the phone. Listening to Paul divulge some more details, Lamore learnt of the death of the twins. Her perspective altered immediately. She had lost her son because of a dark secret, now the twins. Enough was enough! How was she going to keep things under wrap though? She still had her loyalty to consider. Finally, Lamore relented to a visit from Paul in two days.

As Paul explained, it all depended on the flight not being delayed and then travelling to the rural village of McLean in Saskatchewan. Agreeing to telephone Lamore before he set out on his journey to McLean, Paul felt pleased that Ben's Mom was willing to meet with him.

Putting down the telephone receiver, Lamore wiped her eyes. She knew that a duty had to be performed. Picking up the phone, she dialled a number, very dear to her heart and not known to anyone else.

Wrapping up the day, Paul was satisfied now that some progress was beginning to take shape with the case.

Donna had made copious notes and then typed up some pages with details regarding their research so far. She then placed them on a board in Paul's office with tape and they began to piece together this jigsaw. Ever the efficient secretary, even if she did use a pencil and outdated note pad! Donna made a flight booking for Paul to depart at 7.45 a.m. the following morning to Vancouver, with North by North West Airlines. Then she phoned for a taxi to collect Paul from his Beachcomber Sands apartment early, for the drive to the airport.

Whilst Donna was busy attending to these matters, Paul was studying the map of Canada.

It sure will be a long journey. Better get there by the Canadian Pacific Railway, rather than drive all that way to McLean, Paul thought as he traced his right index finger on the map to the small rural village from Vancouver.

The day had filtered away with so much activity. Five o'clock came upon them sooner than they realised.

On impulse, Paul asked Donna if she would like to go out for dinner.

'Yeah, that would be great, boss!' Donna replied as she pulled Paul's loose tie.

'How about that new steakhouse, Riccardo's, up on National Pacific Concourse? You know the one, on the ridge overlooking LA? They say it is excellent.'

Donna looked up to Paul with a lustful look. 'Alright, big boy! What time are we hitting the road?'

'Let's say I pick you up at a quarter to seven, we can have some drinks at the bar and eat around half past. How does that sound, super sleuth?' Paul laughed.

'Fine by me!'

'Right, I shall make a reservation,' Paul smiled wickedly. 'Oh Donna, I'll leave the spare set of keys for Mach with you, in case you require his services! I will get a taxi home and call for you later by taxi. Mach will be okay in the undercover secure parking bay,' informed Paul.

'I hope you know what you are doing leaving your dream machine in the hands of a woman!' laughed Donna.

Paul just chuckled and called for a taxi to take him home to change.

The evening was divine, as they sat outside on a balcony overlooking the twinkling lights of Los Angeles and beyond. The scene was awe-inspiring and gave the viewer an illusion of a fairy town, miles away in the distance.

Apart from idle chitchat, they both laid out their plans for tomorrow. Donna was to collect the cigarettes from Mr Al Bazoukia. It was also agreed upon that she would watch any visitors coming and going from the palace of sinister activities, namely Lorraway.

Knowing that she could be observed, Donna was given some tips from Paul to ensure her concealment.

Paul was to make a voyage to Canada. A place he had never been to before. Paul was looking forward to the trip, but more importantly, to obtain some in depth insight concerning this complex web of incidents, producing horrendous outcomes.

CHAPTER 9

A WARNING MESSAGE

Without any effort, the Boeing 707, North by North West Airlines flight 909, swept into the air stream and made its way north wards to Vancouver. Paul settled back in his seat and contemplated his meeting with Lamore Driscoll.

Meanwhile, as the morning gradually ticked away, Donna tidied up some paperwork on Paul's untidy desk. Completing her desired tasks, Donna now made ready to collect the cigarettes from Mr Ibrahim Al Bazoukia in Palm Ridge. It was fortuitous that Donna chose to take Mach for a spin today!

Parking the Mustang a few doors away from the tobacconist shop, Donna walked towards the entrance.

A pair of threatening eyes watched Donna enter the tobacconist shop from a safe distance.

'Good morning,' said Donna to the gentleman behind the counter. 'I'm Mrs Weston, you have a package for me. I spoke to a Mr Ibrahim Al Bazoukia on the telephone two days ago,' she enquired.

'Yes, Mrs Weston. How are you? I'm Ibrahim Al Bazoukia, the proprietor. Pleased to oblige!' Mr Al Bazoukia bowed his balding head graciously to Donna. 'Now, I have the cigarettes here as you ordered, all specially wrapped for your husband. I'm sure he will enjoy them. Is it his birthday, Mrs Weston?' asked Mr Al Bazoukia.

'Yes, it's next week, so I thought of coming here after Mr Peterson's recommendation,' Donna replied in a convincing way. After making payment, she thanked Mr Al Bazoukia and left the shop.

As the door closed to his shop, Mr Ibrahim Al Bazoukia, Tobacconist, had a conceited look on his weather-beaten face. He knew it wouldn't be long before Donna opened that package. Then she would see what else was in there.

The 100 dollar bill had been very much welcomed by the older man. Detective Sergeant Karl Peterson had been very generous. But Mr Ibrahim Al Bazoukia was not all he claimed to be. Given to black market trading, and dealing in contraband items, this had been his specialty for some years. "You rub my back and I will rub yours", he would often say. Yes, the "arrangement" with Detective Sergeant Karl Peterson had worked very well for both parties.

Leaving the Palm Ridge locality, Donna commenced driving towards the freeway access for West Hollywood, which was some six miles away. Mach purred along pleasantly, with Donna guiding him with one hand on the steering wheel and the other holding the package just collected.

Pulling over to have a closer inspection of the package,

Donna parked in a laundromat parking lot. Curiosity getting the better of her, she unwrapped the package. There was a black coloured box with a silver ribbon surrounding it. An envelope was under the box, with handwritten Gothic style lettering in ink, with the wording, "To Whom It May Concern".

'What in the world is this?' Donna muttered under her breath. Her inquisitiveness was aroused. Opening the envelope, she took out a gold coloured card, edged with a black fluted border.

YOUR NEXT!

The words hit her like a ton of bricks but she knew she had to remain calm. She decided to head back to the office quick smart. She couldn't phone Paul, he was on his way to Vancouver.

Starting Mach, Donna edged back into the line of traffic and made for the freeway access. Checking the rear vision mirror, all seemed okay. However, just to be sure, she pressed the switch for the telescopic camera to operate. Her eyes were lowered onto the screen placed above the centre console. For the next few minutes, all went well, and Donna started to relax – no one was following her. Then, looking closely into the rear vision once again, Donna saw it.

Having been told by Paul about Karl Peterson's car, Donna suspected that a white Chevrolet Camaro was following her about 100 yards back. Checking the screen above the console, Donna saw the enhanced features of a man driving the vehicle. A cigarette was hanging out his mouth. The camera provided a remarkably visible picture of the driver.

'Peterson!' Donna cried. Keeping her speed level, Donna showed no impulse to put her foot down on the accelerator. She wanted to, but instinct told her to do otherwise. The Camaro was now less than fifty yards behind Mach. The exit to the freeway was still some way off yet. Donna had to keep her feelings under control.

The features of the male motorist were now quite clear. It was definitely Karl Peterson. Donna could determine that the man was intending to do something to distract her and cause her to have an accident. The Camaro was less than 10 yards behind Mach, Donna had to react to this dilemma or face possible death. Putting her foot down on the pedal, Mach surged forward, the Ram Air Induction kicked in, and the car edged away from the speeding Camaro. Glimpsing at the camera screen, Donna was startled to see another figure now following her, directly in front of the Camaro. It was a motorbike. She couldn't see clearly who the rider was, but she thought it was a man. Dark wrap around sunglasses obscured the identity of the bike rider. Donna quickly named the mystery figure as the "Batman Biker".

Down the road the three sped like wild fire. Donna changed lanes quickly to over take a slow moving Cadillac. Within seconds the bike and the Camaro had done the same.

Donna steered Mach down the inside lane, hotly pursued by Batman Biker and the Camaro. Engines roared and wits were being tried to the ultimate. She swerved to avoid a truck; another car honked its displeasure at the sudden appearance of Mach. Batman Biker and the Camaro were close on Mach's tail again!

On the screen Donna could still see Batman Biker but where was the Camaro? Nowhere to be seen. Just as she went to change back to the inside lane, knowing that the freeway ramp was coming up soon, she turned her head and saw the Camaro hurtling directly alongside Mach.

The three lanes were soon to converge into two. Donna had to react quick to avoid a possible disaster. Lessening the speed of Mach, Donna had fallen prey to the Camaro. The 393 cubic inch motor of the Camaro was proving to be a challenge to Mach. The passenger window of the Camaro was wound down. Steeling her emotions to keep concentrating on the busy thoroughfare, Donna kept her eyes fixed on the road ahead. Swerving recklessly back into the inside lane, the two cars were now travelling level with each other. Donna did not see the silver, deadly glint in the morning sunshine. Poised ready to strike, the gloved leather hand was aiming a weapon straight at her.

Suddenly catching a glimpse of the deadly gun, Batman Biker drove fiercely towards the Camaro. Sizzling up between the Camaro and Mach, the biker outstretched his leather clad hand and snatched the gun from the stunned driver. Caught off-guard, the Camaro slackened its pace, and thereby allowing the two vehicles to race ahead.

Donna continued her speed and reached the exit for the

freeway. Screeching his tyres, Mach out ran the Camaro, and the white flash disappeared further along the commuter road to North Hollywood. Mach growled fiercely, making the bend in the freeway entrance seem like an effortless manoeuver.

A sweat had broken out on Donna's forehead, and her faculties had been tried to the limit. Her arms were shaking like leaves, and aching with tension. Batman Biker was nowhere to be seen either. Donna had not seen the saving grace performed by the unknown biker, but the action certainly allowed her to live another day.

***

Donna sat slouched forward over the steering wheel. She was exhausted, but grateful to be safely returned to the relative sanctuary of the building – or so she thought. Mach had certainly earned his weight in gold this morning.

Making her way upstairs to the office, Donna flung herself down onto the customer sofa and breathed a heavy sigh of relief.

'You okay, lady?' came the rocky deep voice from somewhere in the office.

Donna shook herself into gear, and looked around the office space.

'It's okay, lady, I'm not here to harm you. Just wanted to make sure you are alright after our little race this morning …'

The voice was coming from inside Paul's office.

Donna staggered herself up and carefully walked to the doorway. Sitting on the customer chair was a very tall, scruffy looking male. Long reddish-blonde hair cascaded over the broad shoulders. The dark wrap around sunglasses had been removed. A nasty looking scar was evident below the left eye. His hands were like a giant, swollen in appearance and were adorned with silver rings of a large size.

Dressed in the tell-tale biker gear, Donna straightaway assumed that it was Batman Biker 'Are you the bike rider who was following me this morning?' she asked with caution.

'Sure am, lady!' came the rapid response. The voice was not actually harsh, but very prompt and definite. His tall 7 foot frame lumbered over to Donna. 'That guy in the Camaro was after you lady. I think he meant business.' With that he pulled out from his studded biker jacket a gun.

Donna gasped, and walked back a few paces.

'It's alright lady, I won't kill you, but that other guy certainly was about to. Do you know who that guy was?' the biker said, scrutinising Donna's alarmed face.

'I'm ... ' Donna paused, she wasn't sure if she should reveal her suspect. 'I'm not one hundred percent sure who it was, but I have a good idea,' she stumbled out with cautiousness.

'Care to share the name with me, lady?' came the hasty reply.

Donna blinked and swallowed hard. She decided to play safe and steer the conversation onto another matter – no way could she risk telling the bike rider that it was undoubtedly Karl Peterson.

'Don't fret, lady. I know who the bastard is. You don't have to tell me, 'cause I know!' the man then touched his crooked nose.

Donna touched her forehead, and walked over to Paul's desk, and held onto it for support.

'Why don't you sit down? You probably could do with it!' Batman Biker suggested.

Donna was still coming to terms with what the biker had just said. 'I'm sorry, but I am still taking all this in. Are you saying that the guy driving the Camaro was going to kill me with that gun?' Donna's eyes were bulging with surprise.

'Spot on, lady. I grabbed the gun off that guy just as he was aiming it at you through his car window. Nasty piece of equipment this is,' he said as he turned the weapon over, casting his blue eyes over it.

Donna shuddered, and pulled her arms around her body. She felt a cold shiver suddenly and went and sat herself down. Then, realising the obvious question, she fixed her gaze on the biker. 'How did you get into the office, it was locked?!'

'Easy, that lock isn't foolproof. Better get your boss to have it changed, but then I would still get in!' A smile had appeared on the biker's large face. 'Where is the big boss? I need to have a talk with him.'

'Oh, um, well, he is away at the moment. I'm not sure when he will be back,' answered Donna quickly, speculating why the biker wanted to know.

'Okay, but I will come back.'

The biker went to leave and Donna followed the man out.

'Well, can I have your name so I can tell my boss to expect you again?' asked Donna meekly.

'No, I'll come back soon though. In the meantime, keep a low profile. Here, this is my number, call me, if you think you might be in danger,' came the biker's warning advice. He then gave a mock salute with his right hand, and left Donna standing in awe.

'Thank you!' Donna called out to the retreating figure.

Locking the office door, she sat herself down at her desk. Closing her eyes, Donna dosed off.

After some time had elapsed, Donna was feeling more composed and unwrapped the package. As could be expected, it was empty – filled with strips of paper and nothing else. She picked up the piece of paper given to her by Batman Biker. The telephone number was handwritten in ink, in a large style. It was scratchily written, as though in a rush, on a small piece of notepaper.

'No name though,' muttered Donna, staring at the piece of paper. Donna immediately identified the paper – Paul had the same kind on his desk. The biker had obviously written the number down while waiting for Donna to arrive back – but how did he know Paul? Her memory kicked in, and she recalled Paul's account of the mystery biker at Seascape Apartments.

Still feeling shaken from the morning's racy proceedings, Donna chose to go home early. Having heeded the wise words of Batman Biker, Donna decided not to expose herself in the neighbourhood of Cricklewood. That could wait. She was in need of a hot, soothing bubble bath.

CHAPTER 10

A CANADIAN ADVENTURE

North by North West Airlines slid smoothly onto the tarmac at Vancouver Airport. The day was cool and somewhat cloudy and a chilly breeze was blowing in from off the Pacific Ocean. Paul made his way out of the terminal building without delay.

After taking a taxi to the imposing Victorian era railway station, Paul made a reservation for an overnight compartment on the Canadian Pacific Express train. Thinking ahead, he booked a return fare from McLean. He was fortunate that the train was departing in just over an hour's time.

Seeing a row of phone boxes, Paul chose to contact Donna. *She might still be at the office, or I will get her at home,* Paul thought as waited for the Canadian operator to connect the phone call.

'I'm sorry sir, but there seems to be no reply on that number. Would you like me to try again?' came the efficient lady operator's voice.

'No,' replied Paul. 'Can you try this landline number?'

A tired yet somewhat refreshed Donna answered the phone. She recounted her exploits of the morning to Paul in detail.

'Are you okay, Donna?' came Paul's voice of concern.

'Yes, I am. I was shaken up initially but I am fine now. I won't have a nosy around Lorraway, for obvious reasons.'

Paul agreed and suggested that she do some more research on the missing Clarene Cremorne .

'This Batman Biker guy said he would get in touch again when you return.'

'He did, huh? Well, that's something new! And he was alright to you, not menacing?' Paul asked.

'No, he was quite okay with me. I'm sure that he is onto Karl Peterson though,' Donna said in a hushed voice.

Keeping Donna up to date with his movements, Paul said that the train would arrive at the village of McLean the following day.

After exchanging some more words, Paul terminated the call. He could discern that Donna was in need of time to herself. He then telephoned Lamore Driscoll to advise her the approximate time the train would arrive at McLean. Lamore Driscoll said she would meet Paul at the station with her car. Her manner was cheerful and Paul was hopeful that it was not all a façade.

The rail journey was comfortable and scenic, as Paul sat peering through the panoramic glass windows, taking in the splendour of the Canadian scenery. The landscape altered dramatically after leaving the picturesque city of Vancouver. The rapidly moving train swept along as the larger towns gave way to isolated localities. The movement of the train induced slumber and contentment to the tired Paul O'Shea.

Following a restful overnight sleep in his sleeping compartment, Paul felt ready for his meeting with Lamore Driscoll. Once the train had left the outskirts of the city of Regina, the capital city of the Province of Saskatchewan, Paul knew that it would not be long before the train would arrive at McLean station.

Our drama moves on now and the fast train stopped briefly at McLean station to let Paul disembark. He was the only passenger to do so. Carrying minimal luggage, he made his way outside the small station building, and saw a dark haired woman standing just outside the entrance.

'Mr O'Shea, is it?' The woman's face had a joyful disposition.

'Yes, hello,' replied Paul, offering his hand.

Greetings over, Lamore directed Paul to her 1963 Dodge Phoenix.

The village was quiet, compared to the environment that Paul was accustomed to. No traffic to deal with and the locals waved to each other in a friendly disposition. The pace was leisurely and refined, a far cry from the streets of Los Angeles and beyond.

The home of Lamore Driscoll was modest from the outside, yet its size was deceiving, as the house spread down the block. Next door was a sizeable ranch, and healthy cattle munched away on the emerald green grass with pleasure and satisfaction.

Lamore welcomed Paul into her home warmly. Seating themselves in the front living room, Paul could now see the lady who possibly held a vital key to solve this tragedy of circumstances. *Lamore Driscoll must be close to seventy by now,* thought Paul, *but her sprightliness gives the impression that she is younger by far.* Her hair was dyed a dark brown, and the diamond earrings sparkled in the sunlight entering the light and airy room, where they both sat. Lamore's amber eyes were kind, but Paul detected a reservation in her manner, perhaps even a stiffness. Her outward appearance was kindness, but inwardly she was wrangling with emotions from the dark past. *What information will she let out, after all these years?* Paul wondered with trepidation. *Does Lamore really know where Maryanne is?* Paul knew he had to start somewhere, so as Lamore poured some percolated coffee, the first in a series of questions were asked of Lamore.

Thinking of a way to commence his words, Paul said, 'Ben was cruelly killed, Lamore, as we both know. I knew Ben very well, having worked together on the force. He was a real pal to me, and I valued his friendship. I am hoping that you can shed some light on who might have had a grudge against Ben or wanted him dead? You are aware that Tryphena and Tryphosa Bentine were murdered the other day?' Paul halted his speech and waited for a response from Lamore.

Sipping her black coffee, Lamore's eyelids fluttered a little. Her face hardened momentarily, then softened, as though she had a million thoughts spinning through her mind. She knew she had to play ignorant on this subject. 'No, I had no idea! They were such a lovely pair. I had not seen them for years, but they were quite adorable. So innocent and naive. Yet, for all that, they were not any fools either!' Lamore finished her sentence, hoping that she had concealed her prior knowledge of the twins' death.

Truth be told, Noreen had let slip that "some twins" had been killed. Her distressed telephone conversation with Lamore last night, had been very unsettling. Unable to recall the names, Lamore did not need to know. The penny dropped instantly – Lamore felt grief stricken.

Paul's intuition told him that Lamore already knew about the deaths. *Noreen, quite likely, or was it someone else?* Paul thought quickly. 'I understand that your late husband, Richard, was also known as Buswell Clancy. Is that correct Lamore?' he asked, speculating just what her response would be.

'Yes, that is right,' Lamore smiled. 'It was a nickname adopted by Charles Osborne. Apparently it was a character that Charles had played himself in a long ago film. There was a manservant called "Buswell Clancy", and Charles dubbed Richard with this name. It was just a joke really, but the name stuck with him for years! Many people thought I was Mrs Buswell Clancy!' she laughed openly.

Paul had to ask the next probing statement with dexterity. 'So, it was your late husband that verified the witness accounts visiting Charles Osborne, the night he died?'

'Yes, that is so,' Lamore answered without reservation. 'The only person he could not vouch for was Maryanne, which you would be aware of. The police thought that Maryanne went there later, and shot Charles Osborne.' Her eyes were centred right upon Paul's face, waiting for the next arrow to hit her.

'Yes, I read that in the records. Richard must have left some time before the arrival of Maryanne,' Paul replied with a pleasant expression. *So far, so good*, he thought. *Will it continue?*

Lamore adjusted herself in her chair, sitting opposite Paul. Her composure was only skin deep. She didn't know how much more she could take – first her son's death and now the twins.

Paul sensed Lamore was exceptionally guarded – she was being helpful only on the surface. He opted for another tactic.

'Okay, Lamore. I'm not going to ask you any further questions. Can you bring yourself to tell me what exactly happened on that night?' Paul asked. 'I appreciate it will be mentally painful, but after all, Ben's life was callously taken. He deserves to be vindicated and I am sure you have love and tenderness towards Noreen and the girls, to expose whoever is behind all this.'

Lamore dropped her head, and sighed deeply.

Stillness enveloped the room, as both individuals had a myriad of thoughts racing through their heads.

Bracing herself, Lamore spoke calmly and quietly. 'Mr O'Shea, what I have to tell you may seem lengthy. To understand the events leading up to the night of August 4,1922, I shall have to explain in some detail.'

'Take all the time you need, Lamore. Please, call me Paul,' he said meaningfully to the woman seated facing him. She gave a smile, and for the first time in their meeting, Paul detected a lowering of her defence.

'To begin with, I was born and raised in this town. My family name was Bostock. There have been Bostock's farming here for generations. When I was 14, my wealthy Aunt Eleanor took me for a holiday of a lifetime to Hollywood. It was like stepping into a world of Alice in Wonderland. I was smitten, and determined to return as soon as I could save enough money. The calling of becoming an actress was just out of this world, to me, at that time. You know, Paul, when you are young, you are focused on being something and proving yourself to others ...'

'I see ...' Paul listened carefully.

'Every aspect of my life was intent on becoming a successful actress. I was lured to Hollywood from the day I stepped foot into the town. In those days, it was only small. Now, it's a hive of activity. Well, I scraped hard, and with some help from Aunt Eleanor, I departed to Tinsel Town, to make my mark! Just how immature and foolish I really was! My dear parents were not pleased, but relented for me to go. I was taken on by First National Pictures Corporation in the summer of 1916. I was allowed to retain my name of Lamore Bostock. The studio sanctioned my name without the need to alter it, as this often happened.

'It was there, that I first met Maryanne, who had also started her career. We became firm friends and helped each other out. Life was not all it was painted to be, I can assure you Paul. Young ladies like us were prey to the foul desires of men, who held high places. Producers, directors, cameramen, studio bosses and any male who thought they could abuse us girls sexually. You either obliged, or faced ruin. It was simple as that! We stuck together, Maryanne and I. We saw many a girl's life shattered through the harsh treatment of working under tyrannical overseers. Us girls were considered little more than objects of petty desire. Drugs became the norm, along with drink ...' Lamore paused to sit up further in the chintz coloured chair. Her ability to express feelings that had been locked up for over forty years, had surfaced with a burning passion.

'Take your time ...' Paul encouraged, eager to hear her story.

'Charles Osborne was our saving grace, Paul. He came to work at the studio in 1918. He was an older man, and could see the workings of the studio for himself. Charles was an experienced actor and wise to the actions of studio bosses. For instance, those publicity shots that were emblazoned on theatre posters, weekly magazines and newspapers, were just a glorified picture that the studio wanted the public to see. Adoring fans lined up to buy a copy of whoever it was, but once that shot was taken, you were sent back to literally sweep the floors, clean out mess laden studio rooms or be summonsed to the boss for a "quickie go over"! People thought we were the sex sirens of the silver screen. Some girls became pregnant or were afflicted with syphilis, venereal disease or had been so badly physically interfered with, they were dumped somewhere outside the studio confines. I know of some who died or simply disappeared!' Lamore wept. Grabbing a handkerchief from her skirt pocket, she composed herself to continue her discourse.

Paul felt skirmish and sickened within. He had no idea of all this. Yes, he had thought the same as anyone else. His now deceased mom, had told him glamour stories of stars from her days. How she lined up to watch the flicks on a Saturday night, with her hard earned wages. It was a treat to see a matinee idol rescue a tragic heroine from near death or a fragile rosebud open it's petals to show the world that beauty was still secure in the arms of a handsome male. "Hollywood heart throbs" were the caption of the day!

'Are you okay to carry on, Lamore?' asked Paul with caring concern.

'Yes, I shall be alright. It is just recollecting those memories, it is difficult, but I have to deal with it,' Lamore said with a degree of agony in her voice. Sniffing away her tears, she carried on. 'So Charles took us under his wings, and became our guardian angel. Over time, Maryanne was cast in a number of films, and became attached to Johnny Appleseed. It was as though they were brother and sister.

There was nothing between them in the sense of being romantically involved. Maryanne was acutely worried with Johnny's drug addiction, and tried to wean him. He was really a loveable man, but so very unwise to the world.

'He had started acting at the age of four. By the time he was 20, Johnny was worn out! So, in order to stay on top of things, he turned to cocaine for security. Maryanne tried vainly to help him, but alas Johnny fell further into an abyss, and he died heartbreakingly young. Maryanne was almost hysterical with his death. I comforted her and gradually she regained her strength. The press were very cruel as were her family. They did not approve of Maryanne's involvement with Johnny at all!'

'I see …"' encouraged Paul, eager to hear the rest of the story.

'I only went twice to Lorraway, but it was made quite clear to me that I was not a "suitable companion" for Maryanne. Felinda had taken over the running of the house, and all things pertaining to the lives of everyone under its roof! The parents were not, how shall I say this, mentally with it. They lived in their own world of Roman and Greek plays, acting out countless parts with finesse – totally oblivious to anything going on around them. They were quite harmless really! It was the actions of Felinda that kept Maryanne away from her own home. That is why she rented a small bungalow on Beverly Boulevard. At least she had privacy from the snooping eyes of Felinda and that despicable Jedson – '

'Jedson!' Paul interrupted with a startled manner. 'Was he there all those years ago?'

'Why yes, didn't you know? They were married. Yes, a

most unusual arrangement if ever there was! Jedson suffers with Parkinson's disease. It was diagnosed not long after they were married. He was very young to be stricken with the incurable illness. Felinda never accepted it, so made him the butler instead! Jedson was the eldest son of a lawyer from Chicago – quite well off, so Maryanne informed me. He was also training to be a lawyer, but his disease put paid to that! That type of illness in those days was considered almost like having leprosy! It was his money that propped up the finances of the Bentine's to keep that mausoleum going. She kept him under lock and key, well almost. Wouldn't let him out of her sight, in case someone saw him, and the Bentine name would be tarnished! Peculiar woman, Felinda. Ruthless to a tee!'

Paul smirked internally. *She sure is!*

'Maryanne said that Felinda refused to divorce. It was out of the question, as that would blacken the family name. Felinda was acutely protective of her reputation. The twins were another issue she had to hideaway, in case the outside world found out. Oh yes, she had a lot to suppress – what with the parents and all – then the untimely death of Alyssa, and then poor Maryanne's involvement with Johnny Appleseed. Then came the ruinous thing of all. The death of Charles Osborne being attributed to Maryanne …'

Paul nodded slowly as he waited for Lamore's next words.

'It was during all this, that I met Richard. He was also working at the studio, as a handy man come jack of all trades. We fell in love at first sight, but it was very difficult to keep our feelings hidden. There were spies all around the studio complex, so we communicated through Maryanne and Charles. Eventually, Charles could see that Richard and I were unable to see each other, so he made Richard his manservant. This worked very well. I could go to see Richard when Maryanne visited Charles. Richard and I kept our secret from the studio.

'Charles was extremely helpful to Maryanne and myself. He placed us in various roles that steamrolled our careers into highly paid actresses. As fate often has the last say, Maryanne's career was abruptly finished once the Osborne scandal destroyed her name. Her last film was in 1924, when her contract expired. After that, no studio would employ her again. Her name was blackened throughout Hollywood! Richard and I were married by then, and once my contract ended in early 1923, I retired to have a family. Ben, our only child, was born in June '23. We moved completely away from the area to San Francisco. Neither of us had happy memories of our days in Hollywood. When Richard died in 1964, I returned here to McLean, to my family home, left to me by my late mother.'

'Can you tell me about that night, August 4?' asked Paul, looking at Lamore with a slight annoyance in his face. *Lamore had deliberately avoided mentioning that night, WHY? Plus she MUST know the whereabouts of Maryanne,* thought Paul. He wished he had a crystal ball for that night, to open up the hidden sequence of events that had changed the lives of so many people – not just Maryanne Myles Morrow, but the entire Bentine family, Jedson, and the Driscoll's also. They had been plagued with dark thoughts that must be veiled, never to be exposed.

Lamore's shoulders dropped with bewilderment, a sour look forming on her face. Paul had to shake the shield of defence that Lamore had placed between them.

'What actually happened on that night, please Lamore,' Paul pleaded, stretching out his hands in mock earnestness.

'On that night, August 4, 1922,' Lamore commenced painfully to make known the night she wished had never come to pass. 'Richard and I had arranged to go the movies at 8 p.m. It had to be that time, as I had been working late on a film. We never knew what time we were ending our day. You were just expected to act or work from sun up to sun down, and not complain! As I already knew I would be finishing late, I told Richard that I couldn't get to Charles's home prior to 7 p.m. We wanted to go and see *The Land of Never Ending Glory*, with Richard Bartlemass and Vena Prentiss. Maryanne had something to discuss with Charles, regarding a part in her latest film. She told me that she would go to Charles's home herself, and not to wait for her at the studio. I was fortunate in that I had some rooms in a boarding house nearby. Well, when I got to the Osborne house, Maryanne wasn't there! I became worried and phoned the studio, just in case she was still there. I was told that she wasn't, but had left some time after 6 p.m. Maryanne had her own car, it was a Chevrolet.'

Interesting, very interesting, thought Paul.

'I then phoned Maryanne's home – no answer. I then remembered that Maryanne had given her staff the night off. Naturally, the three of us were concerned. So I left by taxi, to try to look for Maryanne. Charles was expecting some visitors, as I will relate in a moment. I went back to the studio. Now according to Richard, Norman Lindsay arrived just before 6 p.m. Drunk as a skunk, Richard said. He left about 15 to 20 minutes later. Dreadful man, in charge of costumes. Loved to get under any female's skirts, that one! Then Clarene Cremorne arrived just after Lindsay departed and stayed until approximately 6.45 p.m. Then as Clarene was leaving, the Hummersteins were arriving. They left at 7 p.m. and Richard told Charles that he was going to look for me and then hopefully go to the movies ...' She paused.

Paul nodded slowly, waiting for Lamore to continue.

'Charles Osborne ... he ... he was alive and well when Richard left, he assured me that, Paul! Well, Richard found me outside the studio. I was besides myself with worry. He tried to sooth the matter over, saying there must be an explanation why Maryanne had not arrived at Charles's bungalow. We went to the cinema, and Richard took me back to my lodgings. Then Richard went back to Charles's place, and we know the rest. By morning it was all over the newspapers, what had taken place. Richard found Charles in the living room sitting on the sofa, shot twice through the chest. That was about 10.30 p.m.

'When I saw Maryanne the next day at the studio, she seemed confused, I couldn't get her to tell me where she had been. She was very upset with Charles's death and the police took her into custody for questioning. By the following day, the police were charging Maryanne with Charles's murder!' Lamore sat back and lowered her head in mental anguish.

Perhaps if I can use another line of tactic, she might let something else slip, Paul thought with anticipation before saying, 'What can you tell me about Clarene Cremorne? Did you know her well? There doesn't seem to be any trace of her since the time of the Osborne murder.' Paul stared at the pensive woman opposite him.

Lamore was reawakening all her acting skills now – talent that had laid dormant for many a year, but today would prove to be her crowning glory. She had shined as a young actress in her hey day, crowds flocked to see her gorgeous face grace the screen.

'No, I didn't know Clarene that well,' Lamore said carefully. 'She worked at the same studio of course, but there were so many of us girls there, it was difficult to keep up with who came and who went.' She calmly outstretched her right hand to deliver her final words in a carefree manner. 'I don't think that Maryanne or Richard knew her very well either. Richard came to work for Charles in late '21. As I said earlier, Maryanne and I kept to ourselves as much as we could. What happened to Clarene, is anybody's guess! She quite possibly had another name, and when her contract finished, she reverted back to her real name. They often did that.'

'Well how about the Hummersteins, did they have a grudge against Charles Osborne, or any of those people who visited him that night?' Paul was clutching straws now, Lamore had closed ranks and was playing hard to get at!

'No, of course not! Charles was well liked and respected in the movie industry. It was probably some miscreant who just happened to be passing by. Charles let this person in, and they shot him for money!' Lamore gave Paul an indignant look.

Not a good question, pal, mused Paul. Adopting his severe method of interrogation, Paul struck back. 'Come on Lamore! I don't believe a word of that! Charles Osborne would not have let anyone just enter his home, *IF* ...' Paul paused to create depth to his words, 'he didn't already know them, let alone this unknown person asking for money! I won't buy that! Don't feed me dribble!'

'I ... I – ' Lamore stuttered.

'Now for starters,' cut in Paul, 'you just told me that you had lodgings and Maryanne rented a bungalow on Beverly Boulevard. So how could you both always be together? Answer me that? You couldn't be aware of her movements all the time! So how could the police be certain in their investigation to arrest Maryanne, if she wasn't even at the home of Charles Osborne, according to you anyway?' Paul paused to glare knowingly at the woman opposite him. 'This is not adding up, Lamore. You haven't told me everything, have you? According to the original police investigation, Maryanne left Osborne's home around 8 p.m. So why try to deliberately make out that Maryanne never went there?'

Lamore opened her mouth to respond but Paul quickly

shot another set of words at her.

'Your reasoning regarding Charles's murder is superficial to say the least. Whoever it was, Charles knew personally, to allow entry to his home. It is someone connected with all these characters we have discussed, no outside party! We both know that, don't we?' Paul spoke angrily at the woman who held a pivotal role in the events of that fatal night. 'Whoever it was, came prepared with a gun. Remember that no weapon was ever found. This was probably a premeditated murder, carefully thought out to incriminate Maryanne. I may be wrong there, but, no, I don't believe for one minute that Maryanne committed the murder, but you both know who did!' Paul played his trump card with startling effect.

'Alright, alright! I can't say anymore!' Lamore was teary. Putting her hands up to her head, her facial features were contorted with deep foreboding. She rose her body and slowly walked to a writing bureau situated against the floral wallpapered wall. Opening the cover, she began writing something on paper. When Lamore had completed this, she picked up an envelope and slowly walked over to where Paul was seated. Handing the envelope and the slip of paper to Paul, Lamore seated herself down again. Her eyes were wet with tears and her expression was sorrow stricken.

It seemed to Paul that Lamore had broken a confidence that she had vowed never to break in her lifetime.

Lamore spoke first, her voice was shaky and emotional. 'For the sake of my son and your friendship with Ben, I have given you some photographs of Maryanne with Charles

Osborne. These were taken a few months before this calamity occurred. You may find them useful. My friendship with Maryanne was built on love and admiration for each other. It is up to Maryanne to complete the picture. A scene I cannot recreate or replicate in any form!'

Paul read the neat writing on the piece of fine quality notepaper.

Magdalena Hendon, 3213 Olahparinga Drive, Gull Rock Gorge, Oahu, Hawaii. Telephone 782 6663.

'Who is this person?' enquired Paul, mystified.

'That is Maryanne. After leaving Hollywood, she wanted to get as far away as she could. So Maryanne went to Hawaii. Changed her name, using one of her mother's names and her father's first name. She has lived there happily away from prying eyes for decades now.' Lamore seemed to have nothing further to say and just looked downheartedly at Paul.

Paul realised that his visit had been a traumatic experience – bringing back the past and digging up knowledge that had transformed the life of a dearly loved friend.

The mood in the sunroom seemed to lift to a brighter level when Lamore had composed herself and said cheerily, 'How about I take you for a tour of the farm and then some of the surrounding attractions. We can't sit here all day mooching around can we? I can drive you back later to Regina, if you wish or you could stay overnight. Let me know either way Paul. Yes, Ben often spoke of you. I think he missed your companionship on the beat. Things were never the same after you left, Ben said.' Lamore gave a sincere smile. Her reserve had been taken away, and she was being herself. The "actress" had been tucked away once more.

Soon, the pair were out and about, having an inspection of the adjoining farm. Lamore explained that the Bostock family had been farming for three generations and this farm had passed to her. A manager had been installed to keep the farm functioning, as Lamore was past this now. Cattle and some sheep roamed the lush paddocks, and another large area was for maize and corn growing. The farm paid a lucrative return. Winter was always a time for getting jobs done in the barn ready for sunnier days. Heavy snowfalls were recorded as the onslaught of winter hit Saskatchewan.

Their time together past quickly and Paul enjoyed seeing another side of life that he had never imagined before.

Such a vast difference to the glitz and glamour of Hollywood and the grit and fast pace of Los Angeles, Paul thought later. *The people are actually friendly here and have time to stop and chat with you.*

As Paul had booked a return ticket in Vancouver, he stayed overnight at Lamore's home. The conversation between the two had improved vastly over the evening. Lamore showed Paul family snaps of Ben in younger days when the Driscolls lived in San Francisco.

* * *

Morning came. A heavy dew had moistened the ground overnight and sparkling drops glistened on the grass. The sun had risen to proclaim another day, and bring with it the warmth and vitality of life itself. Bird song awakened Paul from a deep slumber. He rubbed his eyes and peered out through the lace curtains. Paul's perception of life had taken on a new meaning in just his short time here.

Reflecting on all that had been told him by Lamore, Paul perceived that he was still along way from the truth. One quality that Paul had been blessed with was patience. As they say, "Patience is a virtue that is often sorely tried but seldom understood".

Sitting up in bed and bringing his knees up to his chin, Paul was lost in thought. *The bond that existed between Maryanne and Lamore was strong and abiding. They had endured their younger years in fear. Their dreams of stardom were nothing more than a falling star that one endeavours to catch and hold onto for eternity; yet is just beyond your grasp! Would Maryanne or Magdalena, as she was now known, open the door to the actual series of deathly circumstances? One death had now brought four more deaths. Had there been any others prior? Only by speaking with Maryanne, could this case be untangled.*

Paul was sorry to leave McLean and Lamore. He had enjoyed his brief stay immensely. Waving to her from the train window, Lamore blew Paul a kiss and disappeared from view.

The train rolled along smoothly towards Regina and then on to Vancouver. Paul glimpsed out the window and smiled. *What had initially been a challenging meeting with Lamore, had resulted in a good outcome,* Paul thought, and sat back, closing his eyes with contentment.

CHAPTER 11

NEW DEVELOPMENTS

Determined to discover the whereabouts of Clarene Cremorne, Donna had made another visit to the City Records Office. Unfortunately, this determination had not paid off. She knew Paul wouldn't be happy with this.

There had been a phone call from the illustrious Mrs Andersen at 4 p.m. the previous afternoon. She had just arrived back from Las Vegas, and she wanted answers, quick smart! Not happy with Donna's reply that a deposit was required before proceedings could begin, Mrs Andersen informed Donna that Paul could "shove it up his backside!" Paul wouldn't be happy about that either, Donna figured.

Driving Gerty the Chevrolet Corvair, to the airport to meet Paul, Donna waited in the Arrivals Lounge. Soon the figure of Paul could be seen coming through the throng of other passengers from the flight. An enthusiastic kiss from Paul gave Donna a welcome surprise, as they walked out to the parking lot.

On the drive back to the office, Donna was able to inform Paul that her research on Clarene Cremorne had definitely drawn a blank.

'Oh, Mrs Andersen phoned as well,' she added.

'What did she have to say for herself?' asked Paul with an uncaring attitude.

'Well, she told me to tell you to "shove it up your backside!"' Donna turned her head to face Paul.

'Did she now, that's good! Let her stew in her own juice. We have enough to deal with at the moment without Mrs Andersen barking out orders!' replied Paul with a voice of pleasure.

'So, how did it all go with Lamore Driscoll? Any success, Paul?' Donna asked with curiosity in her silken voice.

'Yes, I have with me the address of Maryanne, now known as Magdalena Hendon. She lives in Hawaii. I have the telephone number too. So, I will contact her to arrange for us to pay her a visit. It would be prudent for you to accompany me, as I do think this is going to be a very sensitive matter to say the least! Your presence will help soften the delicate situation.'

'That is marvellous Paul. So this lady is still alive? Living a recluse no doubt, changing her name to conceal her identity. Who from, do you think? Felinda Bentine?' queried Donna.

'Quite possibly, or some other person. I am not sure, but certainly Felinda Bentine has driven Maryanne or now Magdalena, to extreme circumstances. Lamore Driscoll took some time to break under pressure. Her devotion to Magdalena is acutely strong. It seems that they both endured hardships at the studio they worked at. Then came the Osborne murder, and ranks were closed and sealed over, never to be broken. I admired Lamore's faithfulness and love for her friend,' Paul concluded.

'I see ...' said the intrigued Donna.

'But I still am not satisfied that Lamore Driscoll has been entirely honest with me,' Paul spoke on, with a disconcerting tone. 'There was something else that occurred that ill-fated night *or* there was another event that took place *prior* to that shattering night. I do believe that there were a number of people who were involved either indirectly or directly with the murder of Charles Osborne. Lamore Driscoll knows more, but for the sake of Maryanne aka Magdalena, she avoided telling me. I must give her full marks for the way Lamore steered the series of events so remarkably well. Her husband, Richard, also knew the real story, I am sure of that!' Paul was now very deep in thought as Donna drove Gerty back to the Parkside Business Centre.

Donna could determine that Paul was piecing every piece of the jigsaw together. She chose not to interrupt his thoughts. Yet for all that, Paul still lacked some vital pieces!

We may now pause and reflect for a moment, before the narrative is gradually exposed.

Human nature can be terribly vain and foible and satisfaction is often obtained by the most unspeakable methods. We can only ask ourselves the most open question – "Do we really honour and revere our fellows, or are our inmost passions driven to the extreme of hurting them physically and mentally too?"

Evil works in a variety of ways, sometimes swift and other times, slow and painful. The latter can drain and empty a human of their dignity, taking them to depths of despair and the lack of self-preservation, resulting in the most disastrous consequences. We can become victims entrapped in an intricate web of deceit and horrendous happenings. Vainly we endeavour to escape its clutches, but nothing we do, will release us from the dire actions perpetrated by an outside entity.

Now we resume our story, but have our feelings open to inspection and truthfulness!

Settling back into his routine again, Paul discussed the next step they would take to unravel this puzzling secret.

Paul opted to telephone Batman Biker. *What does he know about all this? Probably a lot more than we do, truth knowing!* He laughed inwardly to himself, as he dialled the phone number.

Speaking to some blatantly rude female wretch on the

other end of the line, Paul eventually was able to talk to Batman Biker.

Successful to set up a meeting with Batman Bike at a coffee shop in West Hollywood, just minutes away from the office, Paul was keen to revisit his notes to ensure that his information was accurate. He detected that Batman Biker was pleased that Paul had taken the initiative to make contact first. *It's a positive step in the right direction,* thought Paul.

After lunch, Paul resolved to walk to the coffee shop while Donna remained behind to type up some of Paul's notes from his Canadian journey.

A little after 1 p.m., Paul entered The Coffee House on Mendoza Ramble. Batman Biker was nowhere to be seen. Taking a seat against the back wall, Paul thought this was best, rather than be too obvious at a window table. *You never know who may be following me,* Paul thought.

Minutes ticked away, Paul watched the second hand move around the Tissot watch face. Declining to order a coffee, Paul chose to wait.

Shortly after 1.10 p.m., the door opened and in walked Batman Biker. His long strides took him effortlessly over to Paul's table.

Sitting down with a lumbering manner, Paul felt dwarfed by the figure opposite him. *A tall muscular guy for sure, wouldn't like to meet this one in a dark alley,* he thought. *Even his hands are huge and get a load of those rings. Wow, one smash in the face, and you would be cactus for sure!*

'I'm – '

'Yeah I know who you are. Known for some time where you hang out,' interrupted the deep booming voice of Batman Biker. He leant forward, and spoke with a reduced audibleness. 'Your lady friend had a close shave the other day. She drove that Mustang real well though, outran that bastard!'

'I understand that you really saved her life. Who was in the Camaro? Peterson?' asked Paul, waiting with great anticipation.

'Yeah, that was him alright!'

Nothing more was forthcoming, so Paul knew he had to delve further to get to the essence of their meeting.

'Donna said that you wanted to speak with me.'

'Yeah, that's right. Look pal, I will be open with you, as I think that I can trust you. You worked with Driscoll on the force. He was a good bloke but got shafted by that rat Peterson. I came back from Vietnam in '62 just days prior to the death of Marilyn Monroe. I was badly wounded by some snipers who got at me one night in the jungle. My wounds were painful and I resorted to drugs to kill the pain. At the same time, I started up a biker gang, all of us guys were ex Vietnam veterans. Most of us were all into drugs for various reasons. The group was called the Rebellion Rebels. A few years later, some younger guys joined us, not Vietnam veterans, you got the drift?' said Batman Biker.

Paul nodded his head in comprehension.

'Well, one of these idiots took it upon himself to challenge me to the leadership of the Rebellion Rebels. A fight broke out, I was rewarded with this …' he pointed a thick finger at the ugly scar below the left eye. 'Broken ribs, fractured arm and kicked senseless, I was dumped at a waste disposal site. Anyway, I managed to drag myself back to civilisation and seek treatment. At the Mercy Hospital in San Clemento, I get a visit from shit face Peterson and Driscoll, with the boys in blue! I got done for possession and dealing by Peterson. Peterson told some lie to Driscoll, about my previous drug history. Driscoll naturally believed Peterson, and had me charged!'

Hanging off the biker's every word, Paul continued to listen carefully.

'That was bullshit, I didn't have any drugs on me. Someone from the gang had grassed on me! I got five years for that. I should have been out in '67, but I escaped in '66 and was on the run as a fugitive for five months. I got betrayed by some gas station owner in Sacramento, and I had to do more time. I have not long been out and since then I have been trailing Peterson. He is cunning and a killer cop! He killed Driscoll and that janitor for sure! Peterson is hiding something big, you can count on it! I reckon it's drugs. How can he afford to buy a new Chevy Camaro on his salary. No way, Peterson is as crooked as my arm since it was beat up!'

'So where do I fit into all this?' asked Paul with caution.

'I followed Peterson the day he brought some package to you. He sat out in the car fiddling with it for a while. With binoculars, I could see that Peterson had opened the package.

He was reading some letter, then he resealed the package and took it into you. It was from Driscoll, wasn't it?' Batman Biker heaved his frame closer to Paul, speaking in his quietened tone, yet breathing heavily and studying Paul's face.

'Yes, it was.' Paul was unsure and chose to play safe. *Should I say anything about this Osborne murder, or see what else this guy has to say?*

'Well, come on, man, can't you say what that letter said?' asked Batman Biker in a slightly angry tone. His eyes searched Paul's face with annoyance.

Okay, play the game, don't hold back, thought Paul. Paul spoke honestly and replied, 'There was a tape from Driscoll, regarding a murder of a man named Charles Osborne that took place way back in 1922. A woman by the name of Maryanne Myles Morrow was charged with the murder, but was acquitted before the case was brought to trial. There were some witnesses who verified that Osborne was alive when they left his home but Morrow could not verify her whereabouts for the time of the murder. Hence the police were sure that she had murdered Osborne. Since then there has been the deaths of two ladies who were sisters of Maryanne. Their deaths are definitely suspicious, murdered no doubt by some accomplice of Peterson … ' Paul halted his words, and looked directly at Batman Biker. Continuing his explanation Paul spoke on, 'Yes, there was a letter in the package, containing a message in relation to the possible whereabouts of Maryanne Myles Morrow. That aspect I am still working on.'

The man sat back and gave Paul a stare of contemplation. 'Charles Houghton Osborne was my father. I was adopted as a baby,' he said. 'All I ever knew was that my mother wanted me called "new man". I have been trying to trace my mother since I was a kid. A mother I never had. I was deprived of a normal childhood. It was only by coincidence that I learnt who my real father was. When I joined the army for Vietnam service, you had to fill in some forms about next of kin. Well, I had no one. My adopted parents had died, so I left it blank. The duty officer took pity on me and did some research, how, don't ask me! By this time I was on active service. A letter arrived from this officer telling me who my real father was, but he couldn't give me any lead to who my mother was. Life has been nothing but hardship. I have had to fight to exist, I learnt boxing and martial arts when I was a teenager. This helped me to protect myself otherwise I would have been six foot under! Shunted around from one place to another after my adopted parents were killed in an automobile accident when I was 11. Treated like scum and often locked away for days on end by institutions for homeless kids like me. Beaten most nights and sexually interfered with ...'

Paul listened carefully. He could see the pain on Batman Biker's face as he spoke.

'Suffered from lack of food and warm clothing. Foster parents were much the same, made you feel worthless and unwanted,' the biker continued. 'Starved of love and decency, I tried to kill myself many times, but was never successful. I thought by joining up, I would get away from the life of being a vagrant. I went from place to place and job to job. Accused of theft and being a serial killer, I was in the lockup more times than I can remember. Peterson must have done a background check on me, and found out who my real father was. So he was all out to have me put away! Then I got done by Peterson. So I retaliated, and escaped. Fought my way out of jail, so I became a wanted man!

'All I wanted in life was to be accepted as a real person, who had a father and mother. But all that had been taken away, and I was just a number in a huge void that couldn't care a damn shit! My last stunt in jail gave me the time to think that my whole purpose in life was to now search for my mother. As I now know that Charles Osborne was my real father, then I will not rest until I find who my mother is. Alright, she might be dead, but I deserve to know brother!' With that, Batman Biker completed his life account, pointing a shaking finger to Paul's face. The man was determined and clearly upset.

Paul did feel genuinely sorry for this man sitting opposite him. Regardless of the beefy biker's size and apparent abruptness, he carried an empty heart. Joy had been extinguished and any family ties had also been fragmented at an early age.

'How can I help?' Paul asked with deep regard.

Giving Paul a defiant glance, Batman Biker gruffly said, 'You went away. What for and where?'

'I went to Canada to meet Ben Driscoll's mother, Lamore.

She is a friend of the lady accused of your father's murder. Her name was Maryanne Myles Morrow, but she has since altered it to disguise her identity. She might know some more to help you find your mother,' replied Paul openly. Paul knew he had probably told this man too much, but instinct had taken over his impulses, and the words came tumbling out. Revealing the new name of Maryanne would have been unwise, so Paul carefully avoided mentioning it.

'Where is this lady?' the stocky biker asked hurriedly.

'For the moment, let me speak with her first. I shall keep you informed, and I'll keep my promise. Remember, this woman has been through a lot herself. Her career was cut short in the film industry and her family cut ties with her. She was accused of murder and made a laughing stock by society. I understand that this lady is a recluse and would not take kindly to anyone just appearing at her doorstep asking questions. We have to tread prudently to achieve results. Okay?' Paul sat back and waited for a response.

Staring long and hard at Paul, the eyes of this man were summing Paul up.

Without hesitation, Batman Biker said harshly, 'Alright man, but the minute you have anything, I want to know pronto! No messing me up or funny business, you understand or I shall make a nasty mess of your handsome face, got it?! I don't take kindly to being fucked around pal. Kick ass is a specialty of mine, okay buster?' The man's face was hard and his eyeballs seemed to glow with acute glee at the prospect of administering some facial alterations to Paul's outward appearance.

'Sure, I comprehend. Can you at least tell me your name, that may prove helpful?' Paul asked, hoping that his face would not be rearranged.

'My name is Neumann Riessler. My mother got her wish to name me. My adopted parents told me that I was the 'new man' in my mother's life and that is why she wanted me named that way. The spelling is a bit different that's all.' He then spelt his first name for the benefit of Paul. Batman Biker gave a brief smile. 'The Riessler bit is from my adopted parents.'

'I shall do my utmost to find out all I can and let you know, Neumann. Give me some time, I have to make another trip. Thanks for taking care of Donna, I do appreciate it.' Paul put out his hand to shake.

Neumann gave a nod and likewise shook hands firmly with Paul.

'Can I get you a coffee?' asked Paul.

'No man, I have some stuff to do. Don't drink it anyway, I only drink beer. Used to be an alcoholic, but got it under control now.' Neumann Riessler lowered his large head and leant over towards O'Shea.

Speaking with a softer tone of voice, Riessler said, 'I was late coming here, as I left a package containing the gun I snatched out of Peterson's hand that day he tried to knock off your gorgeous secretary. Have it checked out to see if the bullets match the bullets that killed Driscoll.' With that, Riessler got up, nodded and walked out of the coffee shop.

Paul saw him get on his black 750CC Indian motorbike and roar off. The steel was polished to perfection. *Well, that was an interesting encounter,* Paul thought. *Another spoke in the wheel, what will be the next?*

Walking back to the office, Paul continued to mull over his meeting with Neumann Riessler.

This man had been sorely rejected by society, treated with contempt and set up for a felony he did not commit. Why did Peterson want Riessler out of the way, when he had him put away on trumped up charges? Using Ben as the tool to implement what Peterson wanted! Did this Magdalena Hendon know anything about this son of Charles Osborne? There has to be a connection. The gun theory is worthwhile following up for sure.

The questions kept mounting up, and the answers were not coming as quick!

Donna had completed her task and placed the typed sheets on Paul's desk. She had tried to lay them in chronological order to make it easier for Paul to follow the series of happenings.

'How was the meeting with the biker chap?' Donna was keen to know.

Before Paul could answer, Donna told him about the package that Batman Biker had left.

'Yes, he did tell me about that. The package contains the gun that Peterson was going to use on you. This chap suggested that the police examine the bullets to see if they correspond to the bullets that killed Ben Driscoll. This could prove to be very interesting indeed Donna. If they match, then we have Peterson in our hand,' said Paul excitedly.

"That is a good idea. It probably is the same weapon that Peterson used to kill Ben. Anyway, what else did 'Batman Biker' have to say?' queried Donna, eager to hear more.

'It was enlightening, but I must say it went quite well Donna. His name is Neumann Riessler, and get this, his father was Charles Osborne.'

'No way!' ejaculated Donna, with a stunned look on her face.

Paul explained the content of the appointment with Riessler.

As Paul completed his last words to Donna, he thought of something significant. 'Donna, can I see those photos of Maryanne with Charles Osborne again?'

Donna retrieved the photos from a file, and handed them to Paul.

'Hmmm. There is a definite likeness between the two men. Look at Osborne. He appears quite tall and muscular and his colouring is a light shade too. I appreciate that it's difficult to say exactly from these three black and white photos, but you could certainly say that they were related.'

Donna studied the photos herself and agreed that there was a distinct similarity.

'Do you think that Maryanne, as we know her, may be this guy's mom?'

Before Paul could answer, Donna said with elation, 'If that was the case, then Maryanne may have been pregnant when Osborne was murdered. Unless the mother was someone else. Perhaps Maryanne discovered that Osborne had played dirty on her, then that would give her the motive to kill Osborne!'

'You could well be correct in that assumption, Donna. Our visit to Magdalena Hendon will only cement our thoughts into place. I think its time I contacted her,' Paul said before reaching for the phone.

Donna hovered close by to determine what reaction Paul would receive.

'May I speak with Magdalena Hendon, please?'

'No, Mrs Hendon is unable to come to the phone right now," came a lady's voice, her response stiff. 'Can I take a message?'

Paul then mentioned his name. This proved to be successful, and he was told to wait on the line.

'Hello, this is Magdalena Hendon speaking,' said a mild female voice.

Coming straight to the point of his phone call, Paul asked if Donna and he could come to visit her to discuss the Osborne murder.

'Lamore Driscoll kindly gave me your details, as you are no doubt aware,' Paul said, winking at Donna. Speaking on, he then tactfully said, 'I have some information that you may be interested in.'

There was a definite quietness from Magdalena before she granted a meeting with them.

Confirming her address, Paul said they would convene tomorrow, possibly in the afternoon, but he would confirm this when they were in Hawaii. Paul perceived that Magdalena was cautious and reluctant to open up old wounds that had been nursed for many years.

Donna made reservations for them on an early flight to Hawaii leaving tomorrow morning, including accommodation at the Intercontinental Hotel upon arrival. Paul suggested that they hire a car for convenience. All was set for their next phase in solving this network of treachery and deception.

On his way home that evening, Paul met Detective Sergeant Bruno Capezio at a pre-designated place. Paul discreetly handed Capezio the package containing the deadly revolver. The task was now up to the police to verify the ballistics report to the bullets in the gun belonging to Peterson. Capezio departed with a definite smile on his dial that late afternoon.

CHAPTER 12
PACIFIC INTERLUDE

Sunset Pacific Airlines Flight 101 point 9, glided smoothly onto the runway at Honolulu Airport at precisely 11.29 a.m. Flying time had been approximately six hours.

The day was bright and the sun's intensity was already quite strong. Some humidity was evident in the atmosphere as Paul and Donna emerged from the airport complex.

Hopping into their rental car – a flashy Ford Galaxie convertible – Paul and Donna drove straight to the hotel. The pair had a quick bite to eat before studying their route to Gull Rock Gorge.

In preparation for their discussion, Paul advised Donna on the technique of words to use. Diplomacy was imperative, to be able to extract as much information as possible, given the sensitive nature of the subject. Donna had an important role to play, and Paul expected her to execute this part professionally.

Paul contacted the nameless female voice at the Hendon residence, to inform her of their pending arrival.

Gull Rock Gorge was situated at the bottom of the island of Oahu, in an inlet of secluded beaches and sand dunes. Waving palm trees and sweetly scented oleanders lined the road. With the ocean breeze blowing Donna's hair like sea foam on translucent ribbons, Paul drove the convertible down the freeway. The view was vividly glorious and intoxicating. Homes were perched on spectacular sights overlooking the Pacific waters.

Approaching Gull Rock Gorge, they were amazed to see how quaint this part of the island was. The homes were older and had expansive well tendered gardens. A serene sense of respectability gave the new arrivals a fresh perspective of the neighbourhood. Traffic was minimal and after a pleasant drive, the convertible was turning into the driveway of the Hendon home. A circular driveway gave access to the older style wood structure.

The house was painted a pure gleaming white. A single storey residence with a wrap around verandah painted in a shade of emerald green. Wide window frames gave the viewer an unobstructed vista of the distant ocean. A separate double garage could be seen a short way from the home, also painted in the same colour scheme.

Paul gaped at the magnificent blue and white trim automobile parked just outside the garage. 'Look at that machine!' he called out. His eyes were bulging out of his sockets as he brought the Ford Galaxie to a stop.

'It's just an old car, what's the big deal?' asked Donna.

'That happens to be a really rare car, Donna. Do you know what it is?'

Donna shrugged her shoulders with a "don't know, don't care" attitude.

'That is a 1931 Marmon V16 Town Car. Like hen's teeth! You just don't see them anymore, not many were ever made!'

'Paul, we haven't come here to see old time cars, remember dear?!' said Donna decisively, and guided Paul firmly towards the house.

The double front door had been opened by an elderly woman in her sixties. A face of hardened steel adorned this woman. Her silver hair was severely tied back into a matronly bun. Wearing a dove grey pinafore with a white short sleeve blouse and low-heeled black lace up shoes, one got the impression that she was formerly a head mistress of a girls' school. A very brief smile came and went as she stepped outside for the pair to enter.

Stepping up onto the verandah, Donna and Paul walked across to the door opening and went inside.

The interior was cool and tranquil. Sparsely furnished yet with items of an antique style furnished the large room. The polished boards gleamed in the sunlight streaming through the long windows.

'Please, take a seat. Mrs Hendon will be right with you.' Another forced smile lit the face only momentarily. The woman left the room by one of the three doors leading from the room.

Donna sat down but Paul chose to stand and await Magdalena Hendon. The sage green double sofa was expertly made and there were two more single chairs in the same fabric. Pacing around the room, Paul became anxious and unsettled.

'Paul, come and sit down. There is no point wandering around like a caged lion, she won't come any quicker,' Donna said reprovingly.

'Yeah, alright,' Paul's eyes were taking everything in. 'Nice place she has. Did you notice those paintings on the wall over there? I think that they are originals and signed by Magdalena Hendon herself. I can see an easel through those French doors. There's a painter's palette and paints on a table. She must be an artist,' Paul said as he walked toward the French doorway entrance.

'You are very correct, Mr O'Shea, I am indeed an artist. Would you like to see some more?' came the velvety voice of a woman who had entered the room from the corner arched doorway. 'And you must be Donna?' she greeted.

The woman was small in stature but commanded a presence in the room. Not the glitzy "look at me" factor, but a lady who gave an aura of dignity and immense charm. A certain grace endowed her beauty to anyone beholding her for the first time. The colour of her eyes were an intense yellow shade and merriment danced within their depths. Hair the colour of a snowdrop was neatly arranged, falling just to her delicate shoulders. A long heavenly blue dress was worn with style. It was well cut and a double strand pearl necklace hung around her throat. On her small sized feet were white sandals.

A sincere smile from the lady made Paul and Donna feel more at ease.

'Come this way, and I shall show you some more paintings, if you are interested of course?' offered the lady, looking for confirmation from her visitors.

'Yes, we would love to see your paintings, Mrs Hendon,' Paul stumbled out.

Magdalena Hendon walked to the French doors and opened them, followed by Paul and then Donna.

The airy room was an artist's haven. Finished works were hung on the white walls or on ornate easels. A work in progress comprised of a bowl of rich crimson tulips against a background of sunlight cascading in through an opened window. For a humourous effect, a small snail had been included, making its labourious way across the table to the bowl of tulips.

Paul admired a painting on an easel tucked away at the far end of the extensive room. The long windows opened up onto the porch, where wicker chairs and table were placed.

Magdalena Hendon gradually walked in Paul's direction.

The painting in question was of a young girl, possibly no more than 16 years old. It depicted her standing by a set of long narrow windows, and looking into the room, as though someone had just entered and disturbed her thoughts. A smile of welcome and joy lit her youthful countenance. Closer inspection, Paul realised that it was an old painting. Some of the oil had slightly cracked and the frame was of a heavy wood, intricately carved and painted gold and white. The girl wore a three quarter length exquisite lace dress, and had on shoes with the matching lace. The golden hair radiated in the sunlight that streamed into the room, tied back with a vivid blue ribbon. A glow of warmth enveloped any person casting their eyes upon this work. In the bottom right hand corner Paul could just make out the artist – MMM 1918. Knowing immediately who this was, Paul drew back for Magdalena to come near.

'Yes, that was my only painting of my youngest sister, Alyssa. She was 17 years old then but sadly died two years later. We were particularly close. Even now I still miss her. To think what might have been, poor child.' A hand of gentleness caressed the canvas around the facial parts. Magdalena seemed distant in her thoughts as she spoke, recalling a time that was painful, and better to be forgotten.

Paul saw Donna standing just a few paces back, listening to the words of Magdalena.

'Well, we must make you comfortable and I shall have some refreshments brought in by Audrey. You met Audrey, haven't you? She was my maid in Hollywood, and I had her come with me – a loyal and wonderful friend. Audrey has been a rock through many years of turmoil. I would be lost without her.' Stretching out her arms towards Paul and Donna, she stood in the middle and walked with them back into the front room where they had first encountered this woman who exuded love and compassion.

After having drinks supplied by the silent Audrey, Magdalena sat back in her chair and let Paul do the talking.

Attempting to be as concise as possible, Paul spoke of his visit to Lamore Driscoll. He excluded the earlier events but knew in time that he would have to broach the subject of the deaths of Tryphena and Tryphosa. It now became increasingly challenging to Paul as he relayed the details of the death of Ben Driscoll, and now the meeting with Neumann Riessler.

Donna heard her cue and took over the conversation with ease. 'A man has come forward and told us that his father was Charles Osborne. He is searching for his real mother.'

Magdalena listened intently to the confident voice of Donna.

Donna took a breath and carried on, with a caring attitude. 'Apparently his mother requested he be called a certain name. Would you know what that might be, Mrs Hendon?' Donna stopped and stared with extreme wariness at the woman who held so much knowledge to solve all this heartbreak.

There was a slight intake of breath from Magdalena Hendon, her head turned away and she put her hand up to her mouth. Tears rolled down her face like a waterfall that had a never-ending supply of water.

Donna went over to Magdalena, bending down and held the other hand. Magdalena grasped Donna's hand and looked her in the face and nodded her head.

Paul felt that time stood still, as he watched this scene take place. It was very moving, Donna had struck a sensitive recollection. *All we have to do now is wait,* Paul mused.

Composing herself, Magdalena Hendon managed to control her sobs and Donna sat down next to her on the two-seater sofa. 'I wanted my son named "Newman" because he was the new man in my life. Charles had been taken from me and then my boy was taken as well.' Magdalena's voice was tinged with sadness and acute sorrow. Shedding tears, her body shook and her gasps of breath were poignantly sorrowful. 'Where is he, I want to see him, please, please?' Magdalena pleaded with Paul.

Paul swallowed hard, his voice had momentarily shut down. Regaining his vocal chords, Paul uttered quietly, 'You will, I will see to that, Magdalena. His name is Neumann Riessler, and he has been searching for you since he was a boy.' Paul spelt the name phonetically to Magdalena. 'He was adopted by people named Riessler, but unfortunately they were killed in an automobile accident when Neumann was 11 …' Paul paused to allow Magdalena to comprehend all he had just said, before smoothly adding, 'Neumann looks like his father, Charles Osborne.'

'Does he? I am so pleased! I only got a glimpse of my boy when he was born, then they whisked him away. Neumann would be 47 years old now. I have prayed every day that some time before I died, that I would set my eyes upon my child. Now you have brought hope and certainty to me.' Magdalena held Donna's hand tightly, and turned her enchanting face towards Paul, and sighed deeply. Her eyes held an inner wisdom, yet tinged with knowledge that had to be told after all this period.

Paul, daring to break the silence in the room, said, 'What did happen that night, Magdalena? This is not easy for you, and what's more, I can't begin to understand the anguish you have endured for so long. Lamore has lost a son, and Neumann is involved with this complexity of human manipulation. Lives have been taken or destroyed. I know that you didn't kill Charles, but for his soul to rest, the truth must be disclosed. You owe it to yourself and your son.' Paul was wanting to know desperately if Magdalena was pregnant with Neumann the night of the murder, but had to abstain asking any further questions. *Better allow Magdalena to talk at her pace*, thought Paul.

Magdalena smiled weakly. Her heart was aching with remorse, but she knew Paul was right. Charles deserved to be at peace. So much speculation and despicable horror had afflicted, not just herself, but others too. Comforted with the knowledge that her beloved son was alive, and desired to meet his mother, Magdalena replied with a stronger disposition, 'There is much to say. I'm not sure where to begin …'

Donna's words helped the lady to start her story. 'Tell us about your days at Lorraway … ' she said, 'And the good times you had with your family.'

Blinking quickly, and facing Donna, Magdalena replied, 'My life at Lorraway was idyllic and carefree. We were all so happy, six sisters, close in age, with similar interests. Artistic and theatrical parents, who were loving and protective of us.' Sitting back in the sofa, she released her hands from Donna, and cast her eyes onto nothing specific in the room. 'Then as we matured, the lure of films brought problems and jealousy into our home. Rivalry between us grew like a canker and consumed us. Felinda had assumed the role of "head of the household". Life was like living with a cosmic overlord, setting out rules and regulations. Woe betide if you disobeyed! Her wrath was kindled and sparks flew, I can tell you! My parents had become eccentric, caught up with the classic tales of Greece and Rome. They were just ignorant of anything else, dear pair. We all had been taken on by First National Pictures Corporation, even young Alyssa.' Bringing her thoughts back to reality, Magdalena, heaved her body forward slightly.

'I don't know what you have been told regarding Alyssa or what you may have read, BUT ...' she broke off her speech and raised her eyebrows. 'Alyssa did die because she had contracted diphtheria ... she was denied medical treatment, which resulted in her death.'

'What happened?' Donna asked with wonder, not wanting to pry too much.

Magdalena's mind was a jumble of so many things. She knew she had to tell the truth about Alyssa and the pitiful Felinda. 'My dear, you have to understand that Felinda was not one to take second best in any aspect of life. You see, Alyssa and Felinda had been arguing over who was to play Aphrodite the Goddess of Love in a new film. Both were superb actresses, but the studio chose Alyssa. As destiny often has the final say, Alyssa was afflicted with diphtheria very suddenly. We had a telephone, but Felinda refused to call the family doctor. Her reasoning was that she could take care of Alyssa. I was forbidden to use the phone, as I had been caught by Jedson, her husband, trying to contact the doctor. I assume that you have been acquainted with Felinda and Jedson?'

Paul and Donna nodded comprehendingly, neither saying a word about their unpleasant encounter.

'Yes, a delightful couple. I can see that they have left a lasting impression on you both.' Magdalena's voice was tactile as she smiled at them. 'Mother was made known of Alyssa's illness, and told me to paint her throat with Methylated Spirits. According to mother, this was an old remedy used when doctors were not available. This solution of spirits would burn the throat, but also kill the germ. I beseeched Felinda to apply the Methylated Spirits, but she refused to listen. Shut the bedroom door in my face and locked the door! The only person permitted entry was that horrible Jedson. Thought he was so important. Naturally, Alyssa passed away. Married just five months to a man called Grayden Plantoleggia. Well, he committed suicide a week later. So overcome with grief, he took his life. Felinda sailed on, did all the funeral arrangements, took control of everything. She got her own way, but the shock to the studio losing their leading lady, meant that they cancelled the filming. The studio terminated Felinda's contract instantly. You see, I had informed them what had taken place. So then on, Felinda had it in for me.'

Donna and Paul listened carefully, nodding in unison as the lady shared her story.

Collecting her thoughts, Magdalena carried on her account of events. 'Johnny Appleseed had come into my life a couple of years before – a really dear man, so vain and yet unsure of himself too. Wonderful actor, knew all his lines but fell foul to that wretched cocaine! I tried so hard to help him, but he couldn't bring himself to stop. After Johnny's death in '22, Felinda tainted my name as much as she could, hoping to bring disgrace to me. I became acquainted with Charles a little later, and we just fell in love. I thought of him as a father figure initially, but then our love grew passionately stronger.

'Charles fathered my child and then he was murdered. I was bereft. I suffered a mental breakdown. My mind was muddled, I could not think clearly, and was unable to verify where I was at the time Charles was shot. Naturally the police wanted to charge me with the murder, but my lawyers worked relentlessly to have the case rejected due to insufficient evidence. After that, my name was black! I had to get away, so I came here to Hawaii, and have not regretted the move. The only heartbreak was knowing that I had left my son somewhere, and I could never see or hold him. My only memory I took from Lorraway, was my painting of Alyssa.'

'So you became a successful artist, Magdalena?' asked Paul.

'Yes, Paul. I was professionally trained as a girl, and always enjoyed painting. So in order to earn a living, I resorted to a talent I was endowed with, and have been prosperous.'

Now realising that a crucial aspect needed clarification, Paul introduced the topic of the elusive Clarene Cremorne.

At the mention of the name, Magdalena displayed a hint of recognition, but it quickly faded. 'I can't remember her very well at all. I am aware that she visited Charles on the night he was murdered, but I cannot tell you anything about her, sorry.' The sentence was completed with a definite tinge of "don't ask me again".

'What about the other people who visited Charles, could they have carried out the murder?' asked Paul.

'Oh, I don't think so!' Magdalena said emphatically.

'Lindsay was our costume manager, drunken sex maniac! I doubt if he could have killed anyone. Just loved getting between a woman's legs – that was all he wanted to do! The Hummersteins were very well to do, with connections in Hollywood. They were financiers, and were well spoken of by everyone. No, I am sure it wasn't them. Charles thought highly of the Hummersteins.'

'Well, we haven't got any other suspects, that we know of. Are you sure that no one else had a grudge against Charles?' Paul asked. 'He was opposed to the narcotics industry that had taken hold in Hollywood. Could it have been someone associated with narcotics, that murdered Osborne?'

Paul was in a quandary. *Surely Magdalena must know something more!* he thought. *What is not being told?! This Clarene Cremorne holds a key to resolve the chain of events. If you were pregnant with Neumann, had Osborne asked your hand in marriage? Or, was he having it on with Cremorne?*

Tackling the matter from another angle, Paul screwed up his face and said in a questioning tone, 'Was Clarene Cremorne a drug user?' Paul sat on the edge of his chair and waited for a reply.

Magdalena Hendon made no attempt to answer, it seemed as though she was thinking up an answer – indeed she was. 'Not that I am aware of,' she replied. 'As I said previously, I hardly knew her. I mean, she could have been, but I really couldn't say, Paul.' Magdalena shrugged her shoulders to pass the matter off.

Paul became frustrated, he was being played for the fool. 'I gather that you have been told that your sisters, Tryphena and Tryphosa were horribly murdered just days ago?' he asked. His words were intended to sting the woman sitting opposite him.

'Yes, I know! They were so pure and uncorrupted by the outside world,' Magdalena said no more, clasping her tiny hands together.

Opening his arms wide, Paul had to overcome this tangle of deception, he was getting nowhere. 'Magdalena, there have been four deaths. Two are your blood sisters, and another is the son of your dearest friend. You are talking around a matter, or series of happenings, to get rid of me. That's the bottom line, isn't it? So why was your child taken from you? I will tell you why!' Paul's eyes were raging with exasperation. 'Felinda intervened for some reason. Was it because Charles and you weren't married? Please help us here! We aren't here to seek self glorification Magdalena, so give us a break and start to come clean with us!'

That was the catalyst. Magdalena could take no more.

Flinging her arms into the air, she altered her manner completely. 'I cannot say anymore! You will both have to leave, now!' Magdalena's face was distorted with a mixture of emotions, her face was flushed and voice almost hysterical,

Before Paul and Donna could say anything, Magdalena hurriedly left the room by the archway entrance and disappeared.

CHAPTER 13

PURSUIT OF TRUTH

The truth can often make us do the most remarkable actions that normally we would never do.

Magdalena's calm had been broken. As composed as she wanted to remain, Paul had entered an arena where no one else had ever dared to step. Was he a fool, where angels would dare to tread? Far from it!

Paul was challenging Magdalena to be honest with herself. Why the constant secrecy, was it to protect someone else? Well, we must read on to discover the hidden truth. How easy it is to lead a life of deception, thinking we have fooled our fellows, yet all the time it is just us, who are being deceived. Our vanity is so paramount, yet we handle it with reckless abandon.

Looking at each other like perennial wallflowers, Paul and Donna were amazed at the unexpected change in Magdalena's demeanour.

'Let's go, Donna. There's nothing more we can achieve by staying here,' Paul quickly said to Donna.

They let themselves out of the house and drove away back onto the main road to their hotel.

Paul was extraordinarily reticent. His mind had been circulating some ideas in his mind. Magdalena Hendon had made one error in her account of her time in Hollywood. *Felinda Bentine had no reason to tell a falsehood on timings, but someone had made a subtle mistake, who was it? Could it be possible? Yes, quite likely, in order to get us off the trail!* Paul was so involved with his powers of reasoning, that he had not heard Donna speaking to him.

'Paul, are you listening to me? What are you thinking? Don't you consider your words were somewhat harsh to Magdalena? She requires time Paul. We can't expect answers right away! Paul, what is it, tell me?' Donna leant over and shook his arm.

'When we get back to the hotel, I shall reveal my ideas. Until then, sit back and enjoy the scenery. I have a lot of planning to do. We shall be quite busy, I will say that!' Paul drove on rapidly and soon they were back at the hotel.

Before they even got out of the Ford Galaxie, Paul instructed Donna to go to their hotel room.

'Why, where are you going? Can't I come too, or am I to be kept in the dark?' Donna sounded irritated.

'Donna, I am going to swap this car for something else. I will explain, now please, just trust me and I will be back shortly.'

Forty minutes later, Paul was relaxing in their hotel room.

The tenth floor room had sweeping views of the pristine

beach and the azure blue of the Pacific Ocean.

Donna had changed into something more comfortable, and had mixed some cocktails for them.

'Okay, fill me in on your illustrious ideas, Mr Private Investigator,' Donna said with great interest. Standing behind Paul, she massaged his neck slowly.

It was soothing to the man, as he divulged his ideas to Donna. Firstly, Paul explained that he wanted to change their hire car to one that was quicker, and less conspicuous too. Paul's choice of a current model black American Motors AMX was to his satisfaction. Especially for the assignment he had purposed for them to accomplish. Going into lengthy detail regarding his theory, Paul revealed his inner most thoughts concerning their visit to Magdalena Hendon. Paul then made sure that Donna had packed the necessary outfit that he had stipulated they each take with them.

'Yes, I did as you said.'

Paul took out two walkie talkies from his suitcase and handed one to Donna. 'You are going to need this,' he instructed. 'I shall clarify what we will be doing.'

In summary, Paul's plan was to return at night to the Hendon residence. Donna was to watch the front of the home like a hawk. Protection was afforded by the screen of Mimosa and Bougainvillea bushes at the front entrance. Any movement in or out was to be reported via the walkie talkie to Paul. Dressed in her dark slacks and sweatshirt, with a dark headscarf and sand shoes, Donna was hopeful to remain unseen from the house residents.

Paul's operation was to watch the back of the home. According to a map he had procured, the Hendon property backed onto a small estuary, before being met by the Pacific Ocean. If anyone was to leave via the estuary, Paul was sure to see this.

There was the distinct likelihood that a jetty with a boat moored, was a means to leave the home unnoticed. Regular contact with each other would ensure that neither came into trouble.

Finally, Paul made an urgent telephone call back to the mainland. They required the presence of this person to assist in breaking the tenacity of Magdalena Hendon. Details were given to the recipient of the telephone call with startling accuracy.

Paul ate hungrily that night in the Bistro located on the first floor of their hotel. Donna was a little nervous, but felt she could achieve what was needed to be done. She knew Paul was relying on her ability to remain calm in the face of possible adversity. If Paul's hunch was correct, then the actions of the night would be worthwhile.

Shortly before 10.45 p.m., the black AMX left the Intercontinental Hotel underground parking lot, with Paul driving and Donna as passenger. Both were attired in black outfits and had their respective walkie talkie with them. Paul had a small Swiss army knife, which he thought may prove to be useful.

* * *

Resting your eyes for a moment, let us consider that people can be driven to desperate measures – especially if truth is to be buried, never to see the light of humanity's understanding or gentle touch. Little did Paul and Donna know what lay ahead of them.

The night drive to Gull Rock Gorge was totally different from their day journey. A windless atmosphere graced the evening, and cicadas told stories to their partners. Scattered clouds had rolled in from the ocean and were partly obliterating the numberless array of stars. A luminous full moon was resplendent this night, which would later prove to be fortuitous to our pair of sleuths. The landing on the moon had not long taken place, and man had now conquered the heavens above. However, had man dealt with his own shortcomings here on earth?

Turning off the car engine, Paul let the AMX roll to a stop just south of the Hendon estate driveway. Leaving the car situated well back from the road, screened by a large oleander bush, they made their way to their site of extreme significance. An owl gave a hoot at the two figures who crept with stealth towards the home.

'All set?' whispered Paul.

'Yes, all set!' Donna muttered inaudibly.

Paul gradually made his way down the left hand side of the property, using the garage as cover to gain access to the back of the acreage. Knowing the land size was large from the diagram on the handy town map he had quickly procured from the City of Honolulu cartography department, Paul could see the estuary in the near distance. When he had changed the hire cars, the Municipal building was right next door, which gave Paul the notion to obtain a map of the Gull Rock Gorge home sites.

An avenue of gardenias in full bloom perfumed the night air. The dark figure of Paul rushed behind these beauties and down the sloping land towards the lapping shore. He could just discern a jetty with a speedboat moored alongside. *The avenue of escape,* mused Paul.

Meanwhile, Donna had positioned herself within view of the front door of the wide home frontage.

Using his walkie talkie, Paul contacted Donna to ensure she was in position. 'Come in, Foxy Lady. Do you read me, over.' Paul had decided on the use of code names for them.

A crackling reply came from Donna, 'Yes, Mach 1. I read you, over.'

'Are you in view of target, over,' came Paul's hurried response.

'Affirmative,' uttered Donna carefully. Should she say "over" or not, Donna wasn't sure?

'Good, let me know the minute anyone leaves the house, roger and out.'

Time marched on, and as we know, time waits for no one. It is relentless in its measured pursuit in any era of civilisation. Then it occurred.

Donna saw a woman's figure materialise from inside the house. The woman was hooded, wearing dark slacks, and carried a small bag. Walking like a bent stooger, the female made her way to the garage. Looking around her with a furtive glance, she opened the garage door. It slid silently open. Two cars were visible.

Donna's eyes were fixed on the garage. Crouching down like a panther watching its prey, Donna observed every movement of our escapee. A nocturnal spotted beetle, enjoying a night flight, appeared out of nowhere, and perched itself on Donna's head. Feeling an irritation, Donna flicked her head and overbalanced onto her knees.

The sound of a purring motor alerted Donna that someone was on the move! The Marmon Town Car had been driven out of the garage, and was gaining speed as it made its way to the driveway entrance. Scrambling up, Donna grabbed her means of contact, and tuned into Paul.

'This is Foxy Lady, suspect leaving in old car and turning south, over!' Donna felt heady and breathless.

Things were moving quickly now. If only Donna knew how quick events were going to snowball that night!

'Keep your position, do not move,' advised Paul. 'That is a decoy. I will let you know if anyone comes my way, over and out.' Paul's mind was ablaze with alertness and possibilities. *So, the old trick of misleading was used was it? Nice try ladies, but it won't work tonight!* He now was acutely aware that someone would be departing from the back of the house, to remain unseen.

The jetty was not long, say 20 feet, but there was a new speedboat tied up at the side of the well maintained jetty. A Mercury outboard motor was attached to the sleek boat, named appropriately "Maryanne".

Well, well, thought Paul, *old habits die hard! Even naming the boat her original name.*

The seconds ticked by, darkness had now enveloped the land but the moon shone its eternal glow on the earth's surface.

Using a limestone embankment as coverage, Paul crouched low and moved slightly to limber up his legs. He waited patiently. Checking the incandescent dial of his watch, the time was now 11.48 p.m. *That's it,* he thought, *a flashlight!* Paul's eyes were focused on someone making for the jetty. Then, without the hint of a sound, a figure came into sight. Walking with confidence, the figure came into view more discernibly.

Like greased lightning, Paul made contact with Donna, and told her to stay put. 'I have suspect in sight now, over and out!'

Paul could see it was a woman, carrying a small torch. A headscarf was tied around the head, and her obscure dungaree clothing was beneficial for her nightly escapade. Onto the jetty the woman marched. He could not see her face clearly, hidden by the scarf, but he had a rough idea who it would be.

Loosening the rope, the woman stepped onto the boat and made her way to the covered cabin.

Whilst our hooded individual commenced to start the motor, Paul had sneaked along the jetty and waited his opportunity. The engine kicked into life. Paul made his dash and clambered aboard the boat nimbly, unseen by our mystery woman. Edging the boat out into the estuary, Paul laid low behind a rear set of twin seats. The boat was making good progress by now, and was heading for land on the opposite side. *Was that the headland or was it an island? Could be an island, that would make sense,* reasoned Paul, as the boat sped smoothly over the shiny water, hallowed by the moonlight.

Five, then ten minutes went past, and the boat continued its way towards the land mass. The woman knew her way, and needed no navigational aids.

Paul peered back in the direction that they had come; the lights of the mainland were dim now.

Presently, the boat reduced its speed, and the unknown "skipper" began to make a bee line to a man made outcrop of rocks. There was a very small area where the boat could tie up. Immediately adjacent to this, was a beach. Quite tiny, yet it was conveniently out of view of any onlooker from the cliff face above.

The night air had made an impact on Paul's nasal senses. A sneeze fragmented the complacent woman into red alert. The darkness had been shattered, and the battle was about to begin.

The woman swung around to face her assailant. Moving forward to face her attacker, she anticipated the unwanted passenger would strike. Her move towards Paul allowed the moon to shine right across her face. Distinguishing her features very clearly now, the woman reacted. She was quick to think, and stepped back to the controls, and put the boat into reverse throttle.

The boat lurched backwards, toppling Paul. He fell and hit his head on the side of the boat, temporarily stunning him. Our female combat fighter took advantage of this, and lunged at Paul with a long piece of wood. Paul thought it was an oar, but his eyesight was unable to determine what it was exactly. Rolling away to avoid a brutal head injury, she still managed to inflict some wound to the left side of his face and forehead. Blood had gushed forth, and was streaming down Paul's face. The boat continued to reverse back into the estuary waters in an uncontrollable fashion. Seeing the rope on the boat's floor, he had to counter attack without delay. The rope had been wound carelessly and there were large gaps in the coils.

As the woman tried to regain her balance, and head back to the controls, she placed a foot inside a coil. Promptly Paul pulled the rope sharply, dislodging the woman. She fell forwards screaming. Now Paul got to his unsteady feet, and endeavoured to pull the woman into the confines of the rope coils. Having some success, Paul was becoming dizzy with the pain in his head. The woman struggled up, with the intention to make her way back to the steering wheel. Managing to move the boat's control into forward from reverse, the "Maryanne" responded and changed course.

Paul dived towards the woman and snatched her left arm and bent it around her back. Wracked with pain, the fighting lady winced with discomfort. Dragging her away from the steering wheel, Paul was successful in pushing the woman further down the boat. Any one viewing the two figures on the boat would think they were a pair of frolicking turnips being tossed about in a sinking saucepan.

Paul's mental stability was stimulated. He had to get this boat back under control. The speedboat was now travelling at high speed, but was veering left and right in acute angles. Pushing his fighting female partner back down a final time, Paul made his way precariously to the cabin and brought the boat to a standstill. The craft lost momentum and gradually began to settle once the motor had been switched off.

Still rocking incessantly with the movement of our female warrior queen "Boadicea", Paul faced the woman directly. Breathless himself, Paul knew he had to break this woman's temperament.

'A nice night for a picnic, pity you haven't packed the hamper basket, Audrey. Or should I say Maryanne?' Paul's voice echoed over the still waters, and the moon had completed its task to reveal our female passenger.

A gasp of breath escaped the mouth of the startled woman. Regaining her senses and sitting down on a rear seat, Maryanne was speechless for a few seconds. Then, as fast as she had sat down, Maryanne got up and said with a voice of panic, 'You can't pin the murder on me! I know who you really are! Working undercover for the police, I

won't go with you. I will fight to the bitter end, you hear me!'
Maryanne's body was shaking with hysteria and physical
instability.

She might fall overboard any minute, thought Paul.
Fearful, and yet a fighting vixen to the last. 'Maryanne, I am
not against you, I am for you! Don't you understand that?!
I don't work for the police, but I believe someone in the Los
Angeles police force is against you! Innocent people have
lost their lives because of this evil heartless creature! Who is
behind it all? Felinda, Karl Peterson or someone else?' Paul
demanded, as held onto the side of the boat to steady his
balance. He was now feeling the effects of the whack he had
sustained. Congealed blood was partly blocking his vision
from the left eye and his left shoulder felt numb.

No response came from Maryanne.

'Your friend back there …' Paul said, pointing over to
the Hendon house. 'She certainly put on an Oscar winning
performance earlier today. I give her full marks for that!
However, she made one slip up! Do you know what that
was, Maryanne?' he questioned, breathing heavily and
ready to pounce. He realised Maryanne was definitely a
stronger woman physically than first impressions gave.
How formidable was she with sentiment and common sense?
thought Paul.

Still no response from Maryanne. Her eyes were fixed
on Paul, knuckles clenched with tension. With a face of a
frightened fawn, she waited for Paul's revelation.

'When speaking with Felinda Bentine, she gave an

account of the early years at Lorraway. She referred to the death of Johnny Appleseed, as occurring in early 1921. Now Felinda didn't have any reason to lie regarding that, although I appreciate she has regarding other matters, but not that date. Your lady friend mentioned that Johnny died in early '22. She was incorrect, wasn't she?'

Silence again.

'Either she did it on purpose, which frankly I doubt, or she made a genuine mistake,' Paul boomed. 'Memory can be trusted too much, and you fed her all the information required for our visit, every last detail, but that one slip up got me thinking. I realised later that if that was really Maryanne or Magdalena, whatever you want to call yourself, it's irrelevant to me, she would remember the year a close friend like Johnny Appleseed had died. Next time it might pay to ensure that Clarene Cremorne has all the right facts! It was a very clever strategy that you both embarked upon. Swapping roles and then the Marmon car leaving the house and finally our meeting on the estuary. Where were you going at this time of night, or was that another tactic to fool us?' Paul was in need of rest, his body was beginning to feel painfully slow to respond to his commands.

Maryanne was still silent, her body heaved with indignation and trembled with fear.

'Okay, no comment is your plan of attack! It won't work, Maryanne. The truth has to be faced, especially for the sake of Neumann. He is going to be here tomorrow, so at least give him a better reception, than tonight's ordeal! You covered every angle with Audrey, every detail about your son, just in case the topic was mentioned. Even to the name of your son, quite admirable!' spoke Paul severely to Maryanne.

'You seem to think you have all the answers, Mr O'Shea. We shall see who is right. Start the boat and bring us back to shore,' Maryanne snapped at Paul.

Paul raised his aching body and walked unsteadily to the controls, starting the outboard motor. The engine roared into life, and the boat turned around.

CHAPTER 14

A WOUNDED SOLDIER AND A CAPTURED SWEETHEART

Paul stood with difficulty as he steered the craft, and Maryanne had her final weapon laid bare. She slowly crept up behind Paul.

'Ah!' yelped Paul as he suddenly felt the object prodding him in the back. Slightly moving to the left, he came face to face with the hand of Maryanne. Her hand was holding a small pearl handled pistol, glistening in the light of the moon. A bluish tinge had now been cast down upon the water, and tranquility had taken hold of the night.

'Hey, easy goes lady, please! I might not be General Custer, but I am certainly not the devil!' Paul glared at the woman, whose face was grim with vexation.

'No funny business, alright? Or I will not hesitate to use this, and then drop you overboard! And, what's more, we knew the pair of you would be back like a bad smell. Hence our little ruse with you both!' she spoke through gritted teeth, like a conspiring convict. She was very desperate to preserve a dark secret.

What was all this about? Paul was trying to think, but his concentration was stretched to capacity steering the speedboat back to the jetty.

After what seemed eternity, Paul and Maryanne disembarked from the speedboat and walked with slow steps along the jetty. Paul trudged with some effort ahead of the impulsive Magdalena Hendon, now exposed as Maryanne. The gun was pointed into Paul's back. The pair made their way up to the house, which now was glowing with internal lights.

Entering the home from a side set of French doors, Paul was closely followed by Maryanne. Down a wide hallway they tramped. Paul was holding back the desire to collapse. His head felt as though it was going to fall off its socket.

The gun was held firmly by Maryanne, and Paul knew how many bullets these guns could hold.

Not many, no more than four, but I dare not risk anything. Maryanne is quite wild, and would stop at nothing, Paul thought, trying to see a way out of the dilemma. He could see the Bentine spirit surfacing here right enough.

Yes, it became more of a dilemma when he walked further into the house and into the living room, to be confronted with the other lady accomplice standing guard over Donna.

Donna's eyes searched Paul's face. She was bound and gagged, feet included, sitting on a spindle back chair.

The woman, who Paul thought was Clarene Cremorne, spoke first.

'Caught this one red handed snooping around out the front. So I have dealt with her for the time being.' This woman was in possession of a double barrel shot gun, and was waving it around as though it was a plaything.

'Well done, we will use her for insurance!' Maryanne gave a grin of satisfaction.

'What do you mean "insurance"?' asked Paul quickly, almost falling over with faintness.

'Quite simple, you bring Neumann here. Until then, she stays with us. Now off you go and don't come back until you have my son!' Maryanne bellowed at Paul

Feeling absolutely bewildered, Paul went to move towards Donna, but the barrel gun was put between them both.

'She will be looked after, you keep your part of the bargain, and we will honour ours. We are not killers, but we deserve to be respected and understood. I trust you comprehend me, Mr O'Shea?!' The words of Maryanne were sharp, yet underneath there was a longing for Paul to bring her son back into her life.

These two women had lived lives of cloak and dagger for so long, their behaviour had become engrained with its wicked touch.

Handing Paul a clear plastic bag, the "Annie get your gun" lady said abruptly to Paul, 'Here, take your toys that you left. You won't be needing them anymore!'

The bag contained the two walkie talkies, one from

Donna and the other that Paul had dropped on his flight to the speedboat.

Paul managed a brief smile and said, 'Thanks sister. Do I get a treat for being a good boy?'

Donna raised her eyebrows and made a sound with her voice, but nothing was perceptible.

Paul started to leave the home, although with staggering movements.

Just as Paul was about ten feet from the ladies and their captive, Maryanne smugly said, 'You were right about one thing, I am indeed Maryanne. Very perceptive of you regarding the dates. BUT ...' she then pointed to "Annie", 'this lady is not Clarene Cremorne!'

'I am Audrey ... but I used to be known as Vena Prentiss, when I was an actress,' the nameless lady informed the room. 'Maryanne, Lamore and I are close friends. We don't intend to have that bond broken by outside interference. Have I made myself clear, Mr O'Shea?' The words were callous and conveyed a message of, "Do not meddle!"

'Message received loud and clear!' Paul gave a police salute, and set out to walk back to the hire car.

Any one watching Paul at this early time of the new day, would say he was a drunken sailor coming back from a midnight ramble. Paul's feet would not step forward in a rhythmic pace, so he had to drag his left leg and shuffle with his right.

'Gee, holy shit, they couldn't even offer to patch me up or give me a drink of water! Pair of bitches!' Paul shouted out loud.

With quite a considerable struggle, Paul walked unsteadily to the hire car. Fiddling with the keys, Paul opened the driver's door. His brain was unable to function normally now, and he just flopped into the driver's seat and went into a sound sleep.

Inside the Hendon house, Donna was given some reprieve and permitted to talk, but her wrists and legs remained tied.

'What happened to Paul, he looked awful! His face has been hit! He can't drive in that condition!' Donna said incredulously.

'Never mind, my dear. Mr O'Shea will take care of himself. If he is half the man I think he is, he will be just fine! Your boss won't be going too far anyway!' came the rapid response from Maryanne.

They both chuckled at each other, with a knowing understanding.

Yes, Paul was in a hopeless situation. Time waits for no man – and in this case, he found that out with a rude awakening.

Paul was startled from his slumber by a loud banging noise. His eyesight was hazy and his mind still clouded. His head gave excruciating pain, as he tried to move forward. There was a small figure standing at the driver's door. The person was saying something, but Paul could not hear. With care, he opened the driver's door. A young Hawaiian boy about ten years of age stood there with a look of concern and wonder.

'Hello mister, can you move your car? It's in our driveway and my Dad has to get to the airport soon,' the boy babbled out.

Paul could see that where he had parked the car, was in the driveway of a property, set back from the road. It had been obscured when Paul and Donna had arrived by the large oleander bush.

'Gee, sorry pal. I will see what I can do,' replied Paul with a grimace.

'Look mister, your tyre is flat!' said the boy in a frenzy.

Shit, that's all I need, thought Paul. Straining to get out of the car, he went to the tyre the boy was pointing at. The rear passenger tyre had been slashed. He didn't need to know who was responsible. Trying to fix his eyes on his watch, Paul could make out that it was nearing 2.30 a.m. As he walked to the trunk to get out the necessary jack and replacement tyre, he saw a large sign advertising "Orchid Oasis-wholesale suppliers of orchids". *So this is an orchid farm,* he realised and touched his head, just to ensure it was still in one piece.

A man's voice could be heard approaching from the driveway. The gravel crunched under the weight of the man's heavy gait.

'Kuni, Kuni, are you there, son? I'm waiting for you!' came the impatient masculine voice.

'Down here, Dad!' Kuni replied, looking at Paul with some doubt.

Out of the darkness, the figure of a tall, solidly built man appeared. 'What's going on here, son?' he inquired.

With difficulty, Paul tried to explain his predicament, but could not complete explaining why the car was parked in the man's driveway. Paul fell forward into the trunk, hitting his head and blacking out.

'Stay there son. I'll get help!'

Paul was being attended to by Mrs Grace Ohahreh, a registered nurse at the General Hospital in Honolulu. She had been relaxing at home in her dressing gown when her husband, Taka, had carried the unconscious Paul through their front door. It was certainly providence that Mrs Ohahreh was not working this particular night.

Extracting a long splinter of wood lodged deeply in Paul's left forehead, Grace applied the necessary dressings. After cleaning up her patient, Grace helped Taka carry Paul into the spare bedroom to recuperate.

Taka kindly swapped the slashed tyre and then moved the AMX. He and Kuni, then had to make a dash to the airport with the orchid delivery, for the requirements of the day's incoming flights.

* * *

Donna had not slept well at all, perched upright in an armchair. Her neck was stiff and her hands and legs had cramp.

Birds were stirring, and began to sing their songs to

welcome the new day in. Night had been tucked away, and the sun had risen with an exquisite array of vibrant colours. A hint of red was splashed across the grey blue sky, and a golden haze was now visible as the sun gained intensity. The giver of all life had shown its face once again to mankind.

The curled up figure of Paul laying on the bed in the Ohahreh home was carefully monitored by Grace Ohahreh. Checking on Paul at regular intervals, she was satisfied that progress was being made.

By 6.00 a.m., Taka and Kuni had returned from making their delivery. Kuni was keen to see if "the man was still asleep!" It was a treat for Kuni to accompany his loved Dad to the airport occasionally to deliver their orchids.

The Ohahrehs stood in the doorway of their spare bedroom, watching Paul sleep like a baby. Taka inspected the dark waterproof jacket that they had taken off Paul. Perhaps there was something to identify this mystery stranger.

Paul's driving licence was there, along with his credentials as a private investigator. Taka showed these to his astounded wife. They looked at each other, trying to work out this unusual fellow they had sleeping in their home.

Sending Kuni off to bed for a short while before being woken for breakfast and the school bus, Taka and Grace wondered what had brought Paul to this part of their world. Going back to sit down in their bright flowery kitchen, they both began discussing some more theories.

'Perhaps when he wakes up, he may be able to tell us. I would not allow him to drive Taka, not with that wound.

There is extensive bruising, and some bleeding under the skin too. He needs rest, and I would say he suffered some concussion from the blow to the head. Really, he should see a doctor,' said Grace with grave concern.

Taka nodded with comprehension. 'When I was moving the car, I saw a bag on the passenger's seat. I did look inside, and there were two walkie talkies. Why would he want two for?' Taka screwed up his dark pleasant face at his equally perplexed wife, Grace.

'He must have been investigating something, to be here in the first place. Plus the hire car indicates he was checking something out!' said Taka to Grace.

'I wonder, Taka ... what's his name again, Paul O'Shea? Well, remember that old biddy up the road taking that huge old car out late last night. Remember I told you, I was woken by the sound of the blue and white car? I know the noise the engine makes, it is quite a distinctive sound. From our bedroom window, I could definitely see a woman at the wheel. The street lights illuminated the car as it drove past our place! What was she doing, going out so late, they never go out at that hour of the night? It was after 11.30 p.m. Then I thought I heard the car coming back past our place a few minutes later. Do you think this guy was watching them? Something happened, and he got hit over the head?'

'Who by, the old lady? No, surely not! They are too nice for that sort of thing!' answered Taka with certainty.

'Well, how did he get the injury? Besides, we don't even know the old ladies well. It is only hearsay from the locals,' said Grace, raising her hands into the air.

'Yeah, it does seem a bit suspicious, doesn't it? The business card says he is from California. Did you notice that he was dressed in all dark clothing, and sand shoes as well?' Taka asked Grace, in a dubious tone.

'Yes, I did consider that too. He must be here for a reason,' said the baffled Grace.

Their conversation was interrupted by moaning coming from the spare bedroom. They both raced to the bedside.

Paul seemed to be semi delirious, and in a fever. His slurred speech was barely audible to be heard – 'G-g-gotta … get … D-Donna … '

Grace leant forward and in a professional tone of voice said, 'Mr O'Shea, what are you saying, can you repeat it please?' She looked anxiously at her husband, who stood over the other side of the bed.

'H-h-have to get D-Donna, at the house!' Paul rolled over.

'Whose house?' Taka raised his voice, and leant closer to Paul.

Paul's comprehension was limited, but a few seconds later he was able to raise himself onto his right side. Vainly trying to focus on the face of Taka, Paul took the man's large work worn hands, and stuttered, 'P-p-please man, gotta get Donna, at the Hendon house, Maryanne.' With that, Paul fell back onto the bed almost lifeless, the physical exertion had been too much.

Grace was the first to react. 'I thought so, he was there, watching those old ladies. This Donna, he is talking about, she must be at the Hendon place. That's why there were two walkie talkies! Get it Taka?'

'Yeah, I do, honey. We better get over there right away and see if this Donna is still there!' Taka pulled his frame up to his 6 foot 5 inch height.

'Hold on Taka, it's still not even 7 a.m. They might not be up yet. We better wait till a bit later,' Grace replied rapidly.

'I don't think so, Grace. This guy is worried about this woman called Donna. We gotta go over there now. We will tell them that Paul is here and was asking about Donna, speak the truth. We have nothing to hide!' Taka moved to leave the room.

'Yes, I guess you are right, let's go now. Just wait while I check on Kuni, then we will go there.'

* * *

'We have early morning visitors, Maryanne,' came the wary voice of Vena aka Audrey, as she watched the Ohahreh's make their way to the front door.

'That's those orchid growers from down the road. What do they want so early in the morning?' said Maryanne suspiciously.

'Well, they haven't got a bunch of orchids for us, Maryanne! I better go and see what they want,' answered Audrey with a querulous look.

Tossing her head back, Audrey made her way to the front door.

Maryanne stealthily gagged Donna as a precaution. After all, you can never tell what your neighbours will discover!

Opening the front door with caution, Audrey gave her charming little old lady smile and said with the utmost loveliness. 'Why, what a surprise, so early in the morning too! You're those orchid growers from down the road. How can I help you?' Audrey scrutinised their faces, endeavouring to detect any possible flaws in their manner.

Taka Ohahreh came straight to the point, 'We have a Mr Paul O'Shea with us. He is saying that a lady called Donna is here. He wants us to bring her back right away.' Taka moved forward into the doorway entrance. He had heard about these two dearies, who came over all sweet and lovely, but had never had the privilege of meeting them before today.

The face of Audrey altered to one of an ashen colour. 'I don't know what you are talking about! There is no one called Donna here, and I haven't heard of a Mr O'Shea, was it?' Audrey beamed at her visitors, with gross insincerity.

With luck on her side, Donna had heard the man's voice, and had cleverly thrown herself on the living room floor. The chair overturned with Donna still secured in its frame, and made a deafening sound! Audrey's attention was momentarily distracted by the loud noise. This was the break Donna anticipated for her rescue!

Taka and his wife, Grace, hearing the heavy crash, ventured further into the living room.

Maryanne had gone to the fallen Donna, and was muttering something about, 'Stupid girl!'

'Why have you got this woman tied up? Is this Donna?' Taka looked menacingly at the pair of elderly women, who stood back, now feeling threatened.

Grace went to the aid of Donna, and undid the ropes and gag with care from her mouth.

Taka stood guard, watching the two elderly onlookers, whose faces displayed alarm and exposure.

Donna was very quick thinking, even though sleep had eluded her. 'Careful, they have guns!' she screamed at her rescuers.

Taka was not a man to be easily frightened, and with a big, warm hearted amusing expression in his deep native Hawaiian voice, said, 'I can't imagine these sweet old ladies having guns, ma'am! We have just come to take you back with us to our place. You can have some rest and then breakfast. My wife here, Grace, she will look after you. Oh, Mr O'Shea sends his regards, ladies!' bowing slightly at the two old ladies standing with glum faces in the corner of the living room.

Taka then assisted Donna to her tottering feet, and with Grace on the other side of Donna, they left the speechless, yet very infuriated spectators. The trio negotiated the steps down the verandah and onto the driveway.

'Those dames are in trouble now!' Taka said to Donna. 'Keep walking, they won't come after us, I am sure of that!' He gave a hearty laugh.

Grace said to Donna, with thoughtfulness, 'We have Mr Paul O'Shea with us, but he isn't too good. He has a nasty wound on his forehead and side of his face. How did that happen? Do you know, honey?'

As they all got into the cab of the Ford F100 pickup truck, Donna, was feeling so relieved with her liberation from the clutches of those demented ladies. She replied angrily, 'I think that Maryanne is responsible for that! Paul followed her onto a boat apparently, and they were gone awhile before coming back here in the early hours of this morning. I had been caught by the other woman, and tied up. Gee, my body is so sore!'

'It's okay, we won't be long, and I shall get you a hot bath and then something to eat. You can stay as long as you need to. I am going to have my doctor check your Mr O'Shea over. He has had a severe injury!'

Donna was so thankful of being alive and away from that house.

Back at the Hendon den, Maryanne and Audrey were not happy girls at all.

'Blast them! They have ruined our plans completely! Our insurance is gone now! We will have to come up with another plan to ensure that Neumann is brought here. Oh, what will we do? I can't bear to think that I might not see my son!' Maryanne gave a high-pitched cry.

'Our carefully devised plan was partially effective. Perhaps it was a bit too ambitious of us! Waving unloaded guns around, still I guess we must see the bright side of it all,' retorted Audrey. 'We did the pair a fright, I'm sure of that!'

CHAPTER 15

RECONCILIATION

Neumann Riessler had now arrived in Hawaii, and had hailed a cab to take him to the Intercontinental Hotel. Before checking in, he asked for the room number of Paul O'Shea, stating he was Neumann Riessler.

'Mr Neumann Riessler,' came the reply from the polite hotel male employee, named Mike. 'Oh yes, there is a message for you sir, from Mr O'Shea. He said it was quite urgent.' Mike handed Neumann a telephone number.

Neumann did not hesitate to dial the number.

Having been informed by Paul what he wanted done, Taka had made the phone call to the Intercontinental Hotel, leaving the message for Neumann Riessler to collect upon his arrival.

Now listening intently to the instructions of Taka Ohahreh, Neumann wasted no time, and hailed a cab for a speedy journey to the Ohahreh home.

* * *

With Donna now soundly sleeping, following a welcome reunion with Paul in private, the Ohahreh household was busy awaiting the arrival of their next visitor.

'What a day this has become!' Taka said to Grace. 'A wounded soldier, and then rescuing a maid in distress, and now another person of interest! Did you notice that Kuni wasn't that keen on leaving for school today?' he giggled.

'Kuni told me it was better than watching his favourite TV program *Lost in Space*.'

Neumann Riessler was swift in his journey, and was sitting at the kitchen table listening to the tale of the early morning escapades with acute attentiveness.

'So, is Paul O'Shea going to be okay?' came the first question from Neumann.

'I would say so. The doctor is coming soon to check him over. Donna is sleeping now after her experience, poor thing,' smiled Grace.

'So, all this took place at a home just up the road. Is that right?' came Neumann's puzzling query.

Taka and Grace tried to explain the whole series of happenings in as much detail as they could.

'Can I see O'Shea?' was Neumann's next short response.

'I'll see if he's awake,' Grace said, getting up and going to the spare bedroom.

Paul was sitting on the side of the bed, rubbing his head.

'Mr O'Shea, I have your visitor here. Mr Neumann Riessler has arrived. Would you like to see him?' Grace asked with apprehension.

'Yes, I need to speak with him right away, thanks.'

The Ohahrehs closed the bedroom door, and left the two men alone.

'Thanks for coming, man. I appreciate your coming here so quick,' Paul said to Neumann.

'No problem.'

Paul had to very tactfully explain the visit of Donna and himself to the Hendon residence in the afternoon. Then Paul informed Neumann about his misgivings concerning the identity of Magdalena aka Maryanne and how their planned night visit had ended going belly up.

'So my mother, Maryanne Osborne, lives in that house? When can I see her, I have to go and meet her!' Neumann was genuinely upset.

'I know you do! This ruse they planned, was part of their operation. Taking Donna as hostage, and letting me go to ensure that I would bring you to Maryanne,' Paul said with some strain.

'I'll go alone, you can't go. You are not fit enough,' replied Neumann.

'I want to go, and see you meet your mom. Maryanne still has a lot of explaining to do concerning that night your father was murdered,' Paul replied more emphatically.

Neumann agreed to leave going to the Hendon home for another hour. This would allow Paul to have a wash and change his blood stained sweatshirt, with the aid of Grace.

Preparations were made for Neumann, Paul and Taka to revisit the damsels at the Hendon estate. Grace remained behind to check on Donna. Kuni had already been collected by the school bus, much to his dissatisfaction.

The three men, one either side of Paul, drove in Taka's pickup truck the short distance to the Hendon house.

Neumann Riessler had taken great care with his outward presentation. The hair had been trimmed to a decent length and he had worn a black and white check long sleeve shirt, with his new Levi boot cut style jeans. He had shaved and overall appeared quite smart. Very overcome at the proposed meeting with his mother, he was not sure what to say.

At Grace's suggestion, Taka had cut Neumann a fresh bunch of cymbidium and vanda orchids, to take to his mother. Grace had wrapped the flowers up into a bouquet to present to Maryanne. After all, it had been 47 years, since Maryanne had last seen her son. The only other commodity that Neumann was taking with him was his aching heart.

Before the men had gone a few paces from the pickup truck, the front door opened.

Maryanne had completely changed from the woman Paul had confronted the day and night before.

It was all a façade! That was a wig she was wearing, and those matronly clothes were all false! Gee, she does look totally different today, Paul thought, as he beheld the woman who now was rushing down the steps, and into the arms of her beloved Neumann.

The reunion of mother and son was particularly emotional. Paul and Taka insisted on waiting outside, to give Mother and son their privacy.

Audrey brought some refreshments to the men, now seated at the wicker setting on the porch. Her mannerism had also altered remarkably. Far from being the sharp tongued bitch, that she displayed the night before, her language was kinder and a genuine concern was shown to Paul's injury.

'We caused you a lot of grief last night, Mr O'Shea. And Donna too! How is she? We had to resort to extreme methods, we thought that you were really undercover police. Lamore told us that you were the perfect gentleman, but we couldn't be sure that it was all true. So we devised this plan of swapping each other's identity. Then, we had the bright idea of the trick performed last night. Maryanne so wanted to see Neumann. It's been so cruel for her! I do apologise,' Audrey finished her words with a face of sorrow.

'No harm done, Audrey. Nothing like a good wallop on the head to brighten me up!' laughed Paul nonchalantly. However, Paul could not help but think what extreme measures these ladies had gone to, just to deceive Donna and himself.

Inside the home, the scene was tender. There was so much to say after so long.

Love never lives on words alone, nor can it be explained by verbal means. It has to come from the depths of the heart, the inner recesses of our thoughts expressing themselves in purity and grace. How the world longs for this virtue of love, yet for all that, we cast this quality aside for our self-satisfied powers of reasoning. Our expectations or hopes are cruelly dashed simply by our own undoing. Love to be true must be without fear, without reserve and without any doubt. Only then can one truly find lasting harmony and peace of mind amongst our fellows.

CHAPTER 16

A SON'S INFLUENCE

Taka and Paul made their way back to the Ohahreh home, leaving Neumann with Maryanne and Audrey. It was agreed that Paul return later in the afternoon, with Donna. Audrey continued to be apologetic, and insisted that they both come back later.

The Ohahrehs organised for their family doctor to examine Paul. Upon examination, Dr Arnold Zuugerheim declared in an honest voice, 'I would say no permanent damage has been done. Keep the bandages on for a couple of days, then have them renewed. Ensure the wound is kept clean, and don't overdo it either. Take some pain killer for the pain. You suffered quite a blow!'

Donna fussed over her beau, which relieved Grace to attend to her own family.

Later at around 3 p.m., Paul and Donna were sitting in the Hendon living room, where it had all began yesterday.

After Maryanne made it clear that they intended no harm

to either Paul or Donna, she profusely expressed regret with her actions, especially towards Paul.

'I do appreciate your situation, you acted out of protection. Look, it's all over now, let's forget it. Donna and I are just so overjoyed that you have finally been blessed to meet up with Neumann,' Paul said honestly.

Maryanne's countenance was one of joy and happiness that only a woman in the same circumstances could understand. Constantly desiring to be reunited with her treasured son was almost a dream she thought would never happen. She was nearing 70 years of age, and time for her was running out.

Neumann took up the conversation, holding his mother's delicate hands tightly. 'Maryanne – I mean, Mom – wants to explain everything now. Go on, tell Paul …' prompted Neumann, looking with affection at his mother.

'I know that Lamore told you practically everything that occurred on the night of Charles's murder. You see, the reason why I went to see Charles, was to tell him that I was pregnant with Neumann. I was already four months with child, and I didn't have the courage to let him know he was the father. I thought he might be angry and not want any further association with me. When I did break the news that evening, Charles was ecstatic! He wanted to arrange a wedding as soon as possible. However, before I could leave, someone else arrived.' Maryanne seemed troubled, and dropped her head, as though the memories of that night were too hard to bear.

'Clarene Cremorne, wasn't it?' Paul inquired. He stared at Maryanne, waiting for confirmation.

'Yes, you are correct. Um …' Pausing again, she eyed Neumann for comfort. 'Clarene had a cocaine addiction. Charles had warned her previously that if she didn't cease using the narcotic, she would be sacked from the studio. That night, she came to threaten Charles with blackmail over some matter that had occurred. I had hidden behind a screen in the front living room, and naturally I heard everything they said. Clarene was malicious in her statement, warning Charles that she would carry through her threat. Charles would not listen to Clarene, and still insisted that she stop the use of the cocaine. Clarene said that there were others using it, and they were all working at the studio! Why target her, and not everyone? Charles tried to reason with her, that he was addressing the issue with these other people, but her wrath was kindled! She told Charles in no mean terms, that he had better rethink, or she would expose him! After that bitter exchange of words, Clarene left in a rage. Richard heard it all to, but alas he is not here now to verify my statement.'

'Why didn't you tell the police all this when they interviewed you? You had nothing to hide. It would have made things so much better for you, if you had!' exclaimed Paul, with wonder.

'Oh, but I did have something to hide – I was an unmarried mother. Charles was dead and the studio were not keen to have pregnant women as their stars! How was I going to explain my pregnancy, that Charles was the father? Did I kill him in a blind fit of hatred? The questions were bound to be asked. No, I had to take the road I did. Hard though it was! The only thing I did was to take Charles's surname of Osborne, even though we had not formerly been married. I felt that somehow I was joined to Charles.

'I was permitted some time away from the studio, because of the scandal and the distinct possibility that I would be charged with Charles's murder,' she continued. 'As time moved on, it became obvious that I was pregnant. I was terribly unwell with morning sickness, and I had to move home to Lorraway. That's when Felinda put two and two together, and challenged me about being pregnant. I told her the truth, that Charles was the father, and I had no regrets. Felinda was absolutely livid! "Unmarried, disgusting", she said. Worried that it would tarnish the family name, she took matters into her own grimy hands. And so when I gave birth, I was restrained. Neumann was literally torn from my arms by Felinda, and I never saw him again. I pleaded with Felinda to tell me where Neumann was, but she told me that I had no son ...'

Hot tears pricked in the inner corners of Neumann's eyes.

'It was all a figment of my vivid imagination. Felinda – such a wicked person – so heartless and uncaring. I was kicked out of the house, and I tried to revamp my career, but it was all in tatters by then. My name had been splashed across the newspapers throughout the country. One headline read, "America's little sweetheart, nothing more than a whore". My last film in 1924, was a disastrous failure. I had to start a new life. I had always wanted to go to Hawaii, and learn how to surf. I loved the water and became quite proficient at surfing. Liking the place so much, I decided to stay. My saving grace, was that Charles had left me his entire estate. So I purchased this place and in time became a professional artist.' Pointing to Audrey, Maryanne said, 'Some years later, Audrey's contract expired with the studio, and as her marriage had ended in divorce, I offered her to come and live with me. When was that, dear?'

'It was in 1931,' replied Audrey. 'I had made a few talkies by then, but the film world was not for me. As Maryanne said, my marriage was over. I had no family, so when Maryanne kindly gave me the opportunity of coming to be her companion, I jumped at it! She has been a wonderful friend all these years.'

Paul was still confused. 'Now that we have established all these facts,' he began, 'why years later would someone entice Ben Driscoll to meet at a specified place, and then kill him? I still can't see the linkage. There must have been something to hide, some event that required Ben to be so coldly cut down! He apparently was in the possession of an extremely important piece of information. I believe because of that, Ben was gunned down!' Paul spoke austerely and his blue-grey eyes were penetrating into Maryanne's face for an explanation. 'Are you afraid of someone? I am not trying to intimidate either of you, but we need your help to stop this tyranny.'

Paul was appealing with all his might, but his words hit a brick wall. Nothing was forthcoming from Maryanne. Audrey was silent, sitting back in her chair.

'Could it be the narcotics? Was it another matter entirely divorced from the cocaine? Can you comprehend what I am trying to say, Maryanne? Did you hear or know of another unspecified incident, that incriminated someone you knew or loved?' Paul urged.

Donna watched the two women with great attentiveness. She realised they knew something – they just weren't willing to spill the beans.

With a tone of certainty, Maryanne replied succinctly, 'I can't think of anything or anyone who would want Ben dead. Or, for that matter Tryphena and Tryphosa. It must be related to another occurrence that I am not aware of. I'm sorry I cannot be more helpful, Mr O'Shea.' Her hands were unsteady, and the voice was shaky.

Bullshit, thought Paul inwardly. Keeping his temper under control, he declared that Donna would accompany him back to California to start examining other leads.

Saying their farewells, the party left Neumann with his newly found Mother and Audrey.

'That was a hasty exit, Paul,' said Donna as they walked back to the Ohahreh home, with decisive steps.

'Yeah, those dames are lying through their back teeth. They know why Ben was killed – and the twins as well! What is it that is keeping Maryanne from telling the whole truth? That was only part of the truth, we just heard! I can't pester them again because of Neumann's presence. We will have to dig deeper, Donna! Let's get back to California and have a fresh perspective on the facts we know. I bet you that Karl Peterson has a big sway in all this haze of smoke. It's like wending our way through a mist, clearing away the trash and holding onto the hard core facts!'

Paul was frustrated, but without clear evidence, their task was proving to be complicated.

CHAPTER 17

A FRESH START

Departing from the Ohahreh family – much to the disappointment of Kuni, who had relished the thought of private detectives staying at his home – Paul and Donna made their way back to Honolulu.

Finalising payment for their hotel room, which they had hardly used, the pair booked seats on the next available flight to Los Angeles. Little did Paul know that during their visit to Hawaii, his office at the Parkside Business Centre had been ransacked by an unknown person. Taking with them some fundamental information, our investigative team would be welcomed to a trashed office. Nothing had been left unturned, an extensive search had been carried out with startling thoroughness.

Hours later, Paul and Donna walked into the unlocked suite and were greeted with the mess.

'We have had an unwelcome visitor, Donna!' said Paul curtly.

'Oh, what chaos everything is!' said Donna, inspecting the mess.

After they both had rearranged furniture and sorted papers that had been carelessly thrown around, Paul and Donna sat down to analyse what exactly had been taken.

'Donna, has that photograph of Clarene Cremorne been taken?'

Checking through what was left, Donna replied, 'Yes, that photograph is not here. So someone wanted that photo very much! That must be the missing link!'

'Yes, I believe so! This would have been the work of Peterson for sure. He had to have that photo and the other information we had obtained, removed for some reason. Peterson is our man! Somehow we have to infiltrate his background to determine if he has some connection to Clarene Cremorne,' ended Paul, scratching his head. It was still sore from the blow Paul had suffered. The wound was gradually healing after his midnight assault courtesy of Maryanne.

Spreading his right arm in mockery at Donna, Paul rambled on saying, 'I go to Canada, and first of all I get the run around from Lamore Driscoll. Then she comes clean, to a point, and gives me Maryanne or Magdalena, whatever she calls herself, her details. Then off we go off to Hawaii and what do we get when we arrive there? I get smacked over the head in a night tryst on a powerboat, you get kidnapped and taken as a hostage for bargaining power! I could have been killed by that whack from Maryanne! What was she going to say if I had been killed?!' Paul paused his normal speech and took on the voice of a dear little old lady. 'Gee, sorry pal! Your head got in the way!' Resuming his everyday voice, Paul spoke on in a disgruntled fashion. 'Maryanne get's her son back and we are basically chucked out to fend for ourselves, and clean up the dirty past. We have just been shunted around like a dog given a bone and told to piss off! Well, we are not playing second fiddle anymore. If we tread on someone's dear little toes, then so be it. We have got to break open this case before everything reverts back to what it was before Ben's death. And that is, shit all! A powerful force keeps lips sealed. Is that Felinda Bentine, Karl Peterson or perhaps this Clarene Cremorne?' concluded Paul, looking exasperated at Donna.

Donna detected that Paul was immensely aggravated. 'What about Neumann Riessler?' she asked. 'He knows a lot more about Peterson. Sure he has a grudge against the guy for putting him behind bars falsely, but there must be some other fact that we are not aware of. You remember, Paul … ' Donna looked long and hard at him. 'When Maryanne talked about this Clarene Cremorne and the cocaine aspect, did it occur to you that perhaps that story was another smoke screen? Put there deliberately to get us thinking it was the narcotics they argued about. What if it was entirely different? Another topic altogether, but whether the blackmail part is true, remains to be proven.'

Nodding his head in agreement, Paul was mulling over the ideas Donna had put forward. They held credence. 'Yeah,

I think you are right there, Donna,' he said. 'What you say could well be the right train of thinking. What I would love to know is, who is Karl Peterson's mother? Could it be this Clarene Cremorne?' Paul raised his eyebrows, and sat back in his desk chair, placing his head on the head rest, trying to sift through the puzzle they had before them.

'How are we going to find that out?' asked Donna with some doubt in her voice.

'Right, I got it!' shouted Paul.

Donna was startled and jumped in her chair.

'I want you to go and get another photocopy of that Clarene Cremorne photo, from the City Records Office. Then ... we are going to make a visit to our friendly Felinda.' Paul smiled cunningly at Donna.

'When, today?' queried Donna with surprise.

'No. Get the photocopy today, and tomorrow we will tackle the Bentine beast! I think she might have her nerves rattled with our unexpected visit, Donna!' Paul was feeling intrepid.

Paul remained behind to organise some details and their plan of attack for their "social call" to Lorraway.

During this time, Detective Sergeant Bruno Capezio telephoned Paul from a call box at the Westmead Amusement Parlour, situated some distance away from the city centre. Capezio chose this place specifically. With so many people milling around the slot machines, it was easy to remain incognito and concealed from prying eyes. Capezio informed Paul that the ballistics report confirmed that the bullets from the gun taken by Neumann Riessler, did in fact match the bullets that had ended the life of Detective Inspector Ben Driscoll, and the janitor. Paul was pleased with this information and thanked Capezio.

Paul O'Shea sat back in his office chair and reflected on the way things were shaping up. *Not bad at all,* he thought. *Peterson has a lot of explaining to do, the bastard.*

Not long later, Donna returned with two photocopies of the Cremorne woman. Donna was also delighted with the news from Capezio, but Paul and Donna knew that there was still a long way to go to finalise this mystery saga.

Making a telephone call to Neumann Riessler, Paul eventually managed to speak to the man. The female voice who answered the phone initially was drunk and her speech slurred. Paul found it difficult to make himself understood.

Neumann Riessler was likewise satisfied with the news regarding the bullets.

The day was now drawing to a close, and our pair of "bloodhounds" went their respective ways home for a well-earned rest.

That evening a summer storm hit the Pacific Ocean region, not sparing anything in its relentless path. The islands of Hawaii were the first to receive the brunt of the fierce weather, before the swirling mass of tempest unleashed its fury on Los Angeles and the surrounding areas with a mighty force.

Cascades of warm rain from the Pacific current were swept towards the coast and saturated the dry ground. Gushes of erratic winds flowed through the populated communities and inland valleys, stirring up swathes of brown dust, before the rains came and settled the earth. Flashes of forked lightning illuminated the heavens. The moon was veiled by heavy cloud, and the twinkling stars were blocked from view.

A number of individuals were sitting in their abodes that night, all associated with this devious scheme of autocracy. Some were of the opinion that they were untouchable. Far removed from reality, totally absorbed in their own pride and lust for dominance.

Why do we make life so hard for ourselves?

Mankind delights in suppressing another's life into such a state of misery, the afflicted feels their life is beyond redemption.

CHAPTER 18

BENTINE BAIT

Morning was a relief for some of the population, after such violent weather. The worst of the storm had passed over the coastal areas and taken itself inland to other parts of the country. Sunshine was partly obliterated by low flying cloud drifts and patches of isolated rainfall continued to moisten the already sodden ground. Muddy pools occupied the shallow depressions, and thirsty birds were gathered around these, replenishing themselves with earth's imperative commodity, water. Commuter traffic was slow and accidents were quick to occur.

Donna was caught up in the morning turmoil and arrived at the office later than normal. Paul was impatiently waiting her appearance, so they could run through their action plan. What a stratagem the pair had concocted.

Once Paul had skillfully enlightened Donna regarding their surprise entry to the Lorraway confines, the pair left in Mach.

As they say, "forewarned is forearmed", however, on this occasion, Felinda Bentine was not going to be prepared like she was on the previous occasion.

Mach took Paul and Donna into the immaculate grounds of the massive domain that was known as Lorraway. *I would love to know how they can afford to keep this place going?* Paul thought as he drove towards the house. *I bet there is some form of fraudulent cash flow coming into the coffers!*

Parking straight outside the imposing entrance, our two love sleuths skipped up the marble steps. Paul pushed the brass buzzer, with firmness. *Now, let's see what fancy Felinda can think up today*, he thought.

"Jack of all trades" Jedson opened the massive oak door.

'Howdy pal, is your missus in?' asked Paul with a cheesy grin and a definite cowboy drawl in his voice.

Jedson was completely taken back. 'W-w-wait here! I shall s-see,' he stammered.

'That's got his feather's unsettled!' Paul laughed.

Jedson went into the Prussian blue drawing room, and announced the arrival of "those nuisances, who were here before".

'Not again, I thought that pair of homeless waifs had been dealt with! They obviously don't know the meaning of the word "unwelcome". What in heaven's name do they want now?' Felinda Bentine was incensed with wrath.

Jedson returned, and opened the door for them both to enter.

Paul and Donna didn't wait for Jedson to show the way. They both recalled the route, down the long wide corridor and the last door on the left. In they walked with a definite purpose in their steps.

'Morning Miss Bentine, or should I say, Mrs Jedson! How is it all going here, keeping things under wraps, are we?' asked Paul, as he sat himself down in the same wing back chair that he was permitted to sit on before. 'Oh, by the way, tell Jedson that he can make an appearance, instead of hiding behind curtained alcoves. He might even hear more that way!'

Before Felinda Bentine could manage to reply, Donna ambled over to the woman, who herself was not seated. Standing directly in front of the Bentine brute, Donna pulled out a pen from her shoulder bag and said in a patronising tone, 'I now have a pen, at your suggestion. Plus, I ditched the outdated note pad and bought a new lined note pad instead.' Donna drew the notepad from out of her shoulder bag, and presented both to the steely face of Felinda Bentine.

'There is no need for sarcasm! I was merely advising you to update your secretarial aids! However, as you have chosen to make a mockery of me, I would strongly advise you to leave these premises NOW!' Felinda bellowed at both of them.

'Shut up, and sit your ass on that comfy chair!' instructed Paul to the angry, yet clearly shaken, Felinda Bentine.

'Jedson!' Felinda screamed. 'Take this pair out of my sight now!'

The slightly stooped figure of Jedson emerged from

behind the brocade-curtained alcove. His face was red and appeared to be twitching a little. The right hand was moving uncontrollably.

'Why, here he is! The lad about town! How does it feel to have disposed of Tryphena and Tryphosa so effectively, eh? Pretty clever way of doing it, pal. Nice and neat, no mess!' Paul crossed his legs and clasped his hands together, waiting for the muse to utter a word.

Shaking like a leaf with violent rage and exasperation, Jedson could not cope with the direct comment from Paul.

Donna sat down on the other wing back chair, and opened up her notepad. 'I will take some notes, boss. You carry on, ask them about Ben Driscoll and the janitor from Seascape Apartments. Jedson may have had a hand in their deaths, who knows!' said Donna sucking the top of her new pen. She looked longingly at Jedson, and gave him a wicked wink.

'I-I didn't kill either o-o-of them!' Jedson wailed. He was clenching his hands and trying to maintain some composure, but his reserve of patience had been diminished significantly.

Once again, Paul presented another trump card, and placed the photocopy of Clarene Cremorne's face on the elaborate coffee table, between Donna and himself.

'Who's this Mrs Jedson? Don't tell me that you don't know. We know its Clarene Cremorne. She around to have a little chat to, eh? I am sure you know where she hangs out!' Paul said with a challenging tone in his voice.

There was literally no reaction from Felinda Bentine but her face shouted fury.

'That's okay. I will just ask Karl Peterson, he would know, wouldn't he?' came the decisive voice of Paul. He stared at the Bentine woman, boring into her soulless eyes with discernment.

'Get out! NOW!' Felinda Bentine screeched loudly with rage.

Jedson was holding onto a table on the far wall for support. Wiping his brow with a white linen handkerchief, he was unable to escort the mischievous pair from the room. He was feeling nauseas and his heart was beating wildly – how much longer could he take the barking orders, the dirty work and the permanent silence?

Jedson had been devoted to the felicitous Felinda when he first met her, so many years ago. He'd been taken not only with her looks, but her leadership with people. Forever conscious of being inadequate, the shy and retiring man had been given a new impetus in life thanks to Felinda. Charles Marcus Jedson's self confidence grew and he soon proposed marriage to Felinda after a brief and unromantic courtship. She had accepted, and the date was set. They were to live at Lorraway, for the sake of her mentally unstable parents.

Having excellent prospects as a lawyer, who would set up business in Hollywood, the stage was set for a brand new life for Jedson. Moving from Chicago, from a wealthy law family, meant status for Felinda would be assured.

Then had come the dastardly news just weeks after the

lavish wedding. Jedson had been diagnosed with incurable Parkinson's disease. The uncontrollable movements of the right hand had become progressively worse in the months leading up to the marital ties. The slight stooping of the shoulders and the head, had become more noticeable. Never imaging such a diagnosis, Jedson had visited the Bentine family doctor for advice. Tests had been done, and the shocking news had changed his life forever.

Referred to a specialist for further diagnosis, Jedson was coldly informed by the lack lustre specialist that, 'Nothing can be done to cure the ailment. It is extremely rare for someone so young, as you, to be stricken with the disease.'

Felinda, always one for superiority and grand impressions, had not accepted the fact that her husband was afflicted with an incurable ailment. She did not attempt to understand Jedson's plight. More concerned with what others would think of her, was her most important desire.

Jedson was rejected by his unfeeling family in Chicago. Cut off from the family he had once loved, the eldest son had now become the son who did not exist. They flung him a one off payment of $100,000 to write Jedson out of the family name. It was a godsend to the financially strapped Bentine fortunes, but it cut to the core of Jedson's heart. Then to rub salt into a weeping wound, Felinda flatly refused to sleep with him ever again. 'Separate rooms,' was the order barked out to the heartbroken young man. Jedson's dream of having children was crushed faster than an insect under one's boot. Finally, in a most deplorable practice, Felinda insisted that Jedson become the family butler.

'Make yourself useful, why don't you? Old Hebden won't last much longer. Start learning something from him! You cannot expect to stay here and have your bread buttered too! Never able to earn a dollar, now just a leech on the Bentine gratitude! Fit for nothing!'

The life of this unfortunate being had been so cruelly changed. We see the total lack of love and compassion being dealt out to Jedson. His plight was indeed sour. Where could he go now? At least Lorraway provided some shelter for him.

So, Charles Jedson had endured almost 50 years of humiliation and snide remarks. His manner and nature had altered substantially during this time. The once happy, yet quiet man, gradually transformed into a bitter and heartless soul. Used as a dirty dishcloth to do any task, over and over again. His patience had now been worn to almost a threadbare condition. Yes, indeed, how much more could this man be asked to forbear?

Felinda, now completely rattled by the morning social call of this painful and foolhardy pair, set to work to eliminate all memory of them.

Paul and Donna left with a spring in their step. Their venture had been successful. The scene in the blue drawing room at Lorraway was one of confusion and consternation.

'They will be dealt with! I shall see to that!' Felinda Bentine shrieked out to no one in particular.

Jedson had scurried away, wary of the wrath of the fearless Felinda.

Her fingers were quick to dial the number of our nameless entity. A traumatic discussion followed between Felinda and the person at the other end. Plans were formulated, and specific details provided for the next phase in their quest for dominance.

That evening in the Lorraway mansion, furious, frowsy-faced Felinda sat on her own. Her thoughts were rampant with revenge and retribution. Champagne Charlie, however, was a quivering wreck! Sitting in the kitchen, with a bottle of French champagne in front of him, the liquid was gulped down in a flourish.

Mach carried Paul and Donna back towards West Hollywood. Paul and Donna had their own tasks to complete too.

On the way back, Paul noticed a billboard advertising the Sidney Poitier film, *In the Heat of the Night*. The film had been a topic of conversation since it's release the prior year.

'I would like to go and see that movie sometime, Donna. From what I have heard, it is real good.'

Nodding in agreement, Donna replied, 'Yes, they say it is well acted. When all this is over, we can make a night to go see it.'

Mach continued to purr along in the direction of West Hollywood.

Already laid out by Paul the day before, Donna now went to work on her assigned task.

Delivering Donna to a necessary establishment, Paul would drive back and collect her later. She would require time to complete her needful, but very necessary commission. Paul had arranged a discreet meeting with Detective Sergeant Bruno Capezio. This was a particularly risky tactic for Private Investigator Paul O'Shea to tackle. Would it work, or could O'Shea be overplaying his hand?

That night some of our characters had a restful night, perhaps some more than others.

It could be said that a handful of individuals were deviously planning their modus operandi – a skillful plan that would work in the favour of a few.

Night came upon Los Angeles and its surrounding districts relatively quick that evening. The hours had trickled away, and day had been conveniently put to bed. The night was a relief for many, giving rest to face another day. Others were out enjoying the bright colourful lights that offered wine, women and song.

The hands of evil are quick to hasten unto death, and the new day would give them their earnest desire.

Let's read on and find out.

CHAPTER 19

TILL DEATH DO US PART

Morning crept in with little warning this Thursday. Soft rainfall overnight had left its trail of crystal beads on leaves, flowers and all manner of living things. These delicate outstretched strands of purest ornamental silk, adorned the grasses and reached far above into the tallest of stately trees. Nothing had been spared the wonder and beauty of the Creator's Hand. The spider's webs were glistening like jewels, crowned with an array of glorious rainbow colours. They hung there waiting for their prey, to make a tasty breakfast snack. Mankind was gradually awakening, rubbing eyes or backs, stretching legs and arms, or just simply yawning. The day began its usual activity of hurried exits from homes or apartments, to commute to places of work, whatever that may be.

By 9 a.m., the figures of Paul and Donna were sitting in the office of the Parkside Business Centre. Donna was at her desk, doing a diverse range of paperwork. Paul was seated at his large black desk, head down, looking intensely at the typed notes of his trusty secretary, and companion in detection, Donna. Neither noticed or heard the office door open quietly.

The handle turned ever so slowly. The black leather gloved oversized hand had now opened the door with great care. A size 14 black lace up left shoe was the first to enter the suite. The other shoe followed within seconds. Standing and watching the first victim with every muscle taut with alertness, an arm was raised, holding a horrendously harmful weapon. This was to inflict the anticipated result with startling swiftness.

The head of Donna was immersed in her work. Suddenly, she slumped forward as the bullet ploughed into her body, draining her of all life.

Whisper quiet, was the pride of this deadly assassin. The equipped silencer had worked its charm very well. Now it's next victim.

All that could be seen from inside Paul's office was the barrel of the wicked weapon. Placed just around the corner of the office door. Positioning the deathly instrument in direct line to its intended target, the fiendish finger pulled the trigger.

SLUG, it went. One bullet had done the deed.

The head of Paul O'Shea fell back with the force, and then his body rolled slightly to the left in his chair.

A smile of satisfaction crossed the face of our instigator. Leaving as quiet as they had arrived, their undertaking had certainly left Paul O'Shea and Donna Weston ready for the undertakers.

The discovery of the bodies of Paul O'Shea and Donna Weston made the evening headlines. During the course of the evening CBN television news, the lady newsreader was handed a typewritten page.

'News has just come to hand, that the bodies of two people have been found dead at the Parkside Business Centre in West Hollywood, late this afternoon. The victims, formerly identified as Paul O'Shea, Private Investigator, and Donna Weston, his secretary, were shot at close range. Police are anxious to speak to anyone who has any information regarding the fatal killings. Please urgently contact the Los Angeles Police Department.'

This, and other media releases soon followed on other channels and the radio. Newspapers had made front page evening editions regarding the shootings.

Capezio had been assigned the case, as the now duly promoted, Detective Inspector Karl Peterson, was already heavily involved with the shooting of Ben Driscoll, the dozy janitor, and the vindictive slaying of the Bentine twins.

The Chief of Police was wanting closure on the death of Detective Inspector Ben Driscoll, as soon as possible. Peterson was promising to resolve the case any day now. Naturally, the man was biding time. He had the case already wrapped up, but needed to tie up a few loose ends. Having a "working relationship" with his immediate superiors, Peterson was able to stall for time. As is often the case, the higher one climbs the ladder in any line of work, the more susceptible one becomes to potentially damaging "enticements".

The dispositions of some of our star personalities were thrilled to say the least, when learning of the deaths of Paul O'Shea and Donna Weston.

The news had reached Hawaii the same time it had been released on the mainland.

In the Hendon home, Neumann Riessler, Maryanne (Magdalena) Hendon and Audrey (Vena) Prentiss, were all devastated with the news they had just heard on the television.

Riessler knew he had to act without delay. He explained to his beloved mother and her companion Audrey, as much as he could regarding his involvement with Paul O'Shea, prior to coming to Hawaii. Then, under cover of darkness, Riessler had made a dash to the Ohahreh residence and informed Taka and Grace of his intended flight to the mainland. Asking them to watch for any unusual visitors to the Hendon estate, Taka and Grace promised to do all they could.

Riessler departed from the tropical paradise, and flew back to California on a late night flight. His discretion was essential, and without wishing to alarm the ladies, Riessler was now focused entirely to bringing justice upon Peterson. Just how was Riessler going to track down Peterson, and then carry out his intention? Yes, Riessler could wait outside the LAPD and shoot Peterson, but also run the high possibility of being caught.

The recent ecstasy and joy of being reunited with his mother, Riessler was not going to jeopardise this for anything. He had waited so long, as well as Maryanne, for this precious reunion. No, Riessler knew that he had to work with silence and skill to expose Peterson for who he really was. Now with O'Shea out of the way, and his luscious secretary Donna too, Riessler was on his own. However, he was not unaccustomed to working alone. He had been a loner all his life. This had held him in good stead. Kept his mouth shut and acted as an individual. He had come through the ravages of Vietnam. Riessler was never reliant on anyone else. That's how he had survived the hard life he had trod these last 47 years.

* * *

Meanwhile, Detective Inspector Karl Peterson drove his Chevrolet Camaro at high speed down the South Coastal Freeway in the direction of Ocean Pacific Downs.

This was a minor yet significantly older coastal area, established at the turn of the 19th century. Having a long elegant wooden pier built in 1898, it boasted the longest pier along the United States Pacific Coast. The pier hosted quality outdoor and indoor entertainment to its mostly elderly retired and grey nomad population. Of recent times, a small pocket of newly built homes had seen a younger generation come to savour the town's ambience from a bygone age. Abandoned warehouses had been converted into up market living quarters for the new breed of younger generation that were flocking to the town. Still within commuting distance of the city of Los Angeles, the town had become a favourite place to live.

Families had made the move there, not only for its quietness, but also the safety it offered to their offspring. Fresh ideas had sprung to light with the vibrant mix of both young and old. This had revitalised the town's fortunes over the last 20 years. A brass ensemble band had been formed about five years ago, and was heralded as the best brass ensemble anywhere in California. Three years ago an annual festival had commenced, attracting other brass bands and individuals to perform their music each year in June. Art had also been included in the festival, which was now a mecca for the avante-garde student and tutor.

Puffing away on his favourite Turkish small cigar stuck in his oversized mouth, Peterson was listening to the car radio. Jimi Hendrix was screeching out one of his well known songs, and Peterson was tapping his fingers on the steering wheel.

'Yep, things were goin' real good now. We have things under control now,' he laughed to himself. A sinister smile crossed his face, and then vanished.

Never one to show his feelings much, Peterson had got where he was in the police force by being a bully. His height and heavy frame intimidated other guys. Generally unfriendly and surly to lower ranked officers, meant that they learnt to fear, rather than respect Peterson, and carried out what he wanted. "Do what I say pal, or else", was a motto Peterson employed with constant success.

Yet for all that, Peterson was petrified of women. He was unsure of them in his presence. There was only one woman in his life and he intended to keep it that way!

* * *

A few hours previously at the LAPD Headquarters located in the busy mainstream locality of bustling Los Angeles, Detective Sergeant Bruno Capezio had entered Peterson's office.

Standing back, Capezio's Italian accent uttered, 'Shame 'bout O'Shea and his sidekick lady. I had to organise the funeral arrangements for the bodies. O'Shea had no living relatives, and Donna's mother is so cut up with the death of her only daughter. Mrs Weston flies in tonight from New Jersey. I made the service a private one. We don't want howling dames everywhere. The funeral is tomorrow at 10.30 a.m. at the Pacific Glades Cemetery.' Folding his beefy arms, he awaited the response from the newly appointed Detective Inspector Karl Peterson.

Peterson glanced up in the direction of Capezio, and muttered, while sucking his 58th cancer stick of the day, 'Yeah, O'Shea was a good guy. Didn't know him that well before he left and took up being a private investigator. Driscoll knew him better than me. Okay, I will be there, Capezio.' Acrid smelling smoke leeched out of his mouth as he spoke to Capezio. Peterson continued, 'Any leads on the homicides yet, Capezio?' with some curiosity in his deep smoky voice.

'No, don't think we will. Covered all angles, interviewed suspects and got statements. Nothin' doin' from any of 'em. Running cold I think, boss,' Capezio replied, unfolding his arms and then casually stretching them.

'Well, if there's nothing doing, put it to bed. Write it up, so we can move onto something else, Capezio,' answered Peterson, with some eagerness in his voice. He knew if he shut those cases away and forgot they existed, that he would have Capezio eating out of his hand. He'd have to make up some story to satisfy the Police Commissioner regarding Driscoll's death.

'Sure thing, boss. Pity we didn't find Driscoll's killer but you win some and you lose some!' Capezio laughed, and strode out of Peterson's foul smelling confine.

Detective Inspector Karl Peterson was more than pleased with this result. Feeling self-assured now that any threat to the well laid plans were not going to be compromised, Peterson opted to take a drive south and have a little break.

Reflect now on the above character, or any one for that matter, and we can ascertain that some lives are not given to mindful advantage of our fellow humans. We become so consumed with our own self-importance and aspirations, that we lose sight of what life is really all about.

And what is that, you may ask?

Well, look around you, beyond the busy street we roam each day or the lack lustre highway we drive daily to some specific destination, or the hive of industry shunting its way towards some specific goal or achievement. Life stares us in the face, yet for all that, we fail to grasp it. Perhaps some words of advice from a gentleman who wrote:

> *To see a world in a grain of sand*
> *And a heaven in a wild flower,*
> *Hold infinity in the palm of your hand*
> *And eternity in an hour.*
> – Author William Blake

Our fellow, Peterson, who thought himself beyond question or answerable to anyone, can be like any one of us.

Are we truthful to ourselves, or is it very convenient to deny that our attributes or inner qualities are in need of redemption?

Change is something that we inertly reject vehemently. Most of us are satisfied with our 'comfort zone'. However, it is only by earnestly challenging ourselves, that we *will* overcome and shed those unsavoury characteristics.

We all long for peace, no matter who we are and wherever we may abide. Lasting and eternal harmony can be achieved. It's up to us to work whole-heartedly, without reserve, to accomplish this end desire.

CHAPTER 20
NIGHT TIME MISSION

Detective Inspector Karl Peterson was nearing his destination. Having turned off the South Coastal Freeway, Peterson guided the Chevrolet Camaro towards its predetermined end of journey.

Swinging into a small driveway, and stopping at what appeared to be just a set of large and weather beaten wood doors, Peterson leant out the driver's window. Placing a plastic card into a slot positioned alongside the wood doors, Peterson awaited the doors to open. Anyone would have thought the doors were part of an old disused warehouse.

Instantly, the doors slid open, and Peterson drove into a different environment than what one imagined from the street entrance. Within seconds, the doors closed as quickly as they had been opened. Peterson had not seen the car following the Camaro, at a safe distance.

Observing Peterson's vehicle entering through the battered looking wood doors, was a vital clue to determine the movements of our Detective Inspector. The address was noted by the viewer with relish. Parking further along the road, our discreet onlooker waited patiently for Peterson to reappear, if he was.

Hours past, and there was no sign of Peterson.

Dusk began to fall upon the area. Birds were taking up their roosts for the night. A couple of tabby cats were having a confrontation in the middle of the quiet road. Squealing at each other like squealing kids, one cat made a daring attack at the other, and managed to give a nasty bite to its ginger-coloured neck. The victim howled, and scampered off to lick it's wound. The victor wandered off, happy with the victory he had won.

Light had diminished entirely now, and the darkness spread across the landscape with startling swiftness. Streetlights flickered into life, and the delightful aroma of food cooking, was wafting through the night air. Stars began to show their faces, twinkling as they do. Some bright, and others were dim. So far away in the universe these stars were positioned, and yet they shone their glory with constant joy upon an earth that seldom beheld their beauty.

Traffic along this stretch of road was minimal, however the street was well lit, affording an excellent view of the driveway entrance. Number 401 Lysander Lane, was no ordinary warehouse. Carefully camouflaged to deceive its appearance, no one gave the shabby doors a second glance. What lay beyond was an entirely different structure.

But we won't reveal too much yet, we don't want to be too nosy do we? Hmmm!

The other premises along the road were nondescript structures from the outside. Now occupied by a younger age group, looking for an alternative abode to the ordinary house. Converted into vibrant trendy apartments, new life had been restored to these once flea bitten vacant warehouses. The beach environment had enticed the younger people to leave Los Angeles and its surrounding districts, and start a new life here in Ocean Pacific Downs. Lights lit up the interiors, as majority of these apartments had no window dressings. The windows were wide and gave an expansive view of the street outside. With luck, some vehicles had been parked along the street, allowing our spectator to have a cursory look at its surroundings, without being seen.

Just after 8 p.m., the doors slid open at the warehouse, and out cruised the white Chevrolet Camaro.

Following the identical route it came in, the Camaro headed for the South Coastal Freeway.

Waiting to ensure that the car did not return, the watcher sprung into action. Stepping out of the plain beige Buick Riviera, the driver stepped back to allow another figure to climb out of the rear of the two-door car. This figure had been concealed during this time.

Both figures looked around with stealth and caution.

The driver went to the trunk and took out a small dark canvas bag, handing it to the other figure now crouching alongside the car. Getting back into the Buick, the driver said some words to the other party.

Starting up the Buick, the vehicle drove away down

Lysander Lane, turning right in the direction of the South Coastal Freeway entry. Rapidly gaining on the Camaro, the Buick hung back when a safe distance had been achieved.

Meanwhile, the dark clad figure negotiated its way over the road and onto the pavement. Walking at a brisk pace, they stopped just before the weather beaten doors of the warehouse.

Peering around carefully, the figure extracted a long rope attached to a hook, resembling a small anchor. Flinging this over the high stone wall, our nameless sleuth tugged on the rope to ensure that the anchor had secured itself. Then, gradually, the person climbed up the wall and over the top.

Jagged glass had been placed along the top of the solidly built wall, as a deterrent to anyone contemplating an entry. Fortunately, our climber had already noticed this little "welcome treat", and made allowance when arriving at the top. The figure disappeared from view, to complete their objective.

Meanwhile, along the South Coastal Freeway, the Chevrolet Camaro continued its journey travelling north. Peterson was oblivious to the inconspicuous beige Buick Riviera following about three automobile lengths further back. The Buick Riviera, ever in sight of Peterson's Camaro, kept a respectable distance. The journey back to the city streets was going to take approximately 90 minutes. The Chevrolet Camaro indicated its intention to turn off the freeway, and headed left. The traffic sign spelt out the areas of Rocky Gully, San Sebastian and Old Tremar. The beige

Buick and its undercover driver, took the same route.

Within 20 minutes, Peterson's Camaro began slowing down. Heading down a few roads, he then turned into a sprawling complex of units in San Sebastian. Operated by a slot card, the gates opened. Peterson was now out of visual.

Pulling up some 100 yards from the complex entry gates, the driver of the 1967 Buick turned off the retractable headlights. Stepping out of the car, the person walked on to the pavement, and headed in the direction of the gates.

The units were all two storey and had views over the San Sebastian Valley. Powerful parking lot lights shone their beam across the tarmac parking area.

Our Buick driver was just in time to see the retreating figure of Peterson stepping up the staircase to a unit.

Skillfully drawing out high density binoculars from under their sweatshirt, Peterson could be clearly seen unlocking the door to unit number 27. A light went on, and the white door was closed.

'Bingo, got him!' said the satisfied onlooker.

Hurrying back to the Buick, the car turned around and went back to join the traffic travelling south along the South Coastal Freeway.

Back at the Ranch, so to speak, our other rock face mountaineer, was able to get a bird's eye view of the house before them.

'Gee, this place is huge!'

The gardens were immense, and the wide Spanish style villa was set back in the elaborate grounds.

Wondering if they could entertain the thought of taking a closer inspection, our nimble alpinist began to creep towards the villa. Using the large shaped hedges as cover, the careful eyewitness could see two cars parked out the front of the villa. Different coloured lights were strung around the doorway entrance to the villa. With remarkable silence, a photo was taken of the villa, on a slim Pentax camera, and then slipped carefully into a hip pocket of the dark coloured track pants. Luck was not going to last much longer for this person!

Hoping to venture nearer, a snapping sound shook the clear night air like a rocket that had just been released. The left sandshoe had stepped onto a large twig, and broken it clean in two.

Jolted out of their self-imposed safety of the large box hedge they were hiding behind, the distinct sound of barking dogs could be heard.

Our nighttime investigator did not wait around to see what would happen next. They were off like grease lightning!

Running like a cheetah at full speed towards the wall, they leapt up the wall, with the aid of the rope. This had previously been made ready by our clever thinking black clad runner. Using all their strength, they clambered up the wall and narrowly avoided being slashed by the glass. Jumping down to the pavement, the bag was gathered up from behind a verge bush. They ran further down the road, and hid in the entrance to one of the up market apartments. Panting, and yet in full command of the situation, they hoped that their mission had been successful. Still hearing the guard dogs barking in the distance, two men appeared from inside the compound. Checking around for any sign of activity, they were satisfied that their visitor was gone, and went back inside.

The rope was still attached to the wall, but there was no possibility of retrieving that now. The men would eventually know that someone had entered the property for sure.

Breathing a sigh of relief, our spy gymnast waited their salvation. It was quite a wait before the Buick appeared coming down Lysander Lane. Slowing down, the driver saw a torch flash quickly about 200 yards away, and drove to the intrepid intruder.

Flinging open the passenger door, the individual got into the Buick. The car edged away and did a U-turn, and made its way back in the direction it had already travelled.

Both parties had much to converse about on the way back to LA. Sleep came upon these two entities very quickly this night, after parting company.

CHAPTER 21

THE DEAD SHALL RISE FROM THE GRAVE

The August morning sunrise was shrouded by a mist. Moving across the land from off the warm ocean, a gentle breeze caressed its swirling progress into the city and outer localities. The sky was shadowed in richly decorated tones of light gray and heavenly blue, mixed with an intense hue of bright pink. Low flying clouds dipped in and out of the mist, as they sailed by to their unknown destinations.

In the grand Prussian blue dining room, Felinda Bentine sat at the polished mahogany table. Sitting alone, she considered with pleasure that the two proverbial pests had been exterminated.

Felinda Bentine munched away on her medley of grains, placed before her by the faithful maid, Evelin Parker.

Parker had noticed her employer's manner to be more than frosty recently – particularly when the private detective and his secretary had called without invitation. She had heard most of the conversation that had taken place. Laughing within herself, she was pleased that someone had reckoned to level with the fierce Felinda.

Jedson was moody and sulky, and had ventured outside. Evelin felt some sorrow for the broken man. She had seen the change over the years in Jedson, but could never say a word.

Evelin Parker was nearing 65 years of age, and had been employed at Lorraway for a period of 28 years. Quite a time to be so poorly treated by the frightful Felinda. She inwardly knew what had happened to Tryphena and Tryphosa – removed before they could speak. They both had confided in her many terrible things that had occurred at the "house of horrors", as Parker referred to the house in her mind.

The day after having spoken to the private detective and his secretary, the twins had told her some more despicable happenings. Unmentionable beyond words, yet apparently they were true. Going to meet Mr O'Shea and his secretary, after having their hair done, the twins were excited that they could at last be heard, without the eyes of Jedson upon them – let alone the unappeasable anger of Felinda. Now sadly, neither were here. They were good company and always so cheerful, despite the atmosphere in the house. Evelin Parker missed them greatly. If only she could take over what they had tried to do – speak to this private detective, and reveal all she had been told.

That morning as Evelin prepared breakfast, she

remembered the business card that Paul O'Shea had left the twins. She had found it in their room, when asked to "get rid of that rubbish in their room", by the snappy Felinda. She knew what she had to do. Evelin Parker, always consumed in her duties and attention to detail, to satisfy the fastidious Felinda, had not heard or read the news regarding the shooting of Paul O'Shea and Donna Weston.

* * *

Mrs Patricia Weston sat weeping in the limousine provided to take her and Detective Sergeant Bruno Capezio to the funeral service. Detective Inspector Karl Peterson, chose to make his own way to the cemetery.

Two gleaming black hearse's arrived precisely on schedule and drove into the cemetery grounds. The limousine drove in behind the two hearses. The service was to be at the graveside for each individual. No church service was requested as the service was to be a private occasion. The coffins were duly loaded onto separate trolleys and wheeled to the already prepared holes. The General Section was grassed and exceptionally neat and pristine. The Baptist minister who was to conduct the service, was standing solemnly at the two gravesides. His long robes billowed in the morning westerly breeze. Each corpse was to be buried alongside one another – a fitting end to such a budding romance.

Mrs Weston, Bruno Capezio and Karl Peterson made their way over to the patiently waiting minister. Each man stood either side of the woman, just in case she needed support throughout the service. Capezio introduced Peterson to the clearly distraught Mrs Patricia Weston.

The six funeral attendants, four male and two female, now positioned the coffins parallel to the deep holes.

The minister began his droll speech. 'The dead in Christ shall rise again … '

Before any further words were said, Mrs Weston let out an unearthly wail. Sobbing violently with despair, she reached over to the hands of Karl Peterson and said with a loud trembling voice, 'Oh, please find my daughter's killer, Inspector. When will you find who it is, please?' She grabbed the lapels of Peterson's jacket and hung onto his stiff frame with all her might.

Peterson's hands were like jelly, unable to move with the sudden reaction from Mrs Weston.

Capezio took his cue with great ease, and reached into his dark jacket, and pulled out a set of handcuffs.

Quickly coming around the back of the startled man, Capezio grasped Peterson's wrists together, and clipped the handcuffs onto the perplexed Peterson's large hands. At the same instant, all the funeral attendants brandished weapons, and pointed them at Peterson. The Baptist minister removed himself surreptitiously, and viewed the proceedings from a safe distance – after all, he had not come here today to be buried himself. Mrs Weston had stepped back, having completed her well played out role, and let the action begin. The coffin lids of both oak coffins, were drawn back systematically. Out popped Donna first.

'Well, hi there Karl!' she exclaimed in a bright tone. 'Nice to meet again after our brief encounter on the road the other day. That tie you were wearing the day you popped into the office with your toy gun, was real cute!' She winked at Peterson and gave a sensuous smile.

Reality had really struck a chord with the perilous Peterson – he had been set up!

'Bastard, you bastard!' he shouted at Capezio.

'Steady, Peterson! Or you will get a bullet in your head, just like the janitor you knocked off!'

Capezio, whilst a smaller man, was also a former heavy weight boxer and martial arts competitor, and seized Peterson's right arm. He knew that Peterson was capable of anything, and was taking no chances.

Peterson tried to kick Capezio in the shins, but the Detective Sergeant was too quick, and kicked Peterson between the legs. Screaming and doubling over with pain, Peterson was wreathing with excruciating discomfort, to say the least. Not a pleasant state of affairs for the confident and sanctimonious Peterson!

The other coffin revealed a fresh faced Paul O'Shea. Looking none the worse for having been "laid up", O'Shea came across to Peterson. Bending down to stare Peterson in the face, O'Shea challenged the self-important officer.

Peterson was still unable to stand up properly, and was

partially bent over. He was looking a little worse for wear,

'You killed Ben Driscoll, then the janitor, didn't you? And you tried to take out Donna too! When that failed, and Felinda Bentine informed you of our morning tea call, you thought you would remove us both simultaneously. Well pal, it has backfired! Where is Clarene Cremorne? Don't worry too much bud, 'cause we might know the answer to that. How does number 401 Lysander Lane, Ocean Pacific Downs sound?' O'Shea stood, arms folded, eager to hear what the huge hulk of Peterson would say.

'Don't know w-w-what you are talking about, man! This is crazy. I d-done nothing! You h-h-hear me! I'm clean, man! You've made a big m-mistake! You will pay for this Capezio, you hear me you r-r-rotten bastard!' The man stammered out his response with visual discomfort and obvious vengeance.

Peterson's face was one of concern and entrapment. He quickly realised he had been followed – but how much did they really know, or were they bluffing? Peterson's brain was working overtime to make a dash for freedom. Trying to thrash out of the vice-like grip of Capezio, Peterson was no match for the experienced martial arts expert.

'Come on, Peterson. Your comin' with me pal!' said the harsh voice of Capezio. Dragging Peterson by the scruff of his solid neck, Capezio nodded to the other officers standing close by. They rushed across, and took the restrained Peterson into custody.

Using the disguised hearses, everyone departed the cemetery leaving the Baptist minister behind. He brushed down his white tunic robe, and then removed it. He had never been entitled to a burial and resurrection all in the space of a few short moments – plus an arrest of a high ranking police officer. He had seen it all today! So he certainly had a lot to tell his parishioners this coming Sunday. The collection bag might be heavier this week.

Peterson was loaded into the back of one of the disguised hearses with two of the male boys in black brigade. All the other company, including Capezio, used the second hearse. Mrs Weston, Donna and O'Shea travelled in the limousine back to the Parkside Business Centre. The ingenious organised plan had been well instrumented, and highly successful. A detailed operation skillfully devised by O'Shea and Capezio, was to come undone very soon.

Yes, you had better read on …

The camera that had been placed inside the office of O'Shea had captured the face of the resentful and smug Peterson entering the suite. The shootings had also been photographed, placing Peterson in a perilous position to answer his reasons for being there in the first place.

Now back at LAPD headquarters in Los Angeles, Peterson was being marched into the building. Capezio at the left side of the tall lumbering Peterson and another officer on the right.

Peterson's mind was working craftily to see a way of escaping custody. Suddenly he kicked the officer on his right first. The man stumbled and lost his balance, sprawling onto the floor. Then acting fast, Peterson turned and confronted

Capezio with a loud crunching head butt. Capezio was stunned, and his body was jolted backwards. Before anyone else came to the aid of the stricken officers, Peterson was off down the corridor. Running had always been a talent of the pious Peterson. As he bolted towards freedom, the escaping convict then proceeded to bowl over another officer . The officer was splayed on the floor in seconds with the sheer force of the Peterson frame. Out the wide sliding glass doors Peterson ran, successfully managing to hail, with both handcuffed hands, a passing Red Cab. Miraculously he fumbled to open the cab door, Peterson bundled himself in, and the cab driver sped off downtown.

CHAPTER 22
FLIGHT TO FANCY

Karl Peterson was a desperado on the run.

At a set of traffic lights at the intersection of Hollywood Boulevard and Ranger's Run, Peterson jumped out of the cab and mingled with the crowd on the pavement – no tip for this unhappy cabbie. Trying his best to conceal his handcuffs, Peterson placed his hands deep inside his overcoat. Knowing the streets of the city like the back of his greasy big hands, he knew he could outwit the police in tracking him down. Walking briskly a few blocks in the direction of where he intended to go, Peterson hailed another cab. Barking out directions to the alarmed, yet obedient cabbie, the vehicle sped off to its destination. Our friend, Mr Ibrahim Al Bazoukia was going to come in handy again.

Arriving at the premises of the black market tobacconist in Palm Ridge, Peterson was duly relieved of the handcuffs. Mr Ibrahim Al Bazoukia was well equipped with tools, and using his sharp bolt cutter, released the frustrated Peterson from captivity. Prompt action from Ibrahim Al Bazoukia secured the deliverance of our escapee. Salvation had come at last.

Making a hasty telephone call, Peterson now waited anxiously.

Not all was going Peterson's way, as we will discover very soon.

* * *

What had become of Neumann Riessler? Had he dropped off the radar for good? No, far from that.

Having arrived back on the late flight into the hungry for action city of Los Angeles, Riessler set about to locate Peterson. Catching a cab to his small and shabby insignificant digs in North Hollywood, Riessler laid on the unmade bed located on the first floor. He began laying a scheme to trap the dangerous and slimy Peterson. Little did he know what events were to take place.

Choosing to venture to the Parkside Business Centre in West Hollywood, Riessler thought that Peterson might be there. The suite had been sealed over by the police and no one was around, so Riessler decided to leave.

By fate, Riessler was too early by about 10 minutes, and was going to miss the returning police limousine, with O'Shea and the two ladies. Riessler's next move was to check out the Bentine hideout.

Having positioned himself within sight of the ornate gates of Lorraway, for just over an hour, Riessler waited patiently. High noon was just coming over the city and its extensive commuter belt. The day was bright, and the sun was warming up the earth. Riessler's skull cap was heating up, and a trickle of sweat fell down his ragged worn features with the intense rays of the relentless sun. Laying across the handlebars of his motorbike, Riessler was able to view the comings and goings at Lorraway undetected. The wrap around dark sunglasses gave Riessler the appearance of a biker from the shady side of town. A row of neatly clipped box hedges lined the perimeter of the Lorraway estate, which afforded protection to Riessler. Riessler longed for a drink, a long cool beer would have been great, but he knew that was out of the question. Then it happened.

The silver blue Lincoln Continental swung out of the gates and drove towards the freeway, linking motorists to the busy city. Riessler could see an older man driving. No one else was in the car. He assumed it was Jedson, the hen pecked bastard his mom had spoken of. Riessler turned his American Indian 750cc bike around and followed the Lincoln discreetly.

The '65 Lincoln drove at a rapid pace towards the city. Indicating to turn right, the large automobile was heading in the direction of Palm Ridge. The high-powered bike of Riessler was not far behind.

After some 15 minutes, the Lincoln drove into a street named Vistula Vista, a wealthy stretch of establishments in the inner city neighbourhood of Palm Ridge.

Coming to a stop, Riessler could see the older man alight from the car. Going to the trunk of the car, a large can was taken out. Carrying this in his left hand, the elderly man began to walk hurriedly up the street, but with labouring steps.

Riessler was already parked some 150 yards further back, and watched with keen interest.

Jaunty Jedson was almost at a run, but decided to halt his progress. Checking around him, he straightened his back and slowed his gait.

Riessler had decided to follow on the pavement within vision of the unloved butler from Lorraway. There were numerous businesses along this road, catering for the wealthy and sophisticated customers that trod their highly polished or plush floors.

Jedson paused outside the premises of Ibrahim Al Bazoukia, Tobacconist and Smoking Accessories. Then, taking a deep breath, Jedson walked inside and disappeared from Riessler's sight. The biker hung back, pretending to window shop. He was now within 50 yards of the tobacconist shop.

After a few minutes, the door opened. Out came Karl Peterson, who made his way to the Lincoln without hesitation. He did not even look up, otherwise he may have seen the figure of Riessler just yards away. Then after a brief interlude, came Jedson, who began a hurried trot towards the Lincoln. The man found it difficult to run, as his legs would not co-ordinate for him. The Parkinson's disease had robbed Jedson of this natural ability to run. Stumbling into the driver's seat, Jedson started the Lincoln and made a quick turn around the street. Just as well Jedson had left the keys in the ignition, otherwise fumbling with keys could have been fatal.

The Lincoln Continental gathered speed and was now out of view of Riessler. Choosing to run swiftly back to his bike and attempt to chase after the limousine, Riessler had made a very wise decision.

What had actually happened inside the tobacconist premises was far from pleasant!

Those minutes before had seen Jedson go to the counter of the tobacconist.

'How may I help you, sir?'was the polite, but cagey, response from the Turkish dealer in illegal imports and anything else along the way. You name it, and Ibrahim Al Bazoukia could get it for you – a handy chap to know.

The gruff and unsteady voice of Jedson said, 'I-I have c-come to collect your p-p-parcel.'

This was a predetermined signal, organised by Peterson and Felinda Bentine over the phone. Peterson had informed Mr Ibrahim Al Bazoukia of the password, and when Jedson stuttered out the words, the proprietor went to the back of the shop via the heavy black curtains.

Jedson's body was shuddering with nerves, his mind focused entirely on the assignment to be performed without failure – Felinda's strict instructions must be adhered to. He waited with anxious anticipation for Karl Peterson to come out from behind the curtained entry. It was up to Jedson to finish off the job.

Seated at a mangy desk, Peterson was breathing heavily – naturally, he had filled himself with no less than two packets of the delightful small cigars he relished like candy. Jedson waited for Al Bazoukia to vanish from sight, and bent down. Placing the can gingerly onto the floor, he waited for Peterson to make his appearance. There was no dillydallying on the part of Peterson. He was out of the shop, leaving Jedson to complete his allotted task.

As Felinda Bentine had arranged with Peterson over the short, but concise telephone discussion, the saviour of Peterson was to be extinguished. Al Bazoukia could not be relied upon to keep his unsavoury mouth shut. Ibrahim Al Bazoukia had served his purpose, and now it was time to blot out his existence for good.

Peterson was mindful that Al Bazoukia would always go with the highest bidder to feather his own pocket.

Jedson saw Peterson out of the shop. Making up an excuse to purchase some Turkish cigarettes himself, the tobacco proprietor and dodgy dealer, went over to his supplies to fetch the requested cigarettes. Jedson bent down and took off the can's lid, splashing the liquid all over the counter and into the direction of the victim. Jedson lit a match and flung it over the shop counter. Out of the shop raced Jedson, and down the pavement in the direction of the getaway vehicle.

Peterson had flung the door wide open for Jedson to jump into the car a bit quicker – nice of Karl Peterson to do that!

There was no time now for the target to escape. Seconds ticked away as the petrol and fire met with catastrophic results. Flames instantly consumed the fittings and curtain. There followed a massive roar as the inferno ate everything in its path.

Jedson had heard the helpless screams of Al Bazoukia ringing in his ears as he made his hasty exit from the building. It was at this precise time that Riessler was running back to his motorbike that all hell broke loose.

The furnace lit up the pavement and surrounding shop fronts with a massive explosion. A woman passing by with her young daughter were engulfed in the inferno as it blasted out onto the street. Neither had a hope of fleeing their violent end. Their torsos were blackened beyond recognition.

Riessler was momentarily knocked over with the force. Regaining his footing, Riessler ascertained what had taken place. Wild with anger, he sped off after the retreating Lincoln.

Pandemonium now rocked the immediate area, as people flocked outside to see the tobacconist shop entirely obliterated in leaping flames. The shops either side were also engulfed, causing human injury of the direst consequences.

Riessler's bike was quick, although a cruiser, it was a mean machine as we have encountered before. However, fate often has the last say. Following the Lincoln Continental for about ten minutes, Riessler began to feel that the bike was riding low at the back. Pulling over to inspect the tyre, revealed that a nail had pierced the tyre wall.

'Shit!' shouted Riessler with annoyance. Instinct alerted him that the two felons were travelling to Lorraway. He had to work quick to ensure his hunch was correct. Knowing the outcome of Jedson's little handiwork at the tobacconist, Riessler was resolute in bringing to justice this diabolical setup.

CHAPTER 23

A MOTHER'S LOVE IS INDEFINABLE

Back in Gull Rock Gorge, Hawaii, our ladies had much to be concerned about.

Knowing that Neumann Riessler had departed swiftly to go back to the mainland, without giving a satisfactory explanation, mother and companion were duly worried.

The Ohahrehs had visited to ensure they were both alright. Taka Ohahreh tried to placate the ladies worst fears, and his wife Grace, offered her motherly advice to them. However, for all their words, Maryanne especially, longed for the comforting arms of her son yet again.

Audrey was also troubled, knowing the danger that Neumann was to contend with. She was worried for Maryanne. Sometimes too much knowledge can be heart wrenching, and Audrey was more than aware of the circumstances. After all, Audrey was there on that night of August 4, 1922. She had shared in Maryanne's tragedy. A mother's love for her son is indefinable, and in this case it was beyond words.

Having met her longed for, and always loved son, Magdalena Hendon aka Maryanne Osborne, was inwardly bereft. Deep inside her heart she knew why Neumann had gone to the mainland. She thought about the bitter malice that had eaten into Felinda and the years that had plagued Magdalena unmercifully. Was it time for Magdalena to speak up? Tears rolled down her still, comely face. The veneer that she had portrayed so well when Paul O'Shea and Donna Weston had visited, was now visibly removed. Whilst her hair was now snow white, it was thick and had a lustre of caring quality. Still capable of physical activity and mental alertness, Maryanne had accomplished her art with skill and much applaud. Her natural beauty shone without the use of makeup. Seeming to be almost ageless, after all she had been through, Maryanne was still a very attractive woman for almost 70 years of age. Having had numerous offers of marriage since residing in Hawaii, Maryanne had refused them all.

Discussing matters with Audrey that evening after dinner, the ladies made their necessary decision. Initially they were reluctant to inform the Ohahrehs of their plans, but on second thoughts, chose to let them know.

Audrey was the one to sway Maryanne. 'Maryanne, out of courtesy, we have to tell Taka and Grace. We just can't up and leave without informing them of where we are going! They have been very supportive to us, and I think it would be very prudent and the right thing to do, to tell them!' Her voice was firm, almost scolding.

'Yes, you are so right, Audrey. It would be thoughtless of us to vanish and not say where we are going. They would be worried too. Alright, I will invite them here tonight. Hopefully Grace is not working the late shift, but anyway Taka should be home,' Maryanne replied caringly.

With luck on their side, both Grace and Taka came without delay to the women to hear their proposal.

Upon listening to the ladies idea, Grace looked over to Taka. Her eyes were sending out a message to her beloved husband. Taka understood immediately. He had been married to Grace for some years now, and had developed a recognition of Grace's features in certain events. This one for sure he knew the answer to, without any unwillingness.

'Right ladies,' Taka said. 'When are we going?'

Following some uncertainty on the behalf of Maryanne and Audrey, Taka won the day.

'I won't have you go alone without accompanying you both. You hear me? Neumann gave me stringent instructions to keep an eye on you. Well how can I, if you are not here? I gotta go with you! Grace will be alright. I can get my brother to look after the orchids while I am away, no problems at all.'

A flight was booked to depart at 5.30 a.m., the first flight of the day to the mainland.

Sleep came easier to Maryanne that night. The heavens were a glorious sight during those hours of darkness upon the sleeping earth. Laying awake and looking out her bedroom window, Maryanne saw the quarter moon lying on its side. She was sure it had winked at her and then gave a smile of reassurance. Rolling over, and pulling up the open weave blanket, Maryanne slept the night away in peaceful slumber.

At the Ohahreh home, Grace was hurriedly preparing a packed case for Taka. Always one to be highly organised, she slipped into bed around 11 p.m. and kissed her much adored Taka goodnight. Grace prayed that the Lord would be with Taka and the ladies on their vocation to search for Neumann.

None of our above mentioned characters knew of the "resurrection" of Paul and Donna.

Yes, Paul O'Shea and Donna Weston were enjoying a meal out at the Palermo Palace in Pasadena that evening.

Mrs Weston had accompanied them, enjoying some quality time with her only daughter. Paul's request for Mrs Weston to come to Los Angeles had been most welcomed. A chance to see her only daughter, and have a return flight ticket paid for, was music to her ears. Celebrating the arrest of Karl Peterson and their well thought out plan, they had not been informed of the fugitive that was now on the run.

Detective Sergeant Bruno Capezio was hell bent on finding Peterson. Nursing a dislocated nose, and his pride, the dedicated officer was determined to redeem himself, after the disastrous occurrence at police headquarters.

An APB had been issued for Peterson, but Capezio was, at this stage, unaware of the shelter offered to the scheming Peterson at the hideaway confines of Lorraway. Capezio had managed to suppress a news release regarding the destructive burning in Palm Ridge that had so brutally taken the lives of 10 innocent victims. This of course included Ibrahim Al Bazoukia. He hadn't asked to die so ruthlessly for all the man's faults. The police were more than well conversant of the business ran by Al Bazoukia. Never able to pin point anything concrete against the villain, had left the police exasperated beyond words.

The night broadcast on television and radio stated that "an explosion had occurred in a tobacconist shop in Palm Ridge this morning. Police were now investigating possible arson or an act of terrorism. Further news will follow once additional reports come to hand".

To overcome panic on the subject of the multiple deaths, no mention was made until Capezio gave the word. The express command of the Police Commissioner was to be obeyed without default. It was going to be difficult enough to conceal such a horrendous event. Yet having a highly ranked officer involved with the atrocity was not something the police were comfortable about.

* * *

The three passengers from Hawaii made their way to the Lotus Lily Lodge in Saint Orlando. Accommodation had been pre-booked by the competent Grace Ohahreh the night before.

Taka went to see if the ladies were settled in. He had thoughtfully contacted Grace, to let her know of their safe arrival.

Knocking on their hotel door, Audrey opened the door for Taka to enter. Both ladies were now anxious to catch a cab to the digs of Neumann Riessler.

By chance, Neumann had given his mother the address of where he lived in North Hollywood. His decision to leave California and make the move to Hawaii and live with his mother and Audrey, was such a joy to both ladies. Neumann had provided his address to his loved mother, more out of love, than ever thinking that she would be making a journey to visit him. No phone number had been given, as Neumann shared the phone in the hallway with the other tenants.

Taka escorted the ladies downstairs, and hailed a cab to take them to the lodgings of Neumann Riessler.

The traffic was quite congested, and it took half an hour to drive to the address given to the obliging cab driver. Taka, suspecting that all may not be well, requested the cabbie to wait for them.

Up the four uneven concrete steps they went, Taka pulling open the brown painted wood door. Paint was peeling off the door in tiny flakes. The outside of the building was certainly in much need of repair and the entrance hallway was dim and smelt like a dungeon. There was no tenant directory board, so Taka peered around to see if there was a concierge or janitor on site. Noticing a partially closed door further down the hallway, Taka indicated to the ladies that he would make enquiries.

'Hello, any one home?' bellowed the booming voice of Taka Ohahreh as he knocked on the dirty door,

'What cha wanna know, pal?' came the whining voice from inside the room.

Pushing the door wide open, Taka could now see a woman doing some ironing. A cigarette hung out of her lips, and a glass of some delightful alcoholic beverage stood on a small battered wood table. A bottle of brandy, almost empty, was the 'fuel' this all sorts creature had been sculling. Her sloppy walk revealed that she was quite the worse for wear. Wearing just a short soiled black mini skirt and a particularly low cut white blouse, that had been ripped, and was blood stained, the woman could barely keep both eyes open.

'I'm looking for Neumann Riessler, is he in do you know?' Taka responded brightly.

'How would I know … Want a drink?' she hiccupped violently, but still managed to keep the almost extinguished cigarette between what was left of her yellow teeth. Her voice was husky and her breath wreaked of liquor.

Ignoring her question, Taka said impatiently, 'What room does he have, please?' with some emphasis on the word "please".

'Ten bucks and I'll tell ya, buddy,' came the spiteful reply.

Holding onto the door for support, the whorish woman swayed towards Taka and began to fiddle with his colourful Hawaiian shirt. Tottering in her red nine-inch heel stiletto shoes, the woman lost her footing and crumpled down in a helpless state.

'Is she drunk?' came the voice of Audrey suddenly in the stale smelling room.

'Sure is, Audrey,' Taka replied before taking matters into his own hands. Lifting up the seedy woman, he sat her down on a broken chair. Pushing her back against the wall and grabbing her by the shoulders, Taka moved his face just inches away from hers. 'Where is Riessler?' he boomed.

'Alright … h-h-he's in room 9 … but he ain't here … he left this m-m-morning on his b-bike 'round 8 o'clock. Now let me go you, you ape!'

Leaving the wretched creature to her own devices, Taka leapt up the stairs, followed by Audrey and Maryanne.

Banging on the door to room 9, Taka called out, 'Neumann, you in there?'

No response, so Taka opened the door and ventured inside. All three could see that Neumann was not in residence. Making a thorough search around the room for any clues as to where Neumann could have gone, revealed nothing to assist them.

'I know where he could have gone!' gasped Maryanne.

'Where?' said the others simultaneously.

'To Lorraway! I told Neumann that it was Felinda who took him away from me at birth. Neumann may have gone there to confront Felinda regarding the horrible act she committed. It is quite probable, as I was very disturbed when I was telling him the circumstances of his birth. He would also know that Felinda would be behind the deaths of Paul and Donna. Neumann did say that he knew where Lorraway was. How, I don't know, but he certainly was familiar with the place.'

'Alright, do you know how to get there, after all this time Maryanne?' questioned the worried Taka, unsure who this Felinda was. He realised he was behind the eight ball with everything that had transpired, but was willing to assist in whatever way he could.

'Well, I know the address in Cricklewood. I could never forget that!' replied Maryanne with a decisive tone of voice.

Bundling the ladies back into the taxi, the driver was instructed to drive to Lorraway. By this time it was nearing 1 p.m. in the afternoon.

Internally, Maryanne was extremely apprehensive. Unpleasant memories filtered back into her confused mind – the tragic and needless death of Alyssa, Grayden's suicide, the taking of her much wanted son, the gruesome deaths of her twin sisters, Tryphena and Tryphosa and the slaying of Ben Driscoll, the son of her much loved friend, Lamore. Yes, Felinda had so much to answer!

The taxi sped towards the home that once had been a haven of love and laughter, but had been so meaninglessly altered into a cold-blooded palace of immense callousness and yes, murder.

CHAPTER 24

ALL ROADS LEAD TO LORRAWAY

Evelin Parker heard the Lincoln Continental come to a screeching halt, outside the west wing.

Standing at the large pine kitchen table, polishing the family silver, she paused her rapid handiwork, and listened. She knew Madam wouldn't like him driving the car like that!

Parker could then discern raised voices, which seemed to be coming further down the hallway. Stepping out into the hallway, Parker now heard a man's troubled voice. It was definitely coming from the Prussian blue drawing room.

The door had been left open, and the loud agitated voice of Peterson was easy to hear.

'Aunt Felinda, I need you to hide me for a while. I escaped from police custody. That O'Shea and his secretary are damn well alive! I thought I had knocked them off. They must have had dummies in the office, I didn't check, I honestly thought it was them. It was all a trap, including the funeral ceremony. The bastards think they can nail me, but they won't get me!'

'Oh no Karl, you can't be serious!' came the vexed reply of Felinda Bentine, 'You cannot stay here. The police or O'Shea may already know of our connection. We cannot take that risk! Listen, take the other car, the Pontiac Parisienne, and leave now! Use the back exit, you know the one, over by the ornamental lake. Drive out that gate, they won't be expecting you to leave that way. Quickly, hurry Karl. There is no time to waste, dear! Jedson and I shall hold them off. Phone me when you get there Karl. Momsie will be worried. We will think of another way to exterminate those two idiots!' Felinda Bentine ordered as she hurried over to a walnut bookcase. Sliding open a top drawer, she drew out a set of car keys. Handing them to the outstretched shaking hand of Karl Peterson. 'Now go, and be careful! Are you armed?'

'No, I haven't got any gun with me. It was taken off me when I was arrested,' said the anxious Peterson. His hands were sweaty and he was feeling the threat of capture at any moment.

He gave the impression of a chastised schoolboy.

'Right, take this,' she instructed, as Felinda walked at a rapid pace to a small side table. Under the parquetry top she popped open a hidden drawer. Taking out a lethal looking 38 calibre gun and a box of cartridges, she brought all this over to Peterson.'This is loaded, and here is more ammunition. Off you go, dear. I will quickly phone Momsie to tell her you are on your way.' Tapping Karl Peterson on his solid shoulder, she ushered the panic stricken man from the room.

Parker withdrew back into the kitchen.

Parker was intrigued. She had heard the twins mention this Karl's name occasionally – he was a big wig in the police force, apparently. She knew he was a nephew of Felinda but who was this "Momsie" person, perhaps his mother? Continuing her silver polishing, Parker was acutely aware that she had to be very vigilant now.

The watchful eyes of Jedson were always upon her. She had to play the game well until her afternoon off.

Sensing a presence in the room, Parker's head turned. There just in the kitchen doorway stood high jinx Jedson, staring at her with malicious intent. Parker reacted to this well.

'Hello Mr Jedson. I have almost completed polishing the silver for you to place back into the cabinet.'

Making no reply, Jedson began to slowly walk over to the woman still standing at the table.

Sensing that Jedson must have seen her snooping, Parker's eyes roamed around for some implement to use as defence. There it was, laying on the scrubbed pine table. The rolling pin that was going to be used to make some pastry for the apple pie, after the polishing. She was going to need this!

'You were eavesdropping Parker, weren't you?' came the unkind menacing words.

Now almost in front of her, Parker saw that Jedson's hands were holding a thin object.

Parker's instinct kicked in. Jedson's arms descended like lightning drawing the deadly cat gut closer to Parker's neck. Without hesitation, Parker grabbed her rolling pin, and walloped Jedson over the head twice. He reeled back with the force, stunned and tossing his head around. Evelin Parker was not afraid of the bully, and then came across and swiftly hit the man in the shins. One and two strikes with the faithful wooden rolling pin!. Down Jedson went. Then to ensure that he wouldn't get up quick, Parker raced over to the kitchen cupboard below the large travertine sink, and got the fly spray. Jedson was moaning and crying out with pain. Parker, using her wits, closed the kitchen door, to stop the groaning of Jedson alerting Felinda Bentine. Then she gave Jedson a nice coating of fly spray right over his long pale face.

'Aaaach, aaahhh!' Jedson screamed like a baby in dire misery.

There was no time for Parker to wait around. Out the kitchen door, and into the back courtyard she ran. Being slight of build, gave the woman a good advantage to run like the wind down the side of the house. Checking her progress, Parker considered that she had not been seen by Felinda Bentine. The maid in distress had to make a break now or never. To be caught would be the end of her, Parker realised this with great fearfulness. Using some of the clipped shrubbery as coverage, Parker ran from one bush to the next. Gradually, she made her way down the driveway. Knowing that she could almost certainly be seen from the front windows, Parker edged further away from the great house. Freedom spurred her on. Her salvation arrived none too soon!

A dark figure on a noisy motorbike materialised out of nowhere. Riding just into the grounds, the bike came to a screeching stop.

Parker was now breathless and almost hysterical with terror.

'You need help, lady?' came the deep voice.

'Please, help me! They want to kill me. I have to speak to a Mr O'Shea and the police urgently!' Parker's legs were wobbly and she was bending forward in a very unstable fashion. Her arms were rising wildly into the air.

Neumann "Batman Biker" Riessler got off his bike and put his supporting arms of strength around the woman's waist.

'No worries lady. You are safe now. Come on … .' Riessler spoke softly to Parker.

'Jedson tried to kill me, but I hit him,' was all Parker could now say. Her physical stamina had been sorely tried, but she had been successful in her flight to freedom.

Just then, a taxi turned into the driveway of Lorraway. The occupants were eyeing the figures near the motorbike.

Neumann's attention was alerted to the taxi, and saw the three familiar faces sitting in the back seat.

'Mom, what are you doing here?'

'I could well ask you the same question, son!' came the sharp retort from his mother, Maryanne.

They all got out the cab, but requested the cabbie to remain.

Neumann explained very briefly the plight of Parker, and

the need to get the poor wretch to safety. Getting Parker into the rear of the cab, Maryanne and Audrey comforted the woman. Taka enlightened Neumann regarding the presence of the ladies.

'That bitch Felinda Bentine is in there!' Neumann exclaimed as he pointed to the long drive towards the prestigious palace. 'I would love to blow her brains out, but she ain't worth it, not yet anyway.'

Then a convoy of vehicles arrived at the gates of Lorraway. Two police squad cars and Mustang Mach parked randomly outside the popular venue. Detective Sergeant Bruno Capezio, Paul O'Shea and Donna, were all present. Much conversation was forthcoming from all parties, and it was agreed to now leave the scene and head back to the LAPD. The appearance of Paul O'Shea and Donna Weston brought much relief to the others. Parker had been able to inform the police that Peterson was no longer there. Needful preparation was necessary to bring down the mastermind gang who thought they were beyond reproach. It had been a day of much activity for all our persons of interest.

Peterson had of course arrived safely into the confines of the fortress at Ocean Pacific Downs, and dear "Momsie" was relieved to see her darling boy. A crafty brainwave on the behalf of Karl Peterson had brought liberty to this dastardly deviant.

Karl was such a treasure!

CHAPTER 25

A DAY OF RECKONING

Each moment of the year holds its own specific loveliness, like no other in all eternity. A scene which shall never be repeated again. A beauty that is ours for the beholding, and in that fleeting panorama, mankind is given the rare glimpse of purity and divine exquisiteness.

The scene mentioned below here is not just the description of the surroundings, but more importantly, the natures and minds of those seated at the round table. Rarely would we see such an assembly of differing individuals, who all had the same common purpose.

This particular night a large gathering of family, friends and acquaintance were enjoying a relaxed meal at The Sizzling Steakhouse in Poloma, overlooking the Pacific Ocean. The evening air was mellow and slightly warm, but a mild breeze was blowing across the sparkling waves.

A table had been booked by Donna for the large number of guests.

Neumann sat next to his beloved mom, who was so relieved to see him again. Maryanne had grave doubts that she would be able to meet up with her son ever again, following his hasty departure from Hawaii.

Donna had asked the American Negro taxi driver, Caleb Johnson, to join them for the meal, given his kindness towards the women in his cab, especially Evelin Parker. He had offered to drive the three women back to the hotel after Evelin Parker's ordeal, for no payment. Taka had rode back with Neumann to the Lotus Lily Lodge.

Maryanne and Audrey had taken Parker under their wings, like two mothering hens. Fussing over their new charge, nothing was too much trouble.

We must remember that the smart thinking Evelin Parker fled without taking a thing, even her precious rolling pin had been left behind. Parker's information had been most helpful to the police. Remembering with detail the automobile used by Peterson to make his getaway, and this "Momsie" person, was of great assistance. Plus, the confirmation that Karl Peterson and Felinda were in co hoots with this conspiracy, and they were also blood related. But who to? Clarene Cremorne? More than likely.

Paul O'Shea, Bruno Capezio, Neumann Riessler, Taka and Donna had much to discuss and plan out.

After details had been laid out systematically, the planners joined in the friendly banter with the others.

Caleb Johnson had never in his life been asked to sit at a white man's table, and share a meal. This was unheard of in Alabama, where he came from. White and black were poles apart, never to be seen together. A man of 35 years of age, and a widower after losing his beloved Winifred in childbirth, some three years ago. Their only son died two days later of complications. Caleb had left to try and forget the past, but it always remained with him. The grief never went away. It was like a weeping sore that would not heal.

Taka sensed that Caleb was initially uncomfortable to accept the invitation, but spoke a few words to the taxi driver, and encouraged him to accept the hospitality. Caleb accepted that Taka was a native of Hawaii, with a moderately dark complexion.

Neumann was talkative and appeared to be enjoying himself amongst people for the first time in his life. Being treated as an equal, instead of a law breaker and homeless criminal, was making inroads into the man's outlook on human nature.

Evelin Parker felt special, compared to being the insignificant char woman who dashed about Lorraway cleaning and scrubbing, running hither and dither. Being rudely spoken to and treated with contempt by Felinda Bentine. Checked on by Jedson at every turn she made, yes indeed the woman was now going to start living all over again. Maryanne and Audrey insisted that she come and live with them in Hawaii.

'It will be our pleasure. There is plenty of room, you can have your own bedroom, and the food there is fabulous. You will love it!' said Maryanne eagerly.

Finally, it was agreed that Taka would leave the following day, taking Audrey and Evelin with him, back to Hawaii. Maryanne, keenly perceptive of her son's wishes to apprehend Peterson, had told her son quite firmly, that she was not departing until he came home with her. Maryanne would not be persuaded otherwise. Deep in her heart, Maryanne knew the identity of "Momsie". An intelligent woman, Maryanne's presence was going to be vital.

Paul reasoned within himself that Neumann was ardent to ensure justice was meted out to Peterson, in particular.

Capezio had some strong words with Neumann Riessler, to confirm that the police would now take over the search for Peterson. The Detective Sergeant could not risk Riessler going off on his own, as a merciless mercenary to hunt for Peterson, and the others involved in this grizzly group of villains.

'We need you workin' together with us, pal. Sure, come along, but please, let us do the work from now on!' spoke Capezio with insistence in his Italian accent.

We know that these treacherous terrorists would stop at nothing to achieve their own foul desires!

Capezio told O'Shea, on the side, that the police had suspected Ibrahim Al Bazoukia of being a front for drug running, besides his other favourite pastimes of weapons, illicit tobacco and other illegal toys.

'Al Bazoukia was conveniently put out of the way, as he could squeal on whoever was the big boss behind the operation. Peterson has to be involved with this, man. I just hope we can break this ring of thugs,' said the indomitable Capezio.

A surveillance team had been carefully watching the stronghold in Ocean Pacific Downs, since Peterson had been seen there. Unfortunately, no appearance of Peterson had been sighted. Yes, the proficient Peterson had made his rushed exit from Lorraway with competency. Knowing that the Pontiac car may be traced back to his Aunt Felinda, Peterson made his way to a butcher shop in South Conway. There, he donned a butcher's apron and cap, and rode in the butcher's van, delivering the weekly meat order to the large compound in Ocean Pacific Downs.

The bashful butcher was under the impression that his law enforcement passenger, was on a undercover mission! So no questions were asked.

We must remember that Karl Peterson still had his police badge with him. Admittance to the place of interest was not queried by the observant eyes of the police reconnaissance team. Who was going to suspect the butcher van giving Peterson coverage into the security of the coastal hideaway?

Things were not too good back at Lorraway. Jedson had bruised knees and an aching head to nurse – plus his eyes were still stinging and sore from the fly spray wielded by Evelin Parker. His ears had been given a belting by Felinda, literally and physically too.

'Complete and utter fool!' she had bellowed. 'Allowing Parker to get away, how could you? The police will be onto ME now!'

The woman was now threatened and deeply conscious of being exposed.

Always the personal aspect was Felinda's foremost concern. Her own position in any circumstance of life was of the greatest substance.

Jedson's mind was made up. It was now or never!

Sympathy was never a quality of Felinda Bentine. In fact she viewed upon it as a form of weakness. Felinda's idea of "time away" from Lorraway, was the ideal situation Jedson needed to carry out his scheme. Felinda Bentine's pride and patience had been sorely stretched to their limits. Her normally brusque confident manner, was gradually changing into one who receives the raw end of the stick. With Evelin Parker gone, and taking with her information that she was not meant to hear, Felinda understood the precarious state matters were now hinged on.

A fervent telephone call that evening, had much heated exchange of words between Felinda and our nameless person. Arrangements were put into place for an exodus the next morning.

Some of our characters slept the night away quite well, but others were disturbed and restless.

Human nature is a fragile attribute. We can use our talents to aid our own intentions, without regard to the consequences we inflict on our fellows.

Three women lay awake that night - Felinda Bentine, Maryanne Osborne (now Magdalena Hendon) and one other female, shortly to be revealed. Sleep eluded them. Each knew the startling reality from many years ago – but how much longer could truth be contained in its secret state?

Dawn drew back the blanket of the night and the brilliant rays of the stars were veiled from sight. The new moon that had shone its opaline blue illumination upon the sleeping earth had moved to another part of the heavens. Its continuing magnificence was to be admired by many in opposite parts of the globe. Worshipped by some and gazed at with wonder and awe by others.

The waking of the morning brought renewed life to each individual. Truly a priceless gift we can each take for granted.

In the remote distance, way off the coast and far beyond the reach of man, the sunrise was producing a remarkable phenomena. A high altitude wind current was being utilised by a lone female short tailed Albatross off the California coast. Soaring majestically with effortless ease, she made her way to a safe breeding ground on a secluded rocky islet off the Pacific shoreline. Ready to commence her role as a mother, she was of age now to produce offspring. The mind of the Albatross was entirely focused on renewed life, and maintaining that existence was vitally essential to ensure a continued generation of future breeding. Mankind can learn much from animals. Their interaction, devotion and love for one another, is exemplary.

So, as we enter into the final stages of our story, hearts and minds will be tested.

Justice is measured out in many ways, sometimes with ugly results.

* * *

The tension at Lorraway was indeed fraught with emotion.

Having packed what they each wished to take, Felinda Bentine and Charles Jedson, were now seated in the Lincoln Continental.

The time had just gone 7 a.m. Ever planning ahead, Felinda chose to make for the road as soon as possible, and avoid any unwanted visitors to Lorraway.

The remaining staff were not enlightened where Felinda and Jedson were going. Felinda Bentine was treading on thin ice now. She sat regally in the back of the limousine, as always, the lady of extreme importance. Jedson was to leave by the rear exit, near the ornamental lake.

Travelling slowly along the drive, Felinda began to feel pleased that she was leaving her home, if only for a brief time. Jedson, however, had his mind conditioned entirely on the deed to be performed. His life was finished. Used like a puppet on a string, he had to do this! Felinda was not the woman he once adored those many years ago. She was void of feeling and remorseless in her quest for glory!

Carefully manoeuvring the Lincoln off the stone drive and onto the manicured grass, Jedson saw out of the corner of his eye, the lake below. The lake had been dug out just after Lorraway was constructed. Being a sunken lake, it was surrounded by embankments on all sides. Pristine garden beds, religiously attended to by the team of gardeners, encompassed the lake. Two flights of stone steps lead down to the lake. Four figures of female Greek and Roman deities were strategically placed around the lake, shaped as a heart.

The Lincoln Continental was sitting on one of these grassed embankments, the engine running. Jedson put the gear into reverse and turned the car, so that its trunk faced the lake.

'Jedson, what are you doing? You are supposed to be heading for the gates over there,' hissed Felinda, pointing her knobby finger. Her shrill voice rang in Jedson's ears for the last time.

Jedson gave no answer, taking his hefty sized foot off the brake, the car careered down the slope. Gaining speed, it was travelling at a good pace. Felinda Bentine waved her arms helplessly into the air, and howled with fright. Jedson closed his eyes and waited for the end to come, it could not come quick enough for him. He longed for peace.

The Lincoln crashed through a small stone retaining wall. The force of its descent dislodged Felinda Bentine from her seat. Wearing no seat belt, a figure was seen being thrown out of the rear window, and then the massive car was submerged below the water. Bubbles rose to the surface, as the vehicle began to take water and sink into the miry depths of the lake of no return.

Two gardeners witnessed the horrific scene, but were unable to do anything but watch the spectacle take place. Felinda Bentine had been flung like a paper doll through the back window, glass severing the Jugular vein – her life was null and void. Jedson did not attempt to struggle. He sat there, engulfed with the blackened waters, and was taken to a restful grave.

* * *

Three cars and two unmarked vans made the journey to Ocean Pacific Downs just prior to sunrise. Having left very early to avoid delays, and to strike the residence unawares, the squad observing the complex, reported no activity leaving the dwelling.

Paul and Donna were in Mach, and a contingent of specially trained armed officers, travelled in the two vans. Riessler and Maryanne, along with Bruno Capezio came in another squad car plus some backup officers in a third car. Capezio had instructed his team with great supervision, every detail had been gone over countless times to ensure a successful operation.

Arriving at the reclusive abode, Capezio minced no matters at breaking through the massive doors. Daybreak was just beginning.

Using a piece of wire, Capezio jimmied the card slot, and in seconds the huge doors began to roll open. Vans and cars rolled in. The house could be seen in the distance, a long avenue of clipped pine trees led the way to the entrance.

Maryanne's nerves were calmer now. It was as though it did not matter anymore. Her fear had gone, her son was with her. She asked for no more.

Capezio had ordered that a van block the route out. Men were positioned around the grounds with silence. Each took their place, awaiting further instructions.

Paul and Donna stood a distance back from the zealous Capezio, who gave the signal to his pair of expertly trained officers. Each man was armed and had the necessary equipment to bash the ornate lock from off the antique Spanish style door. It fell off with a clang onto the stone pavers.

The pair entered, followed closely by Capezio and more armed officers. Yelling out as they ran through the house, pandemonium broke the silent reverie of the still sleeping occupants. Up the wrought iron staircase they raced. Suddenly a man came running out of a downstairs room, looking rather perplexed and alarmed. Whisked off by the remaining policemen, it was ascertained that he was a butler, named Beggles.

The shouting had stirred the sweet dreams of Karl Peterson. Lifting his body off the comfortable king size bed, and putting on his candlewick dressing gown, he just got to the bedroom door as he was pushed back by the advance of

Capezio's taskforce. Caught unawares, the petrified Peterson was thrown onto the bed, and handcuffed. The room was searched for weapons. Finding the gun that was given to Peterson by Felinda Bentine, he was bundled down the stairs to wait in the foyer with two armed officers. Cursing Capezio and the men closely guarding him, Peterson was enraged. His face was twisted with hostility.

A scared woman was then seen coming out of an upstairs bedroom. Brought downstairs, she was shaking with terror. Disclosing that she was a live in nurse, her thoughts were then centred upon her mistress, still upstairs in the end bedroom.

'Mrs Peterson is in her bedroom at the far end of the corridor,' the young woman said in a horrified manner.

Capezio pursued after the four heavily armed officers, in search of the woman. Further down the passageway, was a wide set of closed oak doors. Two men burst into the room.

And there she was – laying upright in bed, propped by a number of pale pink pillows. The bedside lamp was still on. A packet of cigarettes and a lighter lay on the bedside table. There were bottles of tablets, a glass of water and an overflowing ashtray full of small cigar stubs. A half empty bottle of Jack Daniels whiskey lay alongside her. She was semi awake, yet dread displayed itself in her sunken dark expression. A wheelchair was placed beside the queen-sized bed. Her face was one of cynicism and indignation mixed together. The cheeks were hollow and the wispy hair was dyed a dark brunette. A short-sleeved pink satin nightgown just hung on the woman like a bit of rag. Her blood blotched arms were thin, and the skin was pale. Veins almost burst through their tissue paper like covering. The brown eyes were deep set, dark and forbidding. A distinct look of terror was evident, yet a fierce will to resist any intrusion into her past, was the woman's firm resolve. The woman gave the impression of death warmed up. Well, she would certainly be staging out her final performance very soon!

Still coming to terms with her morning visitors, the voice was husky and unfriendly, 'What the hell is going on here? Where is Karl? What right have you got to come in here at this unearthly hour? Karl, Karl!' the woman shrieked.

Dear Karl was nowhere in sight.

Waving the warrant in her face, Capezio informed the angry woman that a search was to be conducted of the premises. Capezio had the nurse come to help the disabled woman into the wheelchair. This accomplished, she refused to leave the room until Karl was brought to her.

'Bring my boy to me now, I say. Get out of my home now, you have no right to be here. Get out!' she raved at the policemen.

Downstairs, Karl Peterson had been seated on a sofa. He saw the elderly woman standing just inside the foyer. Then his eyes rested on Neumann Riessler, standing at the side of Maryanne. Poor boy, he hadn't even had time to have breakfast and a smoke. Still dressed in his flannelette pyjamas and a candlewick dressing gown, the lad was not functioning yet.

Paul and Donna were also in the background. Seeing the

now handcuffed Peterson, Paul was satisfied that the man who had murdered Ben Driscoll, was now to face trial. Peterson was taken upstairs to his mother, under custody.

The stage was now set for Maryanne to face the real brains behind all that had happened. Maryanne stepped forward and softly spoke to one of the police officers. 'You are going to need me now. I shall have to go upstairs. You had better let Detective Sergeant Capezio know.'

The officer went upstairs to deliver the message to Bruno Capezio. Shortly after, Capezio came hurrying down the semi circular staircase. Waiting for Neumann, Donna and Paul to come over, Maryanne opened up. They all listened intently to what Maryanne had to say.

'I now have the opportunity to expose the real killer of Charles Osborne. Please let me speak to her, Inspector? That is the only way to positively identify Clarene Cremorne.'

'Okay, we will be there with you. Mrs Peterson is not too happy at having early visitors!' Capezio chuckled.

Maryanne just kept her eyes fixed on the staircase. Ignoring what Capezio had said, Maryanne knew otherwise. Without hesitation, the woman who had for 47 years been concealing a secret of immense magnitude, stepped up the staircase with mental calm.

Neumann was right beside his mother, followed by Capezio, Paul and Donna.

Police had swarmed the house by now, and had a chef brought to the foyer, along with two other maids. Ground staff, numbering 17 in total, were also herded into a spacious living area, just off the foyer. All were aghast at the proceedings, and could not fathom why such measures were needed.

By this time, Karl Peterson had been ushered back to his mother's bedroom. The handcuffs had been removed. Capezio made it very clear to mother and son, that the place was now being searched with painstaking detail. Nothing would be left untouched! Mother and son were worried; their faces were troubled.

'Momsie wants a drink and a cigar,' demanded Peterson. He still thought he was in control, but this was just a mere cover up, to impress "Momsie".

Peterson's mother snatched the whiskey bottle from her son's hands, and helped herself to a generous swig of liquor. Gulping the alcohol down like it was water, she wiped her thin lips with the back of her sinewy hand. Peterson lit her a five star small cigar, the same Turkish brand that her smug son smoked, and put it into her mouth. Sitting in her wheel chair like some obsolete goddess, the woman had a face of deep premonition, yet for all that, she still thought herself beyond reproach. She puffed away, and helped herself to more of the whiskey.

The solid wood bedroom door was opened wide for the party of people to enter.

At Maryanne's wish, everyone else moved back into the room, against a long panelled wood wall. Maryanne stood alone in the centre of the bedroom. Paul and Donna stood together apart from Capezio, Riessler and the police officers.

Maryanne, now for the first time in all these long years, walked closer to the other woman staring at her.

Peterson had drawn back a little from the wheelchair.

The eyes of the two women were locked in recognition.

'Hello Clara,' came the confident words from Maryanne.

There were gasps around the room.

Peterson was the first to react. 'My mother's name is not Clara. You are wrong lady, get out, leave her alone!' he snapped at Maryanne. Trying to protect "Momsie" from exposure, dear Karl was vainly attempting to undermine Maryanne's statement.

Maryanne Osborne remained where she stood, and still piercing into the face of the woman before her, replied serenely, 'Oh yes, she was when I knew her. Weren't you, Clara? My older sister, that everyone thought was dead! Became Clarene Cremorne when an actress, and then vanished away so conveniently.'

The woman in the wheelchair shook violently with rage and shouted, 'You stole Charles from me, it was you that caused everything to go wrong. I had to go away, I was left with no choice! You thought you could get away with it, but I saw to that!' Puffing belligerently on her small cigar, Clara glared daggers at Maryanne.

Paul and Donna raised their eyebrows at each other in total astonishment. This was not what anyone expected! Riessler was becoming agitated, and Capezio had two men restrain him.

Struggling to get out of their clutches, Capezio barked out

to Riessler, "Back off, man! Cool it, please!"

Remaining unruffled and totally composed, Maryanne spoke on. 'You know that is not true Clara. Charles had played the field. You were already pregnant, and then he got me in the family way too. Yet it was me he chose to honour, and for that, you cruelly killed him. Plus the fact of your involvement with narcotics! That night you came to see Charles, I was hiding behind the screen near the sofa. You know the one, that Chinese red silk screen. I heard what Charles said, he told you that his first love was me, not you. Yes, he had raped you, I am not denying that, but he also knew that you were into drugs and dealing too. I was the unseen witness. You had no idea that I was behind the screen, hearing all that was said. Shooting Charles did not solve your problems, Clara, it only made them worse for everyone, especially yourself. I was the scapegoat that was designed to take the blame. Felinda saw to that, didn't she? Circulating rumours that I didn't know where I was that night, so the police could believe her, and have me imprisoned for something I didn't do. Having my child taken away, was pay back to me. Clara had to be vindicated of any responsibility, whilst I was hung out to dry! Whisked off to Switzerland to give birth, it was there that you met your future husband, the rich Conrad Peterson. You fell onto your feet then, didn't you?'

The discourse carried on. All who observed, were amazed with the previously hidden secret that was now being disclosed.

The woman in the wheelchair was wrathful. Pumping her fists into the air, as though to strike out to Maryanne, Clara's face was etched with fury as she screamed, 'Shut up! The bastard deserved it. He told me that he loved me more than you, you bitch! Thought he could threaten me about the drugs, ha! Double crossing dirty swine! I was more important than you, I was the better actress. Offering you parts in films, when all the time I was the one who should have been on the screen, immortal and wonderful me! It should have been me he married, not you, you tramp! He deserved to die, the rat!' Shaking uncontrollably, Clara drank some more whiskey. 'Lighter!' she said sharply to Peterson.

Karl was alarmed at his mother's outburst of hatred and malice. He couldn't believe what he was hearing. So many thoughts were flashing through the fast paced mind but he obeyed his mother's command.

Grabbing another foul smelling small cigar from the crumpled packet on her bony lap, Clara managed to shakily place the cigar in her wretched and twisted mouth. She opened the lighter but accidentally dropped the whiskey bottle into her lap. Out poured the liquid, she wriggled and made a distressed sound. Her bodily movements were unsettled and her coherency was lacking. Suddenly, she dropped the opened lighter into her lap as well. The combination of naked flame and alcohol was a deadly cocktail. The two elements ignited and the pink satin nightgown went up in flames within seconds. She began frantically flapping her arms around in acute pain and distress.

'Momsie, Momsie!' Peterson shrieked with vexation and anxiety, as he ran to his mother's side.

Clara's screams were deafening, the flames were consuming her like wildfire. Little could now been seen of the dragon drug lady, as the fire licked around her with startling ferocity.

Trying ineffectively to smother the flames, Peterson's candlewick dressing gown caught on fire simultaneously.

Police officers raced to the adjoining bathroom and tried to obtain vessels of water. A blanket was thrown over the pair, but the frantic waving arms of Peterson stopped its usefulness. One police officer tried to rugby tackle Peterson, using the blanket to smother the firebird, but it was beyond control now.

Paul hollowed at Donna to take Maryanne away, the moment the flames began to devour Clara's body. Maryanne was horrified and tried to look back, but Riessler shielded his mother's view of the shocking sight.

Peterson was screeching in agony as the flames travelled through his garments. These were a suitable source for any fire to devour in moments. He was running around the room in complete intense fear. Peterson was gradually being burnt to a cinder. A human torch reeling around the room, aimlessly waving his arms around as the flames licked him to death.

Clara was completely engulfed in the flames, death had come swiftly to this devious devil.

Capezio and his men tried unsuccessfully to arrest the flames, but the satin bed sheets also ignited. The fire brigade had been notified.

Chaos reigned for some period until the charred corpses were carried downstairs. The fire was brought under control before it spread any further.

Some time later on, a motley lot of confused and quiet people sat and stood downstairs. Capezio was disappointed that Karl Peterson was now beyond retribution, as was Paul O'Shea. Maryanne wept openly and was being comforted by Riessler and Donna.

Standing by himself, and reflecting on the dire happenings, Paul noticed a small side table against a long window that led out into the well-kept gardens. He could not believe his eyes. *It can't be, no surely not!* Paul thought as he picked up the photo. It was a colour photo, probably taken not that long ago, of three people, one being Karl Peterson, standing behind Clara sitting in the wheelchair, and a female standing at the side of Clara.

O'Shea recognised the woman. Taking the photo out of its frame, he read the inscription on the back. Yes, it was what he had suspected. He felt sick. What a fool he had been taken for, but who would have ever imagined this to be true! Paul rubbed his hands over his face in dismay and bewilderment. He knew he had to deal with this revelation immediately.

Things were being cleared away by the police. Packages of drugs had been found in a basement cellar, estimated to have a street value of more than USD $20 million.

Clarene Peterson, as she was now known, was the queen of the drug trade along the Pacific West Coast. Dominating the drug business for decades had paid its dividends handsomely – plus, having a son in the police force made it even better. Much evidence was located in a study, confirming contacts and suppliers from Colombia and Peru.

Capezio had at least cracked a big drug syndicate, but the one person he really wanted had escaped.

* * *

Donna, wondering where Paul was, saw the man standing near the long set of windows.

Walking over to Paul, she saw him place something inside his jacket.

'What was that Paul, a souvenir?' laughed Donna.

'No, it wasn't,' Paul replied angrily. 'It is proof of something I never thought possible.'

'What is it, Paul? What's the matter, darling?' Donna said with a concerned expression. Her eyes tried to meet with Paul's, but the man was looking out of the window. A troubled and puzzled countenance shrouded Paul's face.

'I have to make a visit to someone now, Donna. Sorry to leave you, I shall meet you back at the station.' Paul's features indicated that he was clearly disturbed.

'But Paul, can't I come too?' asked Donna, with some annoyance in her voice.

'This is for me to deal with. No one else can do this. I promise to be as quick as I can honey. Don't worry, I shall be okay. Trust me, as you have always done, please Donna,' said Paul with sincerity. With that, he kissed Donna on her lilac pink lips and was out of the house.

Donna sensed that she could not argue with Paul, and watched him hurry away.

CHAPTER 26
THE EXPLANATION

Managing to leave the scene of devastation behind, Paul O'Shea was fraught with sentiment. How little you really know an individual, until an incident occurs that alters the way we think about someone.

En route, the car phone began to ring, surprising Paul from his thoughts.

Picking up the phone he listened to the voice of Bruno Capezio telling him of the deaths of Felinda Bentine and Charles Jedson.

O'Shea terminated the call, as he was nearing his destination. Paul hoped the person would be at home.

Parking outside on the road, Paul paced up to the front door. Pressing the buzzer, he waited for a response. A few seconds went by before the door was opened.

'I have been expecting you, Paul.'

Stepping back into the house, Paul followed the person into the living room.

Noreen Driscoll sat herself down on a sofa, and indicated for Paul to do the same.

Paul declined, and just stood glaring at Noreen. 'Why Noreen?'

'You don't understand, Paul … I had to … the family was at stake … '

'Bullshit, you of all people, knew the risk you were taking. What about the girls, did you ever think of them? Did you, Noreen?' Paul was irate and so disorientated with the woman who sat in front of him now.

Noreen Driscoll, so demure and hardworking. The perfect mother and devoted wife, everything Paul thought a woman should be. Now, he understood that she wasn't even as good as Barbara. Yes, Barbara had her faults with men and money, but certainly nothing in the league of drugs and murder that Noreen Driscoll had perpetrated!

'Of course I thought of the girls! How do you think we managed to keep them at college? Annette wants to go to university next year, how were we going to afford it? They all want to go on summer camps, new clothes and all the other things that they need,' Noreen replied lamely, wringing her hands with nervous tension.

'Don't tell me that Ben was party to this, 'cause I won't buy it! When did he find out about the extra money that was filtering in?' Paul barked out to Noreen.

Looking sheepish, like a muddled schoolgirl who has been brought before the headmaster, she said, 'Ben wondered how we could afford for the girls to visit Lamore in Canada last spring. I told him that I had been saving up. Naturally he fathomed that on my meagre housekeeping allowance it was impossible. I also said that I got lucky with a lottery ticket, and he believed me. We could not have done it otherwise, not in a million years!' She gave a pleading expression to Paul, who was not convinced or deceived by this woman. 'Momsie was always on me to take some money to help with the cost of keeping the girls. Plus, we had the mortgage payments to meet, it wasn't easy!' she said with a message conveying that she was "down and out". 'I refused to take any money, but I know that Aunt Felinda was being paid handsome amounts to keep Lorraway going. Two years ago, things got very difficult financially. So, I relented, and took a lump sum amount. That's how the girls could visit Lamore, and Ben bought the new car last year. He had no idea! He thought it was all the proceeds of the lottery ticket. Ben trusted me entirely.'

Paul was disgusted with the last comment. 'Trusted! Yeah sure, poor bloke trusted you so much, that he was murdered by your brother!'

Noreen stopped for a moment, and then spoke on, staring at Paul. 'Then he got that letter, from the twins. Karl had seen it, before he delivered the package to you. Ben must have done some background study on the old case and the circumstances surrounding the death of Charles Osborne. Whatever he found out, alerted him to a clue that could expose us. I know that, because Ben did confide that much to me. So Karl tried to put Ben off the scent, by warning him with a note under the car wipers. There were some other things, but …' Noreen didn't finish her sentence, and just languished on the sofa. Her body was trembling and her hands were constantly moving. Noreen Driscoll, lowered her head, and then raising it said with tears in her green eyes, 'We couldn't take any chances, so I made the phone call to get Ben to go to the Seascape Apartments. You know the rest.'

'So did Ben finally come to the conclusion that you were receiving the proceeds of drug money, to fund the cost of living?'

Noreen Driscoll did not answer immediately. Turning her head away from Paul she sobbed.

'Well?!' Paul interrogated.

'No!' Noreen let out a scream of emotional torment. Screwing her face up, she said in an agonising tone, "Ben went to the apartment block thinking that he could catch red handed the person behind the letter. He even told me himself. Ben was very sure he would apprehend them. I had him killed by mistake, Karl took matters into his own hands. I wish that I had never become involved with it all!"

'Too late now isn't it, Noreen? Ben is dead because of you. Have you told the girls?' said Paul sarcastically.

'The girls are all I have, how can I tell them?'

'Does Lamore know of all this?' queried Paul. *That could have been why Lamore was initially withdrawn when I went to meet with her*, thought Paul, waiting for an answer.

'No, she doesn't. But Lamore did know about my mother.

You have been to Ocean Pacific Downs haven't you? I know, because I have just had a phone call from Beggles, the butler. He informed me what took place.' Noreen dropped her head and cried openly.

Paul was unable to offer comfort now; his feelings were crushed beyond belief. *To think that she had Ben set up to get knocked off, just to protect some family criminal activity. Then the janitor killed, followed by the twins and then Ibrahim Al Bazoukia. Jedson doing his bit to keep the home fires burning, Felinda making the bullets and having others fire them. Now their both dead!*

Noreen continued to shake uncontrollably.

'How in the world did you keep the identity of your mother from Ben?' queried Paul incredulously.

Noreen swallowed, and replied quivering, 'I always led Ben to believe that Momsie and my father had died before we married. Momsie never knew the girls. It was better that way for all of us. We couldn't let her whereabouts be known. Complete privacy was deemed the necessary means to conceal the drug operation. I had minimal contact with Momsie, to ensure Ben never suspected anything unusual. When I did, it was always when Ben was away with the girls.'

'Ben had certainly been taken for a sucker with you!' Paul responded angrily.

'So, what are you going to do, Paul? Turn me in to the police? When did you know I was Karl's twin sister?' croaked the voice of Noreen Driscoll. Her eyes were timid, and her body shook with the harsh reality of what she had done. She knew that she had lost the respect of Paul O'Shea forever.

Mulling things over quickly, there was only one option open to Noreen Driscoll. If she went to Lamore Driscoll, there was every possibility it could be revealed that Noreen had coordinated the death of Lamore's only son, Ben. Apart from the fact that the three teenage girls would have their lives turned up side down, there was only one way out.

'I will give you 24 hours to disappear. This is for the sake of the girls. You owe it to them. After that, I will come looking for you and drag you into the LAPD myself, so help me I will!' Paul then showed Noreen the photograph that he had taken from her mother's home. 'This was the evidence that clinched your relationship with Karl Peterson, the dirty scum bag!' Paul flung the photo onto Noreen's lap.

Choking with physical and mental tension, she picked up the photo, casting her eyes upon it, and said meekly, 'That was taken last year at Momsie's birthday.'

Paul was not in the least interested when it was taken; it was the final proof he needed to incriminate all three individuals. There was nothing more that he could say. His vocal chords were almost numb with this unforeseen admission of guilt.

Walking to the front door to leave, Paul glanced back at the woman sitting on the sofa. He had never imagined that Noreen Driscoll, who was once the epitome of loving wife and devoted mother, had allowed herself to be manipulated by wicked persons. The lust and greed had also consumed her like a disease, and Noreen Driscoll was to pay the price dearly. The horrid betrayal of her husband, Ben Driscoll, who absolutely adored his wife, was so utterly shattering, caused by her own weakness.

Weeping like a woeful and dejected child, Paul O'Shea hoped that Noreen would do the only logical thing possible to finalise this sordid affair.

Seated back inside Mach, Paul contacted Bruno Capezio at the LAPD. Relaying the details of his discussion with Noreen Driscoll, Paul then made his way into the city.

Noreen Driscoll, now alone in every sense of the word, understood the stark reality of what she had been a party to.

Yes, Noreen had three teenage daughters, but would they comprehend the reasons why their mother had allowed herself to become embroiled into such a wicked scheme?

Lives had been taken, including her own husband Ben, and the girls much adored father.

Going into the bathroom, Noreen went to the cabinet above the washbasin. Peering in, she saw the bottle at the back of the top shelf. Taking this with her, Noreen went to the drinks cabinet in the living room. Finding an unopened bottle of cherry brandy, she washed down two handfuls of the sleeping tablets with the liquid. Filled with grief and despair, Noreen stumbled over to an armchair. Flopping herself down onto it's comfortable cushion, Noreen waited for death to overtake her.

* * *

There was much that Detective Sergeant Bruno Capezio wished to ask Magdalena Hendon, but Maryanne Osborne, as we now truly know her.

Capezio had found out that Clarene Peterson used a company name for most of her business dealings, none other than "Charles O". What better way than to use the name of the man who opposed the use of narcotics?! The man she had cold bloodedly shot all those years ago.

Waiting for O'Shea to arrive back, the others were seated in a room. Once Paul O'Shea returned, he went and sat down next to Donna. Paul was quiet and seemed aloof. Donna extended her hand to him, which he took tenderly. Donna said nothing, but held Paul's hand tightly.

Maryanne was more settled now and started to reveal the hidden facts. 'To begin with,' she said, 'Clara and I had always got on well as girls. Then as time went by, Felinda decided to put a wedge between us. I think Felinda could see that she could not break our friendship, so her evil mind went to work! You could say that Felinda was like a "Jezebel", earnestly desiring to do evil! Fuelling Clara's mind with ideas that I was being favoured over her for film roles, incensed her greatly. Then the worst thing imaginable happened ... Unbeknown to me, Clara had been interfered with by Charles about four months prior to my pregnancy. When Clara confided in me the horrible details of her rape, I was appalled! I knew she was telling the truth. She was starting to show, and suffered some morning sickness, like myself. I then found out that I was also with child, to the same man! The difference was that I was not forced upon, like Clara was. Neither of us were married. There was no mention of a marriage proposal from Charles. I had to know what Charles intended to do. Would he marry Clara, or honour me? Charles had said that he loved me dearly, but no mention of marriage had been forthcoming. I realised then that Charles had lost control of his pants! Had there been others, I had to speak to Charles?' Maryanne smiled ruefully.

Quick smirks shot across the rooms. The only person who didn't was Neumann Riessler.

'So, I went to his house that August night ... ' Maryanne continued. 'I arrived not long before 6.30 p.m. Lindsay had just left, staggering down the path, I saw him go. I altered my arrival time in my statement to 7 p.m., so as to avoid any further suspicion. If I said that I arrived at Charles's home at 6.30 p.m., that was the same time period that Clara chose to come. She arrived not long after myself. Anyway, I came straight to the point with Charles. He passionately held me in his arms, and made a declaration that I would be his wife. I couldn't ask about Clara. I was not supposed to know! Then Richard, you know who I mean, Lamore's late husband, informed Charles that Clarene had arrived. Sorry, I know it is confusing with our names. She was known then as her acting name of Clarene Cremorne.' Directing her eyes around the room, she waited a few seconds. Clearing her throat, Maryanne went on. 'Clara was disturbed when she walked into the living room. I had by this time hidden myself behind the Chinese silk screen, just behind the sofa. I could not be seen with Charles, the whole affair was so delicate. When Charles made it clear to Clara that he was going to marry me, she became furious. It was then that she threatened to expose Charles as the father of her child, how he had raped her. This did not alter Charles's choice, but indicated that he would be sacking Clara from the studio for her drug use. So many of them were using drugs back then, and Clara was dealing too. I was not aware of this, and found it hard to come to terms with. We were not brought up with narcotics. How Clara became hooked, I will never know! Cocaine had killed my friend Johnny Appleseed, provided by Clara. She also dealt in heroin, opium and laudanum. You don't hear of the latter one much now. Oh yes, Clara was the girl anyone contacted for their drug supply!' Maryanne explained. She seemed indecisive, and needed coaxing.

'You are doing well Maryanne, take your time,' Donna said sweetly, with encouragement in her voice,

Riessler hung his head down between his knees. He had already accepted the fact that Karl Peterson was actually his half brother. Neumann's mind was racing with ideas – had he been seen as a threat to the family? Maybe they had feared the truth would come out regarding Peterson's poxy drug queen mother, if he were ever to be located?

Maryanne's words of enlightenment continued. 'Then things heated up! Clara shouted at Charles that she would be back. "You won't get away with this!" she yelled at him, and ran out of the house. Charles was not rattled by Clara's warning. He was quite unmoved, but knowing Clara, I had my misgivings. She could be quite hot headed, if someone or something annoyed her. Then the Hummersteins arrived. They only wanted to invite Charles to a golf tournament the following weekend. After about 15 minutes, they departed too. During this time, I was hiding. I didn't want to be seen with Charles. Gossip was rife in Hollywood, and the merest suggestion that I was at Charles's home, would bring a tale of slanderous lies! Anyway, Charles let Richard have his night off. He was taking Lamore to the pictures. I remained behind to discuss some wedding plans. Well, after about 20 minutes, the doorbell sounded. I hid behind the screen again. Charles answered the door. In walked Clara. She had a long black coat on. Charles offered her a drink. Ignoring this, Clara spat out to Charles that he was a mongrel and would pay the price!' Breathing deeply, and looking up with deep sorrow, Maryanne lingered momentarily.

Rubbing his mother's back, Riessler's throaty voice said, 'It's okay, Mom. You don't have to finish if you don't want to.'

'I must, Neumann ... I must ... ' Maryanne wept. 'C-Clara pulled out a gun from the p-p-pocket of her coat. Pointing it at Charles, he said to her, "Clara, there is no need for this". She laughed like a wicked witch, and stood in front of Charles, waving the gun at him. I could see all that was happening through a gap in the screen. Clara had no conception at all of my presence. I was mortified, and just stared in horror. I think my senses just seized up! Before anything else was said.' Maryanne dropped her head briefly, placing a hand over her lovely face.

Neumann continued to pat his mother's back. Everyone in the room remained dead silent as they waited for Maryanne to continue.

'Clara … she … she shot Charles twice through the chest. Without any hesitation, she then ran out of the house, and I was left. I should have phoned the police, but I knew that it would be difficult to explain my presence there. The scandal of being unmarried would come out. Luckily, I was wearing gloves. Ladies often did, back in those days. Clara had gloves on too. So it made it very hard to get any fingerprints. I just panicked, driving around aimlessly. Then later, I managed to drive to Maybelle Normansen's home in Belvedere, arriving around 9 p. m. She was a friend, not close, but Maybelle made you feel comfortable in her presence. I stayed there for awhile. There was a party, so I just mingled with the guests, and left around 10.45 p.m. I drove around again without purpose and parked somewhere for some time. I tried to sleep but that was impossible so I came home in the early hours of the morning. Everything was in a complete daze, the fact that Charles was the father of my unborn child, and yet he was now dead! Murdered by my own sister! Richard came home later that night, and found Charles dead. I always suspected that Felinda had an inkling that I knew who had really murdered Charles. She was very intellectual. So Felinda was all out to protect Clara and the family name. The rest is all history now, it doesn't really matter anymore. I have found my son, that is all I ever wanted.' Maryanne reached over and took her son's hands into hers, and clenched them tightly. 'If it wasn't for the letter that Tryphena and Tryphosa mailed to Ben Driscoll, I might never have seen my son again. They may have been thought of as simple minded ladies, but their love for me was unconditional. That is true love!' With tears streaming down her face, she cuddled into the arms of her son, Neumann.

Paul broke into Maryanne's tender thoughts and said, 'So, that is when Felinda took over matters. Had Neumann taken away at birth and rubbished your name throughout Hollywood. You had no choice but to leave and find a new life for yourself.'

'Yes, that is correct. Felinda always had a soft spot for Clara. I was never in Felinda's good books. She was always jealous of me. I don't know why. I guess the termination of Felinda's film contract following the death of Alyssa, never helped matters either. Clara was sent away to Switzerland to give birth, to avoid any scandal. By coincidence, Clara met her future husband, Conrad Peterson, an import/export consultant. They married, and he was more than happy to have the twins take his name. He was very well-off financially, and was able to afford the lifestyle that Clara longed for. It has been so horrendous all these years. Hiding a dark secret for my sister, who really despised me greatly. Felinda was ever the self-proclaimed guardian angel, who ensured that the skeleton in the cupboard, never saw the light of day! I was told that if I ever squealed about Clara's drug dealings, I would be "done away with". So, making the move to Hawaii, ensured I was out of harm's way.' Making a fleeting smile of reminiscence, Maryanne wiped some tears away, and said, 'Tryphena and Tryphosa tried for a little while to keep me informed, via Lamore, what was going on at Lorraway. Felinda got wise to their messages, and intervened, stopping any communication whatsoever. Lamore did not reveal that I was at Charles's home on that night. She told you a story to keep you satisfied. Don't forget, we have a strong and abiding friendship, Paul.'

So ended Maryanne's recollection of unpleasant memories.

* * *

And so the Charles Osborne case was now officially closed – although much more could be said regarding each person mentioned in the final stages of this book.

Neumann Riessler and Maryanne Osborne went back to Hawaii. Riessler's life had been found for him. There was no turning back for him, nor for Maryanne either.

Once a woman who lived in fear of her life, she now was free of the clutches of her evil family. A family torn apart by foolish ideals, vanity and a lust for control. All that had now disappeared, and only the gold remained, that being Maryanne Osborne. She had been tried dearly, yet had triumphed over tragedy.

As we wind up the narrative, we come to the conclusion that for love to be true, it must not be tainted by the influences of the world. Paul O'Shea had learnt forbearance through a failed marriage. Now, his heart was prepared to start a new life with Donna. There would be no inhibitions to destroy their love for each other. Donna had declared and proven her innermost feelings for Paul. Her love was impartial, without reservation, pure and totally divine.

The three things we crave for in our lives – happiness, freedom and peace of mind – are only obtained by giving them to someone else.

THE UNSEEN WITNESS

Grant Peake

ISBN 9781925367584   Qty

RRP   AU$24.99   .....

Postage within Australia   AU$5.00   .....

TOTAL★ $_____

★ All prices include GST

Name:...

Address: ....

....

Phone:..

Email: ....

Payment: ❏ Money Order ❏ Cheque ❏ MasterCard ❏Visa

Cardholder's Name:..

Credit Card Number: ....

Signature:..

Expiry Date: ....

Allow 7 days for delivery.

Payment to: Marzocco Consultancy (ABN 14 067 257 390)
                   PO Box 12544
                   A'Beckett Street, Melbourne, 8006
                   Victoria, Australia
                   admin@brolgapublishing.com.au

Be Published

Publish through a successful publisher.
Brolga Publishing is represented through:
• **National** book trade distribution, including sales,
marketing & distribution through **Macmillan Australia.**
• **International** book trade distribution to
    • The United Kingdom
    • North America
    • Sales representation in South East Asia
• **Worldwide e-Book distribution**

For details and inquiries, contact:
Brolga Publishing Pty Ltd
PO Box 12544
A'Beckett St VIC 8006

Phone: 0414 608 494
markzocchi@brolgapublishing.com.au
ABN: 46 063 962 443
(Email for a catalogue request)